KT-195-984

Please return on or before the latest date above.
You can renew online at *www.kent.gov.uk/libs*
or by telephone 08458 247 200

CUSTOMER SERVICE EXCELLENCE

Libraries & Archives

Kent
County
Council

00884\DTP\RN\07.07   LIB 7

C153710871

DEATH'S HALF ACRE

DEATH'S HALF ACRE

MARGARET MARON

THORNDIKE
CHIVERS

This Large Print edition is published by Thorndike Press, Waterville, Maine, USA and by BBC Audiobooks Ltd, Bath, England.

Thorndike Press, a part of Gale, Cengage Learning.

The text of this Large Print edition is unabridged.
Other aspects of the book may vary from the original edition.
Set in 16 pt. Plantin.
Printed on permanent paper.

LIBRARY OF CONGRESS CATALOGING-IN-PUBLICATION DATA

Maron, Margaret.
    Death's half acre / by Margaret Maron.
    p. cm.
    ISBN-13: 978-1-4104-1035-1 (hardcover : alk. paper)
    ISBN-10: 1-4104-1035-8 (hardcover : alk. paper)
    1. Knott, Deborah (Fictitious character)—Fiction. 2. Women judges—Fiction. 3. North Carolina—Fiction. 4. Large type books. I. Title.
    PS3563.A679D43 2008b
    813'.54—dc22   2008036822

BRITISH LIBRARY CATALOGUING-IN-PUBLICATION DATA AVAILABLE

Published in 2008 in the U.S. by arrangement with Grand Central Publishing, a division of Hachette Book Group USA, Inc.
Published in 2009 in the U.K. by arrangement with the author.

U.K. Hardcover: 978 1 408 42153 6 (Chivers Large Print)
U.K. Softcover: 978 1 408 42154 3 (Camden Large Print)

Printed in the United States of America
1 2 3 4 5 6 7 12 11 10 09 08

For Rebecca Blackmore, Shelly Holt,
and John Smith
with deep appreciation
for their time, their wisdom, and their
endless generosity

DEBORAH KNOTT'S FAMILY TREE

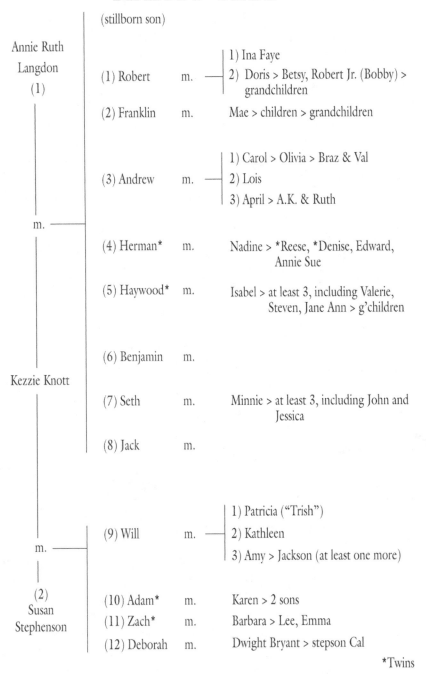

(stillborn son)

Annie Ruth Langdon (1)

Kezzie Knott

(2) Susan Stephenson

(1) Robert   m.
    1) Ina Faye
    2) Doris > Betsy, Robert Jr. (Bobby) > grandchildren

(2) Franklin   m.   Mae > children > grandchildren

(3) Andrew   m.
    1) Carol > Olivia > Braz & Val
    2) Lois
    3) April > A.K. & Ruth

(4) Herman*   m.   Nadine > *Reese, *Denise, Edward, Annie Sue

(5) Haywood*   m.   Isabel > at least 3, including Valerie, Steven, Jane Ann > g'children

(6) Benjamin   m.

(7) Seth   m.   Minnie > at least 3, including John and Jessica

(8) Jack   m.

(9) Will   m.
    1) Patricia ("Trish")
    2) Kathleen
    3) Amy > Jackson (at least one more)

(10) Adam*   m.   Karen > 2 sons

(11) Zach*   m.   Barbara > Lee, Emma

(12) Deborah   m.   Dwight Bryant > stepson Cal

*Twins

Easter Morning

Inside the windowless Church of Jesus Christ Eternal, the Easter Sunday sermon is drawing to a close. Although Mr. McKinney has been known to preach for two hours or more when thoroughly aroused, services usually end around noon. Thinking that she hears a winding-down tone in his voice, the teenage pianist quietly turns the pages of her hymnal to the closing hymn the preacher selected at the last minute. An odd choice for Easter, she thinks. Not that it is hers to question, but the other hymns celebrated the resurrection while this one harkens back to the cross and is less familiar to her than some.

> The thorns in my path are not sharper /
>   than composed His crown for me;
> The cup that I drink not more bitter / than
>   He drank in Gethsemane.

9

She has to squint to see the shaped notes because the fluorescent tubes overhead are flickering and buzzing again. She has been told these are cheaper than regular light fixtures, but the flickers hurt her eyes.

Not for the first time, she wonders why they couldn't have windows here in the sanctuary. Surely God's natural light would be so much better? But Dad says Mr. McKinney vetoed colored glass as too costly, and clear glass would rob them of their privacy.

"I don't think we're likely to have peeping Toms," one of the deacons said when they were first shown the blueprints for their newly founded church, but Mr. McKinney reminded them of the Biblical injunction to pray in secret, "And thy Father, who seeth in secret, shall reward thee openly."

"Besides," said another, "without windows, it'll be cheaper to build and more economical to heat and cool."

All of this her father reported with approval. When their old church split down the middle because the more worldly members wanted to spend the Lord's money on new carpets and pew cushions, Mr. McKinney announced his intentions of building a plain church out of his own money, a church where God would be worshipped in deeds and sacrifice, not with creature comforts and ornamentation. Her dad's favorite saying is "Look after the pennies and the dollars will look after themselves," and he likes it that Mr. McKinney feels the same way.

Her mom is less impressed. She has heard that Mrs. McKinney comes from money and that it is actually her inheritance that built the church even though Mr. McKinney has never said so.

From her seat at the piano, the girl can look out over the congregation while appearing to pay strict attention to the sermon. Last Sunday the pews were filled with dark colors and heavier fabrics. Today the girls and women wear colorful spring dresses and she feels pretty in her own sky-blue dress.

And there is Mrs. McKinney, seated on the front pew, looking almost pretty herself in a neat navy blue suit. The suit itself is old, but her high-necked white blouse is edged in crisp white lace and looks new. Her long brown hair is brushed straight back from her face and held at the nape of her neck with a matching navy blue ribbon. No lipstick, of course. Mr. McKinney does not approve of makeup, though several of the women shrug their shoulders at that and her own parents let her wear lipstick as long as she stays with pastel shades.

Idly, she wonders what it would be like to marry a preacher and always know the right thing to do. Probably nothing like marriage to the tall handsome boy who makes her feel confused and stupid whenever she goes into the barbecue house where he waits tables in the evenings. Not that she is allowed to date yet and not that her parents would let her date one of the Knott boys anyhow. They want someone safe and reliable and average for her.

Mr. McKinney is average — average height and average weight, although he is beginning to get a little potbelly and the shadow of a double chin. He has more hair than a lot of men his age and he is not particularly handsome, but his deep-set blue eyes seem to look from his soul straight into hers and his voice has the range of an organ. That voice can reduce a sinner to tears, it can stir the righteous to anger over society's moral lapses, it can soothe and comfort the afflicted.

As if reading her thoughts, the preacher's voice changes and she realizes that he is not winding down after all. Instead, his voice introduces a new subject and he goes from talking about Jesus's sacrifice and resurrection to the Easter lilies massed around the pulpit, which he compares to the colorful new clothes that bloom on the women today.

The lilies are here to celebrate the rebirth of Christ, he tells them. Pure, white, and chaste. Then, in a voice that holds more sorrow than accusation, he asks the women to examine their hearts. Do they wear their new spring clothes to honor Christ or is it from sinful pride? A desire to put themselves forward?

"Remember the words of Paul." After taking a sip of water, Mr. McKinney turns the pages of the large Bible in front of him and begins to read from Timothy II, " 'Let women adorn themselves in modest apparel with Godly fear.' "

All around the sanctuary, the feminine eyes that had been fixed on the preacher begin to drop. Even the pianist feels a pang of guilt because yes, when she looked at herself in the mirror this morning and was pleased by her reflection, there had been no praise for Jesus in her heart, only sinful pride at her trim waist and the way the dress fit smoothly over her small breasts. Stricken, she looks at her mother, seated near the back in a new pale green suit-dress. She has not lowered her eyes, but continues to look back at the preacher without shame and

13

with nothing but attentive interest on her face.

" 'Let the woman learn in silence with all subjugation,' sayeth Paul. Silence not only of the tongue, but of the body as well, not calling attention to one's dress. 'For Adam was first formed, then Eve. And Adam was not deceived, but the woman, being deceived, was in transgression.' Dear sisters and daughters in Christ, I cannot look into your hearts today and know the transgressions there. Only you and your Lord can say if you dressed with pride or to honor the risen Lord Jesus. I can only repeat the words of Joshua: 'As for me and my house, we shall serve the Lord.' "

He pauses to take another sip of water. "Paul says, 'If a man knows not how to rule his own house, how shall he take care of the church of God?' My own wife knows my thoughts on this matter and dresses appropriately. Proverbs 31. 'Who can find a virtuous woman? Her price is far above rubies.' "

Several eyes turn toward Mrs. McKinney, whose head is bowed now, her face red with embarrassment at being praised and made the center of their attention.

"As a child obeys its father, so does a virtuous wife obey her husband. Whatsoever

14

I ask of her, she will do, whether or not she sees the wisdom of it. Why I could spit in this glass of water and ask her to drink it and she would obey."

Then, to the teenage pianist's horror, the preacher spits into the water and holds the glass out to his wife. "Come, Marian."

From her seat on the piano bench, the girl sees Mrs. McKinney's eyes widen. There is a stricken look on her plain face and she shakes her head in bewilderment as if she cannot understand his words.

"Marian?"

Tears well up in the woman's eyes when she realizes that he is serious. "Please, husband, no," she whispers. "Don't make me do this."

Implacably, he continues to hold out the glass. "A husband does not *make* his wife do anything," he says. "He lets his wishes be known and she submits graciously of her own free will as God has commanded."

The congregation sits in utter silence, holding its breath.

Slowly, Marian McKinney comes to her feet. Tears stream down her cheeks and her face crumples with the effort not to break into sobs. Each step to the altar seems an effort of will. At last, she takes the glass and raises it to her lips, and the girl sees her gag. Then, with eyes clenched tightly shut, she forces herself to drink.

As she stumbles back to her place on the front pew, Mr. McKinney beams. "This is my beloved wife in whom I am well pleased. Let us pray."

His words roll out over the congregation and in their name, he thanks the Lord for the gift of blood that cleanses whiter than snow and for the promise of eternal life to those who love Him and honor Him and keep His commandments.

When everyone stands for the singing of the final hymn, the pianist suddenly realizes that her mother is no longer in the church.

Chapter 1

. . . this is life, and there is no theory for it . . .
— *Fiddledeedee,* by Shelby Stephenson

Nine days later

Tuesday morning's light mist lay over the field of young tobacco. It softened the air and turned the tall pines beyond into gray shadows of themselves. The recently turned earth gave off an honest aroma that was sweet to the old man who stood motionless to take it all in. Another year, another spring. Here in late April, the plants were only knee-high with no hint of the pink blossoms to come, their leaves still small and crisp and deep green. Everything fresh and young.

Everything but me, the old man told himself.

One of two dogs beside him nudged his hand with a muzzle that had, in the past

17

year, become almost as white as his master's hair. The man looked down with a rueful smile. "Yeah and you, too, poor ol' Blue."

He scratched the dog's soft-as-velvet ears, then the three of them ambled slowly on down the lane that circled the perimeter of this field. Cool early mornings used to mean the beginning of another day of hard sweaty work — fields to plow, animals to tend, the hundred and one backbreaking chores that make up a farmer's daily life.

Back at the house, Sue and Essie would be fixing breakfast, rousting the boys out of bed, asking the older ones to fill the woodbox and feed the chickens, sending the younger ones off to school . . .

The whole farm would buzz with meaningful work and raucous laughter.

He almost never thought about his first wife, but Annie Ruth had always liked mornings best, too. More times than he could count, she would be up before him. She scorned mirrors and plaited her hair by touch alone into a long thick braid as she looked out their window to watch the first light define the trees and fields beyond.

"Time to get moving," she would say briskly if he lay in bed too long to watch her.

Now his house was silent and empty every

morning until Maidie came over to make breakfast; and even though he only piddled at working this past year or two, he still felt driven to walk the back lanes each day, to see his fields and woods as fresh and new as the dawn of creation, to make sure that everything was well within the borders of his land. Annie Ruth had usually been too busy to come walking, but Sue used to say, "Now don't you look all the pretty off the morning till I can come, too," and she would often slip away from the demands of the boys and the house to join him out here.

Together they would pause to enjoy the dogwoods that bloomed among the tall pines, to smell the sweet scent of wild crab apples on the ditchbanks or note that the corn could use a little side-dressing of soda to green it up. Away from the house and the boys, they could talk about the larger issues in their life together, the needs of someone in their extended families, or the help they might could give the proud man who was having a hard time of it. They could discuss what to do about Andrew or Frank and whether a good talking-to would be enough to keep those two out of trouble or if it was going to take a trip to the woodshed to get the point across.

Yet they had all turned out well, he

thought, as he ran their faces through his mind, taking stock of his sons as he took stock of his land. The Navy had straightened Frank out; and Sue's patience and April's love had straightened Andrew. There were problems with some of the grandchildren, but they would come out right in the end, too. Of this he had no doubt.

A few feet ahead of him, the younger dog suddenly went on alert. He followed the direction of her point and saw a doe emerge from the woods at the far edge of the field. Behind her two young fawns hesitated, half hidden by the grapevines that hung down from the trees. Ladybelle gave an almost inaudible whine and Blue strained to see what had alerted her. Both of them looked back at him, but he gave the hand signal to stay and they obeyed. Nevertheless, the doe had caught his slight movement and she and the fawns melted back into the trees.

As the sun rose behind the pines and began to burn off the mist, he heard the sound of a motor and turned to see a small black truck slowly easing through the sandy ruts. He stood quietly until the truck pulled even with him and the driver cut its engine. The white man behind the wheel appeared to be in his mid-thirties and wore a gray work shirt with the name ENNIS embroidered in red on the breast pocket. His short brown hair had thinned across the crown but he had not yet begun to go gray.

"Sorry to bother you, Mr. Kezzie, but Miz Holt said you were out here and might not mind."

"Not a bit," Kezzie Knott said politely and waited for the man to identify himself.

"You probably don't remember me, but I'm James Ennis, Frances Pritchard's grandson."

The Pritchard land touched some that he owned over in the next township and Kezzie nodded at that familiar name. "You must be one of Mary's boys."

"Yessir." The younger man got out of the truck and extended his hand.

"What can I do for you, son?"

"It's about my grandmother, Mr. Kezzie. She's about to give away more of our land. Grandy might've left it in her name, but you know good as me he wanted her to pass it on down to my mother. It's been in our family over two hundred years and yeah, nobody wants to farm it any more, but it don't seem right for her to let somebody have for free what the whole family's sweated and bled for all these years. She says she's giving it back to the Lord, but it's not the Lord's name that's gonna be on that deed."

Kezzie Knott lit a cigarette from the hard pack that was always in his shirt pocket and leaned against the truck to listen to a story whose outline had become all too familiar in the past few years. Land you could hardly give away thirty years ago was now so dear that the income it brought in barely paid the rising taxes. The details might be different but the results were often the same — old folks talked out of their land for peanuts on the dollar value while some slick developer made a bundle. The only difference here was that the slick operator was a preacher and not a developer.

"She's always talked about you with respect, Mr. Kezzie. I was thinking that maybe if you could speak to her? It's not just for me and mine neither, but you remember Nancy, Mama's only sister?"

Kezzie Knott nodded. Frances Pritchard's older daughter must be close to sixty now and still had the mind of a sweet-natured three-year-old.

"He's promised Granny he'll take care of Nancy till she dies but you know how much a promise is worth."

"No more'n the air it's written on," the old man agreed. "Now I can't make you no promises myself, son, but I'll look into it for you and see what I can do."

If nothing else, he thought, there was someone in the deeds office that he might could get to lose the papers and snarl up the transaction with red tape for a few weeks.

Mid-afternoon and Cameron Bradshaw firmed the dirt around the last of the purple petunias, then sat back on his padded kneeling stool to admire his handiwork.

It might not be the English gardens he remembered from the tours he had taken with his grandparents before they lost their money, nor the showpiece he had tended before he and Candace split up; nevertheless, its beauty pleased him.

"A poor thing, but mine own," he murmured to himself. He pushed himself up off the stool, straightened his protesting joints, and tried again to remember who it was that said, "What every gardener needs is a cast-iron back with a hinge in it."

The sun was not quite over the yardarm, but he decided he would pour himself a drink, locate his *Bartlett's,* and bring them both out here to the terrace. Nail down that quote once and for all.

He knew from happy experience that one

quotation would lead to another, yet what better way to spend an April afternoon than to sit here in his garden and sip good scotch, to turn the pages at random and let his mind wander through the words of history's great thinkers?

He crossed the flagstone terrace and paused to savor again the beauty of purple petunias, red geraniums, and silver-gray dusty miller. More geraniums and petunias trailed from hanging baskets. White Lady Banks roses were beginning to bud amid the purple wisteria blossoms that hung like clusters of grapes from the trellis that shaded his back door, and terra-cotta tubs of shasta daisies, basil, and dill stood on either side of the gate that opened onto a passageway to the street.

To his dismay, he heard the clip-clop of backless sandals hurrying up that same passageway.

He reached for the doorknob and wondered if there was time to get inside and pretend not to be at home.

As he suspected, it was Deanna.

Other men bragged about their children, he thought wearily — how bright they were, how industrious, how motivated to succeed, how thoughtful of their parents.

He had Dee.

Twenty-two years old. Bright? Yes. But motivated? Thoughtful of her parents?

Ha!

Yet, as he stood motionless under the wisteria vines that grew over the small trellis above his door and watched his daughter fumble with the gate latch, he could not suppress the enduring wonder that he and Candace had produced such beauty.

Today she was dressed in white clam-diggers that sat low on her slender hips, a bright green shirt, gold loop earrings, and gold sandals. He gloomily noted that she had a black duffle bag slung over one shoulder.

Small-boned and deceptively delicate-looking, Dee had the wide deep-set eyes of his family. Their intense green came from her mother, though, as did her long reddish-brown hair. From the genetic pool, she had drawn his thin Bradshaw nose and strong chin. The dimple in her right cheek had skipped a generation and came straight from his late mother-in-law, one of those trashy Seymours from east of Dobbs.

Or so he had been told by white-haired colleagues who sometimes, when in their cups, waxed nostalgic about that dimple and, behind his back, wondered aloud if they had sired his wife.

He himself could not put a face to Candace's mother. Before they lost their money, the Bradshaws had sent their children to private schools, so he had no direct memory of Alice Seymour Wells or her husband, Macon, even though the three of them were native to the county and must have been about the same age.

As the gate finally clicked open, Dee spotted him in the shaded doorway.

"Mom's kicked me out again," she said, her full red lips poked out in a childish pout. She dropped her duffle bag onto the white iron patio table, where her father had planned to spend a peaceful afternoon. "Like it's my fault George puked on her fuckin' couch."

"You let him in the house?" asked Bradshaw, who still winced at the crudities young women so carelessly voiced today. "I thought she told you to quit seeing him."

"And I told *her* I'll see whoever I damn well please."

"Then she said, 'Not in *my* house you won't,' right?"

"Been there, done that, haven't you, Dad?"

"When are you going to quit yanking her chain, honey? If you're really going to drop out of college this near graduation, then

26

don't just threaten to get a job. Do it. Stand on your own two feet."

"Like you do? Taking an allowance from her every month?"

His thin lips tightened. "It's not an allowance, Dee. And it comes out of the company, not from your mother."

"A company you started long before you met her."

"A company I still own," he reminded her. "And one that she helped build up to what it is today."

"So what? She couldn't have gotten her foot in half those doors without the Bradshaw name. And then you just gave it all to her and walked away."

It was an old complaint and one he was tired of hearing, especially since it was not strictly true. Yes, he had handed control of the company over to Candace when they separated, but it was with the stipulation that he would receive a certain percentage of the profits in perpetuity.

"I was ready to retire and it's an equitable arrangement." He brushed away a spent blossom that had dropped onto his white hair from the wisteria vine above his head.

"You sure?"

"What do you mean?"

"She could be cooking the books, couldn't she?"

"Not with my accountant going over them twice a year."

"And how do you know she's not screwing him twice a year just to screw you?"

In spite of her language, Cameron Bradshaw was amused to picture nerdy little Roger Flackman in bed with Candace. She would eat him alive. On the other hand, that last check had been smaller than usual. He had put it down to her preoccupation with her new position on the board of commissioners, but what if she and Roger really were — ?

"So anyhow," said Dee, interrupting his thoughts as she picked up her duffle bag, "can I crash with you for a few days till Mom gets over being mad about the damn couch?"

"Only if you start looking for a job," he said firmly.

"Believe it or not, I think I've already found one," his daughter said.

Some forty-odd miles away, in Durham, Victor Talbert, VP of Talbert Pharmaceuticals, opened the door of the boardroom not really expecting to see anything except the long polished table and a dozen empty chairs. Instead, he found his father poring over a sheaf of surveyor's maps spread across the table.

"There you are," he said. "I've been looking all over for you. What's that? Plans for the new plant in China?"

"Hardly," his father said.

At fifty-five, Grayson Hooks Talbert wore his years lightly. His dark hair was going classically gray at the temples, his five-eleven frame carried no extra pounds, and his charcoal-gray spring suit fit nicely without calling too much attention to its perfect tailoring.

He started to order his son away from the maps. Victor might be curious, but he would obey. Unlike his older son, who would have looked, sneered, and promptly forgotten, assuming he was sober enough to bring the print into focus in the first place. A grasshopper and an ant. That's what he had for sons. One clever and inventive, but mercurial and dedicated to hedonistic self-destruction. The other a dutiful plodder who ran the New York office. Reliable and utterly trustworthy and totally incapable of the flights of imagination and ambition that had built this company into one of the state's major players and its president into a power broker who had the ear of senators and governors.

Victor Talbert looked at the identifying labels and frowned. "Colleton County?"

His father nodded.

"Our subsidiaries are screaming for a decision about our eastern markets and you keep coming back to this? Why, Dad? I thought you were finished out there. You made your point with that bootlegger when you built Grayson Village. You've got a good manager in place and it's peanuts anyhow. Why keep bothering with it? There's nothing for us out there."

"You think not?" Talbert said. He rolled up the maps, gave his son explicit instructions about the subsidiaries, and said, "You going back to New York tonight?"

Victor nodded. "We have tickets to a play. Unless there's something else you want me to stay for?"

"No, I'll be up next week."

They walked down to his office together and once Victor was gone, Talbert told his assistant to order him a car and driver. "And tell him we'll be spending the night at the Grayson Village Inn."

From the windows of her corner office on the second floor of Adams Advertising, where she was a fully invested partner,

30

Jamie Jacobson could look out across Main Street and see the courthouse square, where pansies blossomed extravagantly in the planters on either side of the wide low steps that led down to the sidewalk.

Another perfect spring day and this was the closest she had come to enjoying it since arriving at the office early that morning. Her own pansies needed attention and she had hoped to take off an hour in midday to enjoy the task. Instead, she had eaten a sandwich at her desk and tried to keep her mind focused on work.

A slender woman with sandy blond hair that had begun to sprout a few gray hairs now that she had passed forty, Jamie glanced at her watch and sighed. Five o'clock already and it would take at least another three hours to finish the presentation needed for a client first thing tomorrow morning.

She would have to skip supper and for a moment she considered skipping tonight's board meeting as well. As one of only two Democrats on Colleton County's board of commissioners, she wondered why she kept bothering. Unfortunately, a vote on the planning board's recommendations for slowing growth was scheduled for tonight and she could not pass up one last attempt to accept it, even though she knew Candace

Bradshaw would use every trick in her bottomless bag to vote it down.

Much as Jamie Jacobson hated to admit it, the county's power brokers had planned well when they picked the newest chair of the board. Candace Bradshaw was as cute as a puppy and just as tail-waggingly eager to please the men who had put her in office and who now profited from the five-to-two decisions the board usually made under her chairmanship. A giggling, cuddly woman, she loved being chair. As long as the men pretended she held real power, she would do everything she could to make them happy, and if they wanted a controversial measure passed, she could be as tenacious as a little pit bull on their behalf.

For over three hundred years, Colleton County farmers had wrested a modest living from its mellow soil. Now economists predicted that in another thirty years, the farms might all be gone, bulldozed under and covered with houses and big-box chain stores as farmers took the quick and easy money. Housing bubbles might be bursting all over the rest of the country, but the red-hot market here showed few signs of cooling.

With its temperate climate, low unemployment rate, and even lower taxes, North

Carolina was regularly touted as one of the country's most liveable places and people were streaming in from the old rust belt states. They moved into the cheaply built houses before the paint was dry and immediately looked around for a nearby strip mall and an all-night pizzeria. Happily for the newcomers, local entrepreneurs were right there to service their needs with almost no interference from the local planning boards. Most of the commissioners believed wholeheartedly in laissez-faire, and why not? Most of them were connected either directly or indirectly to the building trades and much of the new money flowed straight into their pockets.

As a battered old red Chevy pickup parked in front of the courthouse, Jamie sighed again and turned away from the window. Tonight's meeting would probably be another exercise in futility, a big waste of time; but for the sake of the people who had voted for her, she would be there even if it meant coming back to the office afterward. Maybe after the presentation tomorrow she could take the afternoon off to smell the flowers in her own garden.

Candace Bradshaw's house was so recently built and furnished that carpets, drapes, and sofas still had that new-car smell. Although it was one of the more modest models in this upscale development — only three bedrooms with two and a half baths — the master bathroom had been designed to her specifications.

To reach it, one walked through a hallway lined on both sides with closets that had sliding mirrored doors. More mirrors paneled all the bathroom walls, including the walls of the walk-in shower. They even fronted the cabinets. The only touches of color were the pink-flowered sink, the dark rose commode, and the matching floor tiles.

And Candace Bradshaw herself, of course, wrapped in a rose bath sheet.

She turned on the shower, dropped the towel to the floor, and smiled at the multiple images of her naked body. Overall, she was entitled to that smile. Poverty and hard work had kept the pounds off when she was a girl; rigorous dieting and three miles a day on her treadmill kept them off as she approached her forty-second birthday. Yes, she saw the slight drooping of her full breasts, and yes, her waist was a bit thicker than on the day she traded her cherry for a gold bracelet to a dirtbag who went off to Duke and came back with his nose in the air, till she won a seat on the board of commissioners and he needed some favors.

Well, that cost him more than a gold bracelet, a bracelet that was long gone anyhow, stolen by her own pa and hocked for a gallon of Kezzie Knott's white lightning, and how Deborah Knott ever got appointed to be a judge by a Republican governor with a bootlegging Democrat for a father she would never understand. Bound to be some dirt there somewhere, Candace thought for the hundredth time, and one of these days she was going to pick up a shovel and start digging. They still had the cleaning contract for Lee and Stephenson, Deborah Knott's old law firm, and —

A small bruise on her thigh distracted Candace Bradshaw's attention. Now how did she get that? she wondered as she went back to evaluating her body. Her legs had always been too short in proportion to the rest of her body and she used to envy girls with longer legs until it dawned on her that men of power were often short and short men did not take kindly to women who towered over them. Much better to be small and cuddly. Besides, her short thighs were fairly free of cellulite and her calves were still shapely, her ankles still trim. She had been good to her body, and in turn her body had been good to her.

Very good to her.

It had given her a free and clear title to this house. It had helped make her a power in her own right. It would help her take care of that bastard who —

Her head turned alertly. Was that the sound of a door latch?

She quickly stooped for the towel and covered herself even though she was supposed to be alone in the house.

"Deanna?" she called. She had taken Dee's house key, but locked doors and drawers had never stopped her daughter. Slowed her down, maybe, but never stopped her. Exasperation tinged her voice. "Is that you?"

Silence.

She walked past the mirrored closets, through her bedroom and out into the hall.

"Dee?"

No answer and a quick look through a front window did not show Dee's car parked on the circular drive outside.

She shrugged and returned to the bathroom. Hot water from three shower heads had begun to steam up the mirrors. She stepped into the stall, lifted her oval face to the needle-fine spray like a sunflower lifting to the sun, and sighed with happiness as water sluiced down her body, pulsating to the rhythm of her heartbeats.

This was her favorite place in the house and it was not unusual for her to shower twice a day. In periods of stress, three times.

Thank God there aren't any calories in water, she thought.

She could win the lottery tomorrow, the party could nominate her to run for governor, and nothing — *nothing!* — would give her the same satisfaction as knowing she could have hot water at the turn of a tap, day or night.

Growing up in a dilapidated trailer with a broken water heater that was never replaced, the only way to get hot water was if she heated it on the kitchen stove. Even then, she would often come back with a final kettle to find her mother sitting in the chipped and rust-stained bathtub she had so laboriously filled. "Well, hell, Miss Prissypants. What's your problem? When I was your age, the only thing we had was an old tin washtub and five or six of us would have to use the same water. It'd be pure black by the time it was my turn. You're lucky you got a tub big enough to wallow around in, sugar Candy, and it ain't like I'm all that dirty or gonna pee in the water like my brothers did."

For a moment, she almost wished her

parents could see her now. That she could show them how far she had come on her own with no help from them. Admittedly, it was only a fleeting wish. The happiest day of her life was when word came that Macon and Alice Wells had died in a fiery car crash, and she was suddenly free to reinvent herself, to legally change her name to Candace and call herself that instead of the Candy on her birth certificate. Not that she could ever pretend that she came from something more than the trashiest trailer park in Colleton County. The communal memory was too long to forget that her mother was a whore and her father a shiftless drunk. All the same, their ashes were now scattered to the four winds and they could never again embarrass her by showing up at her work or by calling her to come bail them out of jail.

She reached for the bar of soap.

Cake of soap, not bar, she reminded herself as she lathered her body in rose-scented suds. Handmade from organic goat milk. And what would Ma have made of paying five dollars for goat soap?

Or twenty dollars for a bottle of herbal shampoo?

She rinsed her hair, worked a handful of fragrant conditioner into each long chestnut tress that was artfully streaked with gold every five weeks at the best hairdresser in Dobbs, then rinsed again. Even when every trace of soap, shampoo, and conditioner was gone, she continued to stand under the pulsing water. She cupped her hands beneath her breasts and lifted them up to the water till the nipples hardened. It was as if they were caressed by a lover's gentle hands, an undemanding lover whose only desire was to pleasure her and not himself. Unlike the brutish pawings she had endured to get where she was today, each pulse was a soft pat that calmed her nerves and suffused her senses with a feeling of well-being.

At last, she reluctantly turned off the taps and toweled her body and hair dry. She smoothed scented lotion on her skin; and when she had finished making up her face, she styled her hair with a hand dryer and a brush until it hung sleek and shining halfway down her back.

It vaguely worried her that women were advised to cut their hair shorter as they grew older, but she figured she had at least another six or eight years before she had to make that decision. Men liked long sexy hair and salesclerks still thought that she and Dee were sisters. Indeed, someone had recently taken a quick look at Dee's hung-over pasty face and baggy eyes and mistakenly assumed that Dee was the mother and she the daughter.

Candace smiled at the memory of Dee's reaction to that.

Satisfied with her looks, she strolled over to the closet and pulled out a favorite spring dress. The white top was a respectable short-sleeved shirt with tiny pearl buttons and a boat collar cut low enough that when she leaned forward to share a confidential aside with one of her fellow board members, he could get a nice glimpse of cleavage. The skirt was green with white polka dots and cut on the bias so that it made a flirty flare at the hemline, a hemline so short that it added an illusion of length to her legs.

The dress made her feel flirty herself and would probably tempt old Harvey Underwood into patting her knees at the board meeting tonight.

As long as his hand stops at my knees and doesn't try to slide on up under my skirt, she thought. If it got her his vote against the planning board's recommendations, what did she care?

Let Jamie Jacobson fume and make sarcastic highfalutin remarks that half the time nobody could understand. She'd teach that long-legged bitch a few lessons about trying to take on Candace Bradshaw.

She carried the dress on into her bedroom and laid it on the bed. As she turned to a dresser for lingerie, a voice said, "Very nice, Candy."

"Don't call me Candy," she snapped as she reached for a robe to cover her nakedness. "And what the hell are you doing here?"

"I came to see you. Although I didn't expect to see quite this much of you."

"How did you get in?"

"You must have left the door unlocked."

Candace gave an unladylike snort of derision. "Not hardly likely. What do you want?"

"Nothing that's not well within your abilities."

Candace flushed, knowing this was a dig at her lack of education. Okay, so she never went to college. Big damn deal. Most of the county commissioners had degrees from State or Carolina and who was their chair? And who ran Colleton County's largest managerial service?

"What's that?" she asked as the other handed her a sheet of paper.

"What do you care? It's a little late to go reading what you're told to sign. Just copy it on your pretty notepaper, okay?"

Candace Bradshaw's eyes widened as she

read the few short sentences typed on the paper. " 'I take full responsibility for my greediness'? 'I apologize to everybody in the county who trusted me'? You're crazy if you think I'll write anything like this. Get the hell out of my house and stay out or I'll —"

Her voice broke off at the sudden appearance of a small pistol. "You wouldn't dare!"

"No?" A pull of the trigger, a soft *pfft,* and a bullet buried itself in the pile rug next to her bare feet.

Candace's eyes widened in fear. "My God! You *are* crazy."

"Not crazy enough to go to jail because you messed up."

"*Me?* You're the one who said nobody would ever find out."

"And they wouldn't have if you hadn't been so greedy that they've started noticing."

Appalled, Candace listened as the facts were laid out — the questions that were starting to be asked, the people who were doing the asking.

Her real desk and computer were in the third bedroom, which she had furnished as a home office, but a jerk of the pistol directed her over to the dainty desk where she wrote personal notes and cards.

It took only a moment or two to copy the

typescript she had been handed.

To whom it may concern:
I have used my position to enrich myself and some of my friends. I acted alone though and I take full responsibility for my greediness. I am sincerely ashamed and I apologize to everyone in Colleton County who trusted me with their well-being.

When she finished, she signed it CAN-DACE BRADSHAW with an angry flourish. "There! Satisfied?"

"Not quite. Not till it's safely locked away."

"I'll tell them you made me write it," she spat out.

"Won't matter. It'll be your word against mine, Candy."

"Don't call me Candy. And put down my robe!"

"Relax, *Candace.* I could ask you to give me your word that you wouldn't call Sheriff Poole and have me arrested before I can put your copy in a safe place and destroy the original, but we both know how much your word's worth. I think I'd rather tie you up for a while, give you time to think things over and realize that anything you say about

43

me will only make people believe it was all your doing."

With that pistol aimed at her chest, Candace stood up as instructed and draped the second robe over her shoulders backward so that her arms were pinned to her sides and held almost immobile when the sash and the empty sleeves were tied in back.

All the while, her mind was racing furiously, weighing her options. The sash wasn't too tight and there was a little slack inside the second robe. It wouldn't be too hard to wriggle free. And then? If things really were coming unraveled, there had to be a way out of this mess. She'd call Cam. He'd help her find a way to throw all the blame on —

Abruptly, something looped her throat. There was a sudden tightening, a constriction that left her unable to breathe. Frantically, she struggled to jerk away, but the pressure increased inexorably.

No way to use her arms or hands to yank it away from her neck. In fear and rage, she sank to her knees and butted backward with her head, her body arching and twisting to free herself, to take one deep lifesaving breath. A quick lunge forward and she felt the cord loosen. For one second, she could almost breathe again.

Oh please oh please oh please —

And then the pressure was back. A frantic twist and something tore in her throat. Searing pain lanced across her dying brain and sparked a last incoherent thought of water . . . her healing shower . . . hot water . . .

CHAPTER 2

All the big apple orchards are gone.
. . . peach trees, old horse apples
that came from Civil War days.
I remember the Indian and Clear-seed
    peach . . .
All that, gone.

       — *Middle Creek Poems,*
        by Shelby Stephenson

Tuesday night

"You ain't never gonna get a man to vote against his pocketbook, Deb'rah," Daddy said, waving a hard roll at me to make his point. "And right now, every one of them commissioners 'cepting maybe Abe Jacobson's granddaughter is either in the building trade or got real close ties to somebody that's making a bunch of money offen the new folks. So lessen you plan to quit being a judge and run for commissioner yourself, you can just suck it up."

46

"I don't want to suck it up," I said petulantly as I dipped a piece of my own roll into the dish of olive oil on the table between us. "I just want them to start thinking about the people of Colleton County. *All* the people, not just the ones that pay for their political posters and campaign ads."

"Oh, I reckon them people's paying for a lot more than that," he said cynically as he waited for our server to bring him some butter.

After finishing up a court session that ran late, I had stayed on in Dobbs to catch up on my paperwork until it was time to meet some of the family for supper. It had surprised me to get to the restaurant and find Daddy there. He doesn't drive at night much any more and I hadn't realized he was coming.

Ferguson's is a little pricy, but their steaks are dry-aged and supposedly hormone-free. Here on a Tuesday night, it wasn't very busy and the waiter had already been around once to refill our tea glasses.

"Anyhow," said Daddy, "when did you start thinking county commissioners oughta be different from any other politicians?"

"Ever since I heard they're letting Nutri-Good build a store at Pleasant's Crossroads."

47

I have nothing against the NutriGood grocery chain, per se. I may not preach the gospel of whole grains and free-range chickens like a born-again health nut, but I do like them; and whenever I'm in Raleigh, I swing past the NutriGood to pick up store-baked bread and organic vegetables that aren't yet ripe in our garden. Hell, I even bring my own reusable cloth tote bags so I won't have to decide whether it's paper or plastic that's going to wind up in our county landfill.

A chain store in Raleigh's one thing, and I can grit my teeth and live with the sprawling commercial mess around the interstate exits several miles to the east of me. But an upscale town store to anchor a strip mall at Pleasant's Crossroads? Only three short miles from my own house? That's a whole 'nother can of something, and no, I'm not talking organic worms.

Pleasant's Crossroads is the intersection of two back country roads that used to go nowhere. Nothing was there except scrubby woods, tobacco fields, and a couple of dilapidated clapboard buildings on diagonal corners facing each other across the two-lane hardtop. One building was a little general store and single-pump service station that old Max Pleasant owned back when my daddy was running white lightning all up and down the coast and needed a safe source of sugar. It's been closed for years. Daddy's name was never on the deed to that store, but everyone knew who bankrolled it and who paid the bills. The other was a barbershop run by one of Max's Yadkin cousins. That's where Daddy and those of my eleven brothers who live out this way used to get their hair cut every four or five weeks until Baldy Yadkin abruptly hung up his scissors, sold out to a commercial builder, and bought himself a place on the Pamlico Sound, where he can fish and crab three hundred days a year.

Bulldozers had already torn out and removed Max's old gas and kerosene tanks and thrown up a berm around that corner so as to provide privacy for a secluded high-end "village" developed and owned by G. Hooks Talbert, one of the movers and shakers in the state's Republican party and a descendant of the original Pleasant who held a land grant from the Lords Proprietor. Talbert's older son used to run a wholesale nursery out there on the other side of Possum Creek from us. In fact, that nursery was responsible for my becoming a district court judge five years ago.

It's a long story, but all you need to know

is that it gave Daddy the opportunity to pressure G. Hooks —

"Pressure?" asked the preacher who lurks at the edge of my consciousness and tries to keep me honest.

"I believe the word you're looking for is blackmail," said the pragmatist who usually approves of euphemisms.

Okay, okay. Technically speaking, that nursery gave Daddy the ammunition to *blackmail* G. Hooks Talbert into asking the governor to appoint me after I lost my first race. Until then, Talbert was famous in our family for saying he didn't care to deal with any ignorant bootlegger. Nobody's heard him say that recently and now it's gotten personal.

To even the score, and knowing how it would gall Daddy to have any kind of a development — even an upscale one — so close to his borders, G. Hooks quietly bought up all the land on the south side of Possum Creek and, even more quietly, got the county commissioners to rubber-stamp his plans to build creekside houses and a tiny village centered around a café and a gift shop that stocked designer jewelry and local pottery. The first thing he did was dredge out a lake on a bend of the creek and put up a picturesque country inn with a gourmet restaurant suitable for formal weddings.

Unfortunately for him, he underestimated the Kezzie Knott grapevine. Someone at the register of deeds office had given Daddy a heads-up before the ink was dry on the first property transfers. Daddy waited until the inn was finished and the lake was already stocked with bass and perch before it was brought to G. Hooks's attention that our line ran along the south bank of the creek and not down the middle of the creek itself as was usual. Daddy could have made G. Hooks tear down his new million-dollar inn and fill the lake back in.

We've heard that several of G. Hooks's attorneys were fired after he was sent a copy of our deeds with the relevant parts highlighted in yellow.

The agreement that our family hammered out with the Talbert Corporation provided that the rest of the creek and the new lake would become a managed greenway. No houses on the creek itself. Instead, there would be hiking trails and bicycle paths on both sides. We don't have to look at the Mc-Mansions that are still going up, and in return, we allow hikers and picnickers on our side of the creek, which, according to Talbert's site manager, is proving to be a big plus in the eyes of potential buyers who have moved to the country because they want to see a little country.

Except for the extra cars that the new village has added to our roads, it's been a good enough compromise, although I suspect G. Hooks is still smarting from being one-upped by an ex-bootlegger. Sequestered behind berms and fast-growing evergreen firs and hollies, there were no visual eyesores to blight the landscape.

Until now. Now a big gaudy sign proudly announces the imminent arrival of our very own NutriGood grocery store. Soon that little homemade barbershop will be swept away as if it never existed.

As if four generations of Colleton County farmers hadn't swapped tall tales and bragged about how many pounds of tobacco or how many bales of cotton their land was going to produce that year.

As if little boys who are now grandfathers hadn't scrunched down on the wooden bench beneath the dangling bare lightbulb to listen while their elders waxed eloquent about the love and loss of a good woman or a good car or a good hound that treed his last possum more than fifty years ago.

It's not that I didn't know how financial magazines regularly rate us as one of the best places to live. But it wasn't till I saw the bulldozers scraping that corner clean that it finally hit home for me that our whole way of life is under attack. Let an ant find one tasty crumb and soon your whole kitchen counter is aswarm with them. People who live in the county's small towns or inside Raleigh's Beltline don't have a clue about the changes out here in the country, of the things we're losing.

Two years ago, tobacco and corn grew behind that little shop. Pine trees have encroached along the back edges where dogwoods and redbuds bloom. The new strip of brick buildings will include a bath and beauty store, a Thai restaurant, a dry cleaner, and God knows what else. The parking lot will hold three hundred cars. Nothing's been said about limiting the light pollution that will wash the rest of the Milky Way out of our night skies. Nothing about requiring trees to shade that much asphalt and help with the runoff that will surely work its way into the creek that meanders through my family's land.

Even though it's downstream from us, we still care. Years ago, my brothers quit farming right up to the edge of the creek and built dikes across the fields so as to prevent fertilizers and pesticides from washing into it. They don't go around hugging trees, but they try to be good stewards of the land and they know that we're all interconnected — not that any of them would put it that way. But Possum Creek flows into the Neuse and the Neuse flows into Core Sound, which used to have the best scallops and oysters my brothers ever tasted. They can remember standing waist-deep in the gentle waters off Harkers Island, feeling for scallops with their bare feet. The big twins can get downright lyrical remembering their salty sweetness.

"We'd scoop one up and wait for it to peep open," says Haywood. "Soon as we saw that ring of shiny blue eyes, we'd slide in a clamshell, twist it open, and eat it raw right there."

"That was good eating, won't it?" Herman always says.

"Real good," Haywood says with a sigh for what's been lost. "Real good."

The Neuse was recently declared one of the most polluted rivers in the country.

I felt a hand on my shoulder and looked up to see Seth smiling down at me. He's five brothers up from me, but there's always been a special bond between us.

"Y'all order yet?" his wife, Minnie, asked.

"I'm hungry enough to eat a cow. Or at least the flank of one that's walked past the fire."

She leaned over to kiss Daddy's leathery cheek and took the chair next to mine.

"Any of the others coming to the meeting?" I asked Minnie, meaning those of my brothers and sisters-in-law who still live out on the farm.

"All of 'em." She put on her glasses and reached for a menu. "Plus some of those new people from Talbert's place. They're not exactly clear on what a stump dump is, but they're pretty sure they didn't pay close to a million dollars to live near one."

Seth grinned as he looked up from his menu. "Not after Minnie finished talking to them anyhow."

Minnie used to be president of the county's Democratic Women and she's shepherded me through both of my campaigns. Comfortably plump and fast going gray, she keeps an eye on the larger community for the family and rallies us to the cause when she thinks we're needed.

"Times like this, I really miss Linsey Thomas," she sighed.

The owner and editor of *The Dobbs Ledger* died in a hit-and-run almost a year ago, a case that remains unsolved despite the large reward posted by his loyal readers. I was still messing around with a game warden from down east then, with no thought of marrying anybody, much less Dwight Bryant, Sheriff Bo Poole's chief deputy; but I remember how long and how hard Bo's whole force worked to find the driver, only to come up dry.

Linsey Thomas was a straight-shooting liberal from a long line of liberals. His grandfather was labeled a commie during the McCarthy era. His father had advocated integration during the civil rights movement, back when the KKK was still active in the county. They burned a cross on the Thomas lawn and shot out all the windows at the *Ledger.* When Linsey took over the paper, he continued their tradition. Didn't matter if the miscreants were Republican or Democrat, the *Ledger* named names and kicked butt whenever county officials favored special interests or began to think no one cared if they bent the rules for themselves or their friends. Linsey cared and he made his readers care.

Regrettably for us, he had been a childless only child and ownership of the paper had passed to a distant cousin down in Florida, who promptly sold it to a conservative conglomerate that looks upon a community newspaper as something to wrap around advertising and two-for-one or ten-cents-off coupons.

The waiter returned with Daddy's butter and took our orders — steak for Minnie and Seth, broiled shrimp for Daddy, grilled chicken salad for me.

"Linsey would have explained exactly what a stump dump was and illustrated it with photographs from the one that caught on fire over in Johnston County," said Minnie, handing her menu to the waiter.

"He'd've printed who was asking for the permit and whether or not an impact study had been done," Seth agreed.

Daddy frowned. "Don't believe I've seen a single mention of it in the paper."

"No, and you won't," Minnie said. She broke a roll in half and shared it with Seth, who grumbled that he was with Daddy when it came to dunking your bread in olive oil instead of buttering it like God intended. "Ruby's not going to rock any boats. Long as the advertising keeps coming in, her bosses in Florida don't care that she can't put together a decent paper."

Ruby Dixon is a tall, horse-faced woman who had been a good reporter till gin got the best of her. Even falling-down drunk, she could write like an angel. Linsey had inherited her from his dad and didn't have the heart to fire her. Before his death, she'd managed to stay sober till late afternoon. After he died, she was handed the editorship and now we hear that she starts her days with a glass of liberally laced orange juice sitting on her desk. The best reporters have drifted away and the *Ledger* doesn't print much substantive news any more.

What saves her is the county's explosive growth. The paper's advertising department sells so many ads that the inserts weigh at least three times more than the eight or ten sheets of newsprint. As long as deaths, weddings, and high school ball scores are reported, and which churches are having revivals or guest gospel singers, which kids have made the honor roll, and what the school cafeterias are serving this week, most people don't seem to care that the *Ledger* no longer takes unpopular stands or tries to educate and inform. There will never be any crosses burned or windows shot out while Ruby's the editor.

"Any word around the courthouse as to how Candace Bradshaw feels about stump dumps?" Minnie asked me.

"However Danny Creedmore's told her to feel," I said cynically. "You know well as I do who pulls her strings."

Daniel Creedmore is the owner of Creedmore Concrete Corporation. He began twenty-five years ago with a single cement truck and made concrete blocks for cheap houses and migrant camps. Now he owns a fleet of trucks and Triple C probably pours at least a third of the foundations for new construction in the county.

Oh, and did I mention that he runs the Republican party in Colleton County?

As for Candace Bradshaw, who now chairs the board of commissioners, maybe if I'd been born poor and raggedy with a slut for a mother, I might have a warped view of powerful men and money, too. At fifteen she quit school, moved in with her grand-mother here in Dobbs, and went to work for Bradshaw Management and Janitorial. She cleaned apartments and scrubbed toilets for a couple of years and eventually took night classes at Colleton Community College till she earned her GED. Two months later, she married her boss and seven months after that, they were blessed with a beautiful baby girl. A real Horatio Alger story, right? With everybody living happily ever after?

Unfortunately, she couldn't help bragging to her best friend about how clever she'd been to notice that Cameron Bradshaw kept books of poetry in his office. She batted her green eyes at him, tucked a strand of her sexy long hair behind her ear, and asked his advice about a paper she had to write. One thing soon led to another, as it usually does with cute young women and naive older men. Even before the baby was born, her best friend had confided in *her* best friend and it was soon all over Dobbs that Candace deliberately got pregnant so that Cameron Bradshaw, a well-regarded businessman more than twenty years her senior, would do the honorable thing and marry her.

Bradshaw Management provides janitorial services for half the businesses in Dobbs, including my old law firm. It also manages a couple of apartment complexes and two rest homes. It took Candace a few years to learn all the ropes, but once she felt competent enough, she pushed her husband aside and took over the business after their separation. Gossip says her goal in life is to be rich and powerful and that she compensates for her lack of smarts by working hard. Gossip also says that she landed some of her biggest contracts by working hard between the sheets.

She ran for the county board of commissioners the first time I ran for judge, which is when I finally became aware of her and heard all the gossip. She won her primary. I lost mine.

Of course, her party bosses had quietly agreed on a single slate of local candidates before the primary so that she could run unopposed, while my primary was the usual free-for-all with four of us slugging it out for the same slot.

It would be hypocritical for me to sling mud at *how* she got her seat. It's what she does with it that tightens my jaws. Yes, Daddy blackmailed a crook to get me appointed, but neither he nor any of my friends or family have ever gotten a cent out of it, unlike the men who put Candace Bradshaw on the board, where she happily does their bidding with girlish giggles and much tossing of her long brown hair.

Our food came and, as we ate, talk turned to the familiar — the children, neighbors, our gardens, and whether or not Dwight and I were ever going to take a real honeymoon. I married him a few days before Christmas and his eight-year-old son had stayed on to spend the holidays with us before returning to his mother in Virginia. Three weeks later, she was murdered and Cal's been with us since January.

"Maybe when school's out," I murmured,

spearing one of Daddy's shrimp.

"You're going to take Cal with you on your honeymoon?" Minnie shook her head as the waiter refilled our tea glasses. "You and Dwight need time alone, honey. Any of us would be glad to keep him for you."

"I know," I said, "and we will. Only not just yet."

Seth looked at Daddy. "Did you and Mama Sue have a honeymoon?"

He gave a crooked smile. "With all of you young'uns? We couldn't farm y'all out to one family and Sue didn't want to split you up."

Every time I get to thinking how hard it is to be a stepmother before I was used to being a wife, I think of those eight little motherless boys: some too young to know what was going on, some shyly wanting to love their daddy's new wife, two or three of them resenting the hell out of her, and all of them as wary as ditch cats waiting to see which way to jump. How on earth did she do it?

"Did you ever tell Mother she wasn't your mother and you didn't have to mind her?" I asked Seth.

He paused with a final forkful of steak and shook his head. "I was too little to remember my own mother. She was the only mother I ever knew."

" 'Sides," growled Daddy. "Anybody sassed her would've had to answer to me. That boy of Dwight's sassing you, Deb'rah?"

"No," I said, reaching across to squeeze his calloused hand in reassurance. "Dwight wouldn't let that happen either. It's just that Cal's so quiet sometimes. I'm never sure if it's because he's missing Jonna or because he wishes I weren't in the picture."

"He probably doesn't know himself," Minnie said briskly. She waved off our waiter's offer of a third round of tea and gathered up her purse and glasses. "We'd better get going if we want to get a seat."

"No problem," I said. "Jamie Jacobson told me yesterday that they'd be meeting in the old courtroom. So many people turn out to speak for or against any of the items on their agenda these days that they haven't met in their own room since Christmas."

Daddy and Seth had their usual squabble over who was going to pay the check. I didn't bother to get into it, because Daddy always wins. I just put down the tip and waited for Seth to give it up.

CHAPTER 3

Fields brown the dozer's tread.
Wood, nails, cement, a pile of bricks —
With every hammer's fall, a cul-de-sac.
My farmboy throws up his hands. . . .
They are farming houses right up to the
　creeks.
　　　Paul's Hill, by Shelby Stephenson

I love the old courtroom where the commissioners were to meet that night. Unlike the modern ones in our glass-and-marble annex, it embodies the weight and majesty of what the law should be. This is where I took my oath of office and, yes, a setting like this makes it feel much more binding when you swear that you will judge impartially without fear or favors. Even hardened criminals seem more subdued here.

The floor is carpeted in deep red and gently slopes so that everyone can see any bit of evidence presented to the judge. The benches, doors, and jury boxes are dark solid oak. No drywall anywhere because the walls are lath and hand-troweled plaster. Plaster acanthus leaves fashioned by craftsmen long dead adorn the high vaulted ceiling. Hanging pierced brass lamps cast a soft golden glow that gives a natural solemnity. It's almost like being in church.

Tonight, however, there was nothing churchly about the indignant buzz that rose from the crowded benches. Some of it came from the people in our community who were appalled that the planning board had recommended approval of a stump dump just west of us. Others were just as upset that the planning board had also recommended a first step toward trying to slow some of the growth until the infrastructure could catch up. Limit growth? How dare they!

It took us a while to get inside and sit down. Daddy doesn't come into Dobbs all that often these days and it seemed as if every other person wanted to speak to him or shake his hand. Once we were seated, a vaguely familiar face down front caught my eye and I nudged Daddy. "Isn't that G. Hooks Talbert?"

He didn't bother to follow my eyes. "Yeah. I seen him when we come in."

"What's Talbert doing here, you reckon?"

"The stump dump probably," said Minnie. "It would affect Grayson Village, too."

The meeting was supposed to start at seven, but while three or four of the commissioners paid court to Talbert, there was no sign of Candace Bradshaw. At seven-fifteen, when she still hadn't arrived, the vice chair, Thad Hamilton, called us to order. Half a lifetime ago, Thad tried to put the moves on me after I dumped his cousin. He's porked up a bit since then, but he still looks good in a white-hair/florid-face Ted Kennedy sort of way. He first ran for the board as a Democrat, lost, changed his registration, and is now into his second term as a county commissioner. The Hamiltons were always comfortably well-off, but the family's building supply business has made so much money these past fifteen years that there's talk they're going to back him for the state assembly.

To my dismay, instead of addressing the stump dump issue first, Thad announced that they would listen to arguments for and against the planning board's second recommendation. Hands went up all around the courtroom when he asked who wanted to speak and eleven names were put on the speaker list.

"In accordance with our usual procedures, we'll limit the discussion to one hour," Thad said. "If my math is right, that means y'all each have five and a half minutes. Be warned right now though that if you try to go over that, I'll cut you off in mid-sentence, okay?"

The planning board's core recommendation was for no more than fifty houses per hundred acres, the lots to be configured however the developer wished within the minimal guidelines already set. Those fifty houses could be built on third- or quarteracre lots and the other seventy-five or eighty acres could become athletic fields or garden allotments or left natural. That was up to the builders.

Three of the speakers would probably oppose the continuation of unmanaged growth, while the rest were from the building trades and real estate industry and would no doubt argue for the county to keep hands off their honeypot.

Both sides were eloquent in their positions. The three who wanted the commissioners to put a few brakes on the runaway developments spoke of vanishing farms, the disappearance of open land, the pressures put on wildlife and wetlands, and the continual need for more multilane roads, schools, and hospitals, which would entail more and more bonds and higher taxes. They asked for impact fees and transfer taxes and adoption of the planning board's recommendation for better land use, none of which they were likely to get from this particular board.

Seven of the eight speakers for unmanaged growth shed crocodile tears for all the poor working-class people who would never be able to afford the American dream of a home of one's own in a bucolic setting if building lots had to average two acres. Crocodile tears because all seven of those speakers were either building or selling houses that sat on a quarter-acre and started at $400,000. They spoke of jobs and the larger tax base. They also spoke of a farmer's right to sell his land to whoever came along with the highest offer because "farmers don't have a 401(k) to fall back on."

"Yeah," said another. "And what if the farmer has only two acres and three kids. You gonna tell him he can't give building lots to all three of his children?"

I wanted to jump up and ask that real estate dealer to name a single Colleton County farm that consisted of only two acres, but except for some under-the-breath muttering to Minnie, I held my tongue.

They spoke of all the paychecks they were keeping right here in the county. No mention that most of the construction crews consisted of Latinos who were sending the bulk of their paychecks home to their families in Mexico and Central America. No mention that most of the high-end new homes were occupied by white-collars who worked and shopped in Raleigh.

No mention, that is, until the last speaker came to the microphone. She was a commercial developer who had moved here from Michigan and she was the most truthful person to speak for the raw hard realities of growth. She had statistics to bolster her contention that the more houses in Colleton County, the more commerce that would come.

"When we do a flyover, all we're doing is counting rooftops," she said. "Doesn't matter if those roofs are low-end starter houses or high-end mansions on two-acre lots. Every rooftop means at least three or four potential shoppers. The more growth, the more businesses you're going to have here and the bigger your tax base to pay for the roads and schools and infrastructure." She glanced at her watch and wound up her argument. "Rooftops, people. The more, the better. I was recently at a commercial trade show out in Las Vegas. When I told them I was a commercial developer in North Carolina, some of those business reps wanted to give me their cards. When I told them I was from Colleton County, they asked for my phone number. They know that this county is one of the twenty fastest-growing in the nation. You start limiting that growth and you're not going to get your Wal-Marts, your McDonald'ses, or your Targets."

The whole courtroom burst into applause and yeah, most of them were in support of her optimistic, single-minded spin on how wonderful unfettered building could be, the rest of us were hoping that such a limitation would indeed slow the invasion of chain stores.

Take that, NutriGood!

After a brief consultation among the commissioners, Thad announced that because they were missing one of their members, they would take the planning board's recommendation under advisement and table it until the next meeting. Half the audience left at that point, having made their feelings known.

Next came the application of one Chester Coburn, who owned eight landlocked acres a half-mile to the west of us. His request to turn those eight acres into a stump dump had originally been approved by the planning board, but their chair was here tonight to point out that they had not realized that his only access to that land was through a thirty-foot wide "cart path" easement and not a fifty-foot easement as required for a real road.

A stump dump is exactly what the name implies — a place where developers can rid themselves of the tree stumps that have been bulldozed up after they've clear-cut a tract of land.

Coburn argued that a wider easement wouldn't be necessary because his would be a puny little stump dump that would probably be open for only two or three years. He promised to follow all the regulations, cover the stumps with lots of dirt, and then grade the land so he could use it for something else. "I'm hoping to open a wholesale nursery and this will give me the seed money to build greenhouses," he said.

Minnie's name was first on the speaker list for this item and it didn't take her long to shoot it down. She merely reminded the commissioners of the stump dump over in neighboring Johnston County that had caught on fire by spontaneous combustion several months ago and was still smoldering despite all the efforts to put it out. "Yes, there are regulations to ensure this won't happen here. Regulations cost nothing. But do we have enough paid inspectors to make sure this stump dump would meet those regulations? Do you know how much it's cost Johnston to try to put out that fire? Do you know how much the dump's neighbors have had to endure living downwind from the smell of burning, rotting wood?"

In case they didn't, she had facts and figures.

Other neighbors spoke of the dust and noise from a steady stream of dump trucks on a narrow dirt road. Then some of the new people from Grayson Village spoke of how they hadn't moved to North Carolina to smell like New Jersey. "We don't want our neighborhood to be known as the armpit of Colleton County, okay?"

Another consultation of the commissioners, then Thad announced that Coburn's application was denied because the easement was insufficient for dump truck traffic.

When they moved on to an application to change the zoning for a lot down near Makely from agriculture/residential to commercial, we got up and left.

As we walked out to the parking lot, I

asked Daddy, "So how you like living in a place where its value's based on how many rooftops they can count?"

"Long as they keep giving us the agricultural assessment, I reckon I can stand it," he said, climbing into his red pickup.

I followed him back to the farm and when he pulled up to his back door and waved good night, I continued on down the lane past the smaller house where Maidie and Cletus Holt have lived for the past thirty or so years. Maidie keeps house for him and Cletus helps with the garden and yard work. About a half-mile farther on, the lane splits. The left one leads to Seth and Minnie's, the other to the house I now shared with Dwight and Cal and Cal's dog, Bandit, a mixed-breed terrier with a mask of dark hair across his eyes, which is how he got his name.

It was not quite nine-thirty when I let myself in and found Dwight at the dining table with a glass of beer and stacks of manila file folders spread out in front of him. Bandit came down the hallway to make sure I wasn't some stranger he needed to protect Dwight from, yawned widely, and trotted back to Cal's room, where he sleeps at Cal's feet.

"Looks serious," I said of Dwight's folders.

He gave me a weary smile. "We need at least two more patrol cars, three uniforms, and two detectives. Bo says he can only pry one car and two men out of the commissioners, so we've got to figure out how to deploy our people for maximum coverage."

"Oh, didn't you hear?" I asked with phony brightness. "All this growth gives us such a large tax base that you can probably get five cars and ten more officers in another year or two. Of course, by that time, the population will have tripled so you'll still be playing catch-up."

He leaned back in his chair and took a swallow from his half-empty glass. "Does this mean the stump dump passed?"

"Actually, it didn't," I said although I immediately began to rant about how we were nothing but a bunch of rooftops these days. "God, listen to me! I'm turning into one of those cranky old ladies who yearn for how things used to be when the world was young."

"C'mere, old lady," he said.

I took a sip of his beer and sat down on his lap. His arms went around me but our lips had barely touched when the phone rang.

Dwight sighed and let me up. "That'll be Will. I told him you'd probably be back by now."

He was right. Will's name and number were on the phone screen.

"Hey, Will," I said. "What's up?"

"How come you don't ever leave your cell phone on?" my brother complained. "What's the point of having one if you don't use it?"

"I use it," I said. "But I use it at my own convenience, not everyone else's. Did you want something or did you only call to bitch at me about my cell phone?"

Will's the oldest of my mother's four children, and like my other ten brothers, he thinks he can still boss me around.

"I was wondering if you've got some free time tomorrow?"

"My lunch hour. Why?"

"Remember Linsey Thomas?"

"Of course I remember him."

"Remember how his cousin came up last summer and took everything out of the house he wanted and sold the rest of the contents to me?"

"So?"

"So I put most of the furnishings in my big fall auction back in September, but now I'm getting around to his books and papers and I found a bunch of files in a hassock and one of them has your name on it. Mostly clippings and stuff. You want to come over to the warehouse tomorrow and pick it up?"

"Sure," I said, waiting for the real reason for his call.

"And there are some court records and stuff that maybe you could look through and tell me if I should toss them or turn them over to the historical center? Shouldn't take you more than an hour. I'll pick up some sandwiches or something."

As I hesitated, he said, "There's a file on Daddy, too. Linsey started a story about you and him three or four years ago."

"Oh?"

"Yeah, but here's what's crazy. It's like he thought you and Daddy had some sort of connection to G. Hooks Talbert before he started buying up the land for Grayson Village. Isn't that weird?"

"Very," I said.

Only three people knew about the devil's bargain Daddy had made with Talbert: me, Talbert himself, and Daddy. How the hell could Linsey Thomas have heard about it? Or was it merely his instinct for taking a closer look at things that might not be what they seemed? I remember his asking me why our governor had appointed me instead of a conservative male Democrat closer to his own political leanings. I had shrugged and made a flip answer about the governor recognizing that the best man for the job was a liberal woman.

After agreeing to meet him at his warehouse at noon, I hung up and Dwight raised a quizzical eyebrow. "What was that about?"

"Will's been going through Linsey Thomas's papers and thought I might want a file he found about me — clippings and things of public record, but maybe I'll start a scrapbook or something. Now where were we?"

He grinned and patted his knee. "You were here."

"Right," I said.

(*Ping!*)

CHAPTER 4

> . . . I was
> born in that house in the hedge, the dog-
>   yard
> outback, the mulestables, chickens run-
>   ning
> free, the hogpen homey with grunts and
> tail-twitches . . .
> — *Fiddledeedee,* by Shelby Stephenson

"Oyez, oyez, oyez!" intoned the bailiff in my courtroom next morning. "This honorable court for the County of Colleton is now open and sitting for the dispatch of its business. God save the state and this honorable court, the Honorable Judge Deborah Knott pleasant and presiding. Be seated."

He paused as if hearing his words on a playback track and looked up at me sheepishly. "I mean, Judge Deborah Knott *present* and presiding."

I laughed. "You saying I'm not pleasant,

Mr. Overby?"

"Not me, ma'am." He cast a significant eye to the side bench where three attorneys waited for their cases to be called.

Two of them had broad grins. The third, the one who was audibly snickering, was my own cousin Reid Stephenson.

"A little decorum here, gentlemen," I said with mock sternness.

Today's calendar listed the usual DWIs, the bad checks, the drunk-and-disorderlies, the shoplifters, and the brawlers. Usual to me, that is, and to the prosecutors and attorneys, and even to most of the defendants. But there are always some for whom this is a first-time event.

About ninety minutes into our morning session, Kevin Foster pulled a shuck and said, "State versus Dorothy Arnfeldt and Monica Udell. Assault and battery."

Both looked to be middle-class white women, late forties. Both were charged with assault and battery, and even though both looked embarrassed to be there, both had facial expressions that proclaimed the righteousness of whatever actions had brought them to my courtroom.

Although they were neighbors, this was clearly not kiss-and-make-up time for either of them. They sat at the defense table with their attorneys, George Francisco and my cousin Reid, between them.

"How do you plead?" I asked.

"Not guilty!" they chorused.

The older attorney placed a calming hand on Mrs. Udell's arm and rose to address me. "Your Honor, my client pleads guilty, but with extenuating circumstances."

"Thank you, Mr. Francisco," I said and looked to the prosecution's table and ADA Kevin Foster. "Call your first witness, Mr. Foster."

A uniformed patrol officer took the stand and swore to tell the truth, the whole truth, and nothing but. Referring to his notes, Officer Maynes described how he had responded to a call about a domestic disturbance on the outskirts of Cotton Grove in February in the late afternoon. Stripped of the formal officialese, he had arrived to find these two women slugging it out in the backyard of the Udell domicile. A dead and mangled chicken was being worried by a dog owned by Mrs. Arnfeldt, whose backyard butted up against that of Mrs. Udell.

"As best I could make out, Your Honor, Mrs. Udell keeps a few chickens in her backyard. Mrs. Arnfeldt said that one of them flew over the hedge that separates the two yards and her terrier got hold of it and killed it. Mrs. Arnfeldt says the dog was in his own yard and she's had trouble with Mrs. Udell's chickens scratching in her flower gardens. Mrs. Udell says the dog was not fenced and came into her yard and killed her chicken. She got the little .22 rifle she keeps to kill snakes and squirrels and was going to shoot the dog when Mrs. Arnfeldt jumped her."

"The dead chicken was in Mrs. Udell's yard?"

"Yessir."

"And the dog was in her yard, too?"

"Yessir."

"Were there any witnesses to the incident?"

"Not to my knowledge. The 911 call came from the Arnfeldt house. I believe her daughter."

On the bench in the front row, a teenage girl in torn jeans and a long-sleeved orange top that showed off her navel ring gave an involuntary nod.

"According to her statement, she saw the altercation from the window of her room on the second floor after it was already in progress."

Again the girl in the front row nodded.

"When you arrived, what did you see?" Kevin asked.

"As I came around the corner of the house, I saw Mrs. Udell give Mrs. Arnfeldt a shove, and their language had a lot of profanity. Both had lacerations on their faces and their clothes had dirt and grass and chicken manure on them."

"Your witness," Kevin said to the nearer of the two attorneys.

Despite his soft voice and courteous manners, George Francisco has the tanned and athletic build of an outdoorsman. He doesn't like to argue criminal cases and I wasn't quite sure why he had agreed to represent Monica Udell.

"Tell me, Officer Maynes," he said. "Is it against the law to own chickens in this county?"

"No, sir. Not outside town limits. Some towns do have regulations, but —"

"Does the Udell residence lie within the limits of Cotton Grove?"

"No, sir. About a quarter-mile outside."

"And is there a leash law in the county?"

"Some of the towns have them, but not unincorporated areas."

"Was the dog on a leash when you arrived?"

"No, sir."

Francisco took an eight-by-ten photo from the folder before him and asked for permission to approach. I nodded.

He showed the picture to me, to Reid and Mrs. Arnfeldt, and to Kevin Foster before handing it to Maynes. "Is this a picture you took of the dead chicken?"

"Yessir. In fact, that's the toe of my shoe in the corner here."

"Your Honor, I would ask that this picture be submitted into evidence as Exhibit A."

"So ordered," I said.

After looking at the picture, I thought I knew where Francisco was going with this one and I was surprised that Reid hadn't caught it. But then Reid was town-raised and maybe a bit clueless about chickens.

"Thank you, Officer. No further questions," he said.

"Mr. Stephenson?" I said with careful formality. Even though I have eleven older brothers, Reid is the closest I've ever come to having a younger one. When I first joined the law firm of Lee and Stephenson, his father, Brix Junior, was still practicing. As soon as Reid passed the bar exam, Brix Junior retired to Southern Pines, where he could play golf every day if he wanted, and left Reid to take his place. Reid's a bright and competent attorney, but he does have trouble keeping his pants zipped, which irritates the hell out of John Claude Lee, his senior partner.

As Dorothy Arnfeldt's attorney, Reid smiled pleasantly at the officer and said, "This is not the first time you've been called to my client's home, is it?"

"No, sir. She's filed complaints about the chickens . . . well, the first time it was about a rooster crowing early of a morning, and a week before this incident, she complained that the chickens were scratching up some flowers she'd just set out in her backyard."

"When you say 'backyard,' Deputy Maynes, exactly what do you mean?"

The officer was puzzled. "You want me to describe them?"

"Just the general size, please."

"Well, the Arnfeldt lot is like most of the new places they're building. Maybe a quarter to a third of an acre."

"It's part of Crescent Ridge subdivision?"

"Yes, sir."

"Where there's a homeowner's association?"

The officer shook his head. "I wouldn't know about that. Anyhow, Mrs. Udell's place isn't part of it. Crescent Ridge backs up on what's left of the old Crandall farm. I'd say it's about two acres."

"And are Mrs. Udell's two acres fenced in?"

"No, sir. Just her chicken yard," he said.

"How high is that fence?"

"About five feet."

"And the hedges that separate the properties?"

"Maybe four feet?"

"Could a chicken fly over them?"

"Objection," said George. "Calls for a personal opinion."

"Sustained," I said.

"Your folks keep chickens when you were a boy?" Reid asked.

"Yes, sir."

"Did you ever see one of your chickens fly over a five-foot fence?"

Maynes grinned. "Yessir!"

"And what about roosters?"

"Well, we kept one to service the hens and —"

"No, I'm referring to their crowing habits. When do they start crowing?"

"Soon as the sky lightens up of a morning."

"Are they loud?"

"I could sleep through it myself," said Maynes, who was clearly enjoying himself, "but it always woke my dad and he woke the rest of us."

"No further questions," Reid said and sat down.

"Redirect, Your Honor," said George Francisco. "Officer Maynes, when you were in the Udell yard, did you see any roosters?"

"No, sir."

"Thank you," said Francisco, and he, too, sat down.

"Further witnesses?" I asked.

"No, ma'am. The prosecution rests."

I told Maynes that he could step down, then asked the defense table, "Who goes first?"

Reid's client rose and crossed to the witness stand. Dorothy Arnfeldt wore a tailored navy blue suit. The neckline of her white blouse had a narrow ruffle and showed a tiny bit of cleavage. Simple gold earrings and gold wedding band. She sat with her shoulders squared and her demeanor was respectful, but by no means intimidated. Although Arnfeldt was her married name, she appeared to be of Scandinavian descent herself: fair skin, thick silver-blond hair, strong nose and chin. Her accent was from "a little further up the road," as my mechanic refers to states north of us, and indeed, after giving her name and address and swearing to speak truthfully, she told of moving down from Detroit when her husband was transferred last fall.

She spoke of how pleasantly surprised they were to realize they could buy a new and bigger house with a bigger yard than they had been able to afford in Detroit. "Then I discovered that we were just a few feet away from a dirty chicken house. And that the owner let them run wild through our yards, too. The lady next door warned me to watch where I put my feet when I walked back where the hedge is, but I stepped in a pile of chicken dirt and tracked it in on my new carpet before I realized, so I went over and very nicely asked her to keep her chickens in her own yard."

"And what was her response?" Reid asked.

"She said she'd try, but that they were used to roaming around before any houses were built there."

"Did she keep the chickens penned?"

"Not all the time. And once when she let them out, three flew straight over the hedge to where I'd had somebody dig a flower garden for me. That time, she said chickens were naturally drawn to freshly turned dirt and that her chickens were doing me a favor by eating all the cutworms in the soil. I told her I could do without the favor and that's when I called to report it."

"What about the rooster?"

"It didn't crow only in the morning, it

crowed all day long. And those hens! Every time they lay an egg, they tell the world about it. So, yes, I've complained about the noise."

"What about your dog?"

"We have an invisible electric fence, so she stays in our own yard."

On the day of the altercation, she said that she heard her dog barking and looked out in time to see a chicken come flying over the hedge. The dog immediately pounced on it. "I rushed out to try to save it, but Pixie grabbed the chicken and squeezed through a gap in the hedge with it. When I got through, I saw Mrs. Udell come out of the house with a gun in her hands and she said a chicken-killing dog shouldn't be allowed to live . . . well, that's not precisely what she said, but I can't repeat the kind of language she actually used. Anyhow —"

"Wait a minute, Mrs. Arnfeldt," Reid said. "Was your invisible fence turned off?"

"It was on, but it's not set very high. We don't want to really hurt Pixie, just discourage her from straying. It's strong enough that she never crosses it when she's out there alone and unprovoked, but if something like a chicken flies into our yard and gets her all excited, then I guess she just charges right across it."

"So what did you do next?"

"What I didn't do is let her shoot Pixie. What sort of neighbor shoots another neighbor's pedigreed dog over a dumb chicken? I offered to pay her for it, but she wouldn't listen. Just kept yelling that she was going to kill 'that damn dog.' Her words, Your Honor, not mine. When I tried to take the gun away from her, she hit me in the face and we got into it. But she threw the first punch. Not me."

"Your witness, Mr. Foster," Reid said.

"Just to be clear, Mrs. Arnfeldt," said Kevin. "You claim that the chicken flew into your yard, your dog killed it and then ran off with it when you came out so that you and your dog and the dead chicken were in the Udell yard when Mrs. Udell came out with the rifle?"

"Yes, sir."

"No further questions."

Francisco stood to cross-examine. "When you were buying your house, Mrs. Arnfeldt, did you look around out back?"

"You mean did I see the chickens? Not really. I thought that little building was a toolshed or something. It was almost dark and they must have already gone in for the night so that rooster could get a good rest before it started crowing."

"But you did drive past farms to get to Crescent Ridge and knew that there were farms around?"

"Yes, of course. That's why we bought out there. So that we could live in the country, but I didn't know that meant I was going to be living in someone's barnyard."

Francisco paused. "Six chickens constitute a barnyard to you?"

"Objection!" said Reid.

"Sustained."

"My apologies," Francisco told me. "Now on the evening in question, Mrs. Arnfeldt —"

"You mean that afternoon?" she asked. "It was still daylight."

My clerk looked up with a small roll of her eyes but the rest of us kept a neutral face. We all realized that it was an innocent question. For us, "afternoon" becomes "evening" around three-thirty or four o'clock, a nuance that takes newcomers a while to pick up on.

"I stand corrected," Francisco said politely without the least trace of sarcasm. "That afternoon. Are you quite certain that you saw that chicken fly over your hedge?"

"Absolutely. And then Pixie grabbed it and —"

"You do understand the penalties for

perjury, do you not?"

"Objection!"

"Overruled," I said.

Dorothy Arnfeldt turned to me indignantly. "Is he calling me a liar?"

"I don't think so, ma'am. I think he's just warning you to be sure it's the truth you're speaking."

Reid's head came up sharply at that. He knows me well enough to read me and the very fact that I'd just overruled his reasonable objection put him on alert that his client might somehow be walking on shaky ground although he didn't know why.

"Please take another look at Exhibit A," Francisco said, handing her the picture after I'd nodded to show he could approach. "Is this the chicken that flew into your yard and that your dog killed?"

With a toss of her pale blond hair, she gave the picture a disdainful glance. "I suppose so. All chickens look alike, though, don't they?"

"Not to people who keep chickens, Mrs. Arnfeldt." His voice was scrupulously polite.

"Look, Your Honor," she said, twisting in her chair to face me directly. I think it was finally getting through to her that she wasn't in Kansas any more. "I really do regret this and if that chicken was her pet, then I guess

I can't blame her for flying off the handle. I'm willing to pay a reasonable amount for what it was worth to her."

"We can discuss that later," I said. "You're not charged with contributing to the death of a chicken. You're charged with assault and battery."

"No further questions," said Francisco. "May I call my client to the stand?"

Baffled, Mrs. Arnfeldt returned to the defense table and Mrs. Udell took her place.

After she was sworn in, Francisco asked her to tell her side of the story.

Monica Udell's skin was the color of wild honey. Her straight brown hair was cut in a no-nonsense bob. A wisp of bangs brushed her forehead. She wore black slacks and a white shirt layered over a red-checked shirt. No jewelry except for a wedding band and a modest diamond on her left hand.

She described how her two acres were all that were left of her grandfather's farm. "You divide the land four or five times every generation and not much is left," she said. "One of my sisters still lives next door, but the others sold out to Crescent Ridge. I've tried to be a good neighbor to these new folks, but I like eggs that have some color to their yolks and aren't full of hormones and stuff and I don't plan to quit just because city's come to the country."

She admitted that her chickens had originally strayed over to the newcomers' yards, "but as soon as they asked me to keep them penned, I did. And when she put the law on me about my rooster, I made a big pot of pastry out of him rather than have hard feelings with her. Once in a while, one would fly over the fence in the morning and head straight for her yard. But her dog was over at my place more than my chickens were over there, worrying around the pen like he hadn't never seen a chicken before. When she complained to me the last time, I quit letting them out in the morning, just in the evening right before dark. They don't get far from their roost when night's coming on. And I clipped the left wing of all five of 'em as any fool can see if they look at that picture of poor Bella laying there dead. So if she says that chicken flew over her hedge, she's just pure-out lying. There's never been a chicken hatched that can fly on just one set of wing feathers. Her dog came in *my* yard and killed *my* chicken right where it had every right to be, and yeah, I might've hit her first, but I do believe she was asking for it when she came over yelling and cussing me out because I was about to shoot me a chicken-killing dog."

Reid immediately asked to see the picture again and his client's blue eyes widened when she saw the closely clipped feathers on the dead chicken's left wing and comprehended the significance. She whispered something to him and he stood. "Your Honor, about my client's testimony . . ."

"About her perjury, Mr. Stephenson?"

"My client would like to correct her earlier misstatement."

"I'm sure she would," I said crisply, "but I've let this drag on too long as it is. Perjury is a Class F felony, Mrs. Arnfeldt, and I could send you to jail for thirteen months. Or, I could cite you for contempt, which carries ten days in jail."

She gave an audible gasp and clutched Reid's arm.

"But I'm going to overlook it this time." Before she could quit looking worried, I continued, "On the other hand, because you did lie to this court, I'm going to accept that Mrs. Udell's is the truthful account and that your dog did go into her yard and kill her chicken. I'm ordering you to keep your dog on a leash when it's outside or else strengthen the charge on your invisible fence. If she had shot your dog, how much compensation would you have asked for?"

She balked at that. "My dog has papers."

"If you're going to live in the country," I said, "then you need to know that some chickens have pedigrees, too, and a lot of them are pets with personalities as individual as dogs or cats. I'm entering a judgment of three hundred dollars against you for the death of the chicken, payable to Mrs. Udell.

"As to the assault and battery, I find you each guilty as charged and sentence you to ten days in jail, suspended for one year, unsupervised probation, on condition that you each pay a hundred-dollar fine and court costs, and that you neither threaten nor assault each other during that year or you *will* go to jail."

It did not immediately register with either woman that Mrs. Arnfeldt was going to be out at least five hundred dollars while Mrs. Udell would break even, assuming her attorney didn't bill too many hours.

With an amused nod of his head, George Francisco said, "Thank you, Your Honor."

He started to follow his client out but I motioned for him to come up to the bench. As Kevin Foster looked through his shucks before calling the next case, I leaned forward and said, "Did you have a pet chicken when you were a kid?"

He smiled. "A white silkie. Her name was

95

Blossom. You?"

"A Rhode Island Red named Maisie Lou,"
I told him.

CHAPTER 5

The relating debris scatters enough tiny
   reckonings to force off a
Remembrance of tomorrows . . .
   — *Paul's Hill,* by Shelby Stephenson

I got to Will's warehouse on the west side of Dobbs a few minutes past noon. It's an old brick building with its own scruffy charm, sort of like Will himself, although Amy — she's his third wife — has done what she could with both of them. Like the wisteria vine she planted in front of the warehouse, a vine that now grows lushly across the whole front right up to the roof and blossoms with great purple clusters, she's given Will the freedom to be himself.

Growing up, his nickname in the family was Won't and not only because it's an easy pun on Will Knott. Our mother was a Stephenson and while Stephensons are quick to anger, quick to tears, quick to forgive, Will was hardheaded as well, always ready to strike out across the field rather than plow a straight furrow, no matter what the consequences.

To the dismay of his first two wives, he was constitutionally unable to hold down a nine-to-five job for longer than six months. We've lost count of how many different things he tried before he finally stumbled into auctioneering, which combines a certain amount of risk, ever-changing novelty, freedom to stick his nose into interesting places, and the possibility of big profits.

Amy's the director of human resources out at the hospital and it's her job that provides medical insurance, buys groceries, and pays their day-to-day bills. Will's earnings are more erratic, but they probably come close to matching hers on a year-to-year reckoning.

He doesn't keep regular hours at his warehouse. Instead, he roams the state as a freelance auctioneer. Your mother's left you a houseful of furniture? Will can come and advise you on whether to hold an estate sale or offer it to an antiques dealer. Even after his commission, a well-advertised sale will usually net you more than a straight cash offer from a dealer.

He doesn't have any training in appraisals, but he does have a good eye for what's quality and what should probably go to a flea market. During the year, the owners will often give him whatever doesn't sell — the odd lamps, tables, mule collars, or mismatched dishes — and he sticks it in his warehouse. Then, twice a year, he holds his own auction. When Dwight was furnishing his bachelor apartment after his divorce from Jonna, he got a box of decent tableware and glasses at one of Will's sales for ten dollars.

His spring sale was coming up at the end of the month, so the warehouse was fairly cluttered when I walked in.

"Will?" I called.

"Down here, Deb'rah."

I followed the sound of his voice back to where he was trying to inventory what was to go into that sale.

A very pretty young woman was perched on a nearby stool. A laptop was balanced atop a file cabinet and she seemed to be taking dictation from him.

"Number 238," he said, hefting a gloomy-looking portrait in a gilded frame. "The Reverend Jacob Saunders."

He looked at a Post-it note on the back. "Native of Colleton County, 1899 to 1980."

The girl's slender fingers darted over the

keyboard. "Nineteen-eighty. Got it."

"Saunders," I said, trying to see a likeness in that grim, unsmiling face. "Any kin to Fred?"

"His granddaddy. Scared the shit out of Fred and his brothers when they were kids. None of 'em want his picture hanging in their house. Nice frame though. You know Dee Bradshaw?"

I took a second look at the girl. Cute, long brown hair, green eyes, short legs? Yes, this could be Candace Bradshaw's daughter.

"I don't believe so."

"I know you, though," she said with a friendly smile. "You gave my boyfriend a prayer for judgment when he got caught for speeding last month."

"I did?"

"Yeah. He's kept it on cruise control ever since."

Will glanced at his watch. "We'll break for lunch now, Dee. Back at one?"

"Sure thing," she said. "Nice meeting you, Judge Knott."

Will watched appreciatively as she threaded her way through a maze of straight-back wooden chairs, her shapely hips swinging provocatively in her tight jeans.

"Quit it," I said.

"What?" He tried to look innocent, then gave a sheepish grin. "I'm allowed to look. Amy doesn't care if I look."

"She's young enough to be your grand-daughter."

"Go to hell!" he said indignantly. "She's almost twenty-two."

"How long's she been working for you?"

"I only hired her yesterday. Nobody else answered my want ad for some temporary clerical work." He peered at the computer screen. "At least she can spell."

"So where are those folders? I have to be back at the courthouse in an hour."

"Still in Linsey's hassock." He led me deeper into the warehouse. "I moved that thing over here after it didn't sell last summer and I knew it was godawful heavy, but I didn't realize the top could open. Then, when I was shifting it yesterday, I noticed a little keyhole up under the ledge."

He pointed to a cube with a cushioned top. The thing was covered in scuffed brown leather. "I tried to pick the lock, but nothing worked, so I finally took a crowbar to it."

Will lifted the hinged lid and I immediately saw that he'd wrecked the lock. "Doesn't hurt the value," he assured me. "It's vinyl, not leather, and ugly as Aunt

Sister's pet goat."

Aunt Sister's a little younger than Daddy and her pet goat died when she was still a child. No one ever took its picture, so we don't know if it really did have bald spots and a misshapen horn that curled in the wrong direction. Nevertheless, it's the standard of ugliness in our family. Aunt Sister swears that Daddy exaggerates the goat's bad features, but we've heard her say things like, "Now I won't say that baby's as ugly as my pet goat, but . . ."

Will cocked his head at that hassock. "I wonder if it came with a lock or if Linsey had it added? For a minute there, I thought I was going to find a real treasure — maybe the Thomas family silver or Confederate gold or something."

I knelt down for a closer examination. "It could've started life as a trunk or a foot-locker that someone upholstered. Who knows? Maybe Linsey bought it at an estate sale himself."

The interior was deeper and slightly wider than the file folders that took up most of the space.

I lifted one and a packet of letters slid into my lap. The pale blue and green envelopes were tied with a faded satin ribbon. "Oh, Will! Look at the return address."

"Meg Woods? Who was she?"

"His wife. She died of a ruptured appendix when she was only thirty. Mother said it broke his heart and he never remarried. These must be her love letters to him."

I opened the file to put the letters back inside and found a photograph of a laughing girl with a pixie cut.

"Wow!" Will gave a soft whistle. "If that's her, no wonder he never married again."

Another folder was labeled DAD and seemed to be letters written to Linsey when he was in school over in Chapel Hill.

And then there was the folder labeled KNOTT.

As Will had said when he called last night, there were sheets of typescript, jotted notes, and several news clippings that chronicled my first campaign, my loss, and then my appointment. The papers were crammed in haphazardly with no apparent order and Will had to flip through to find a scrap of paper that looked as if it'd been torn from a yellow legal pad.

"See this?"

In what looked like Linsey's distinctive printing, my name was circled with several arrows that pointed to different names: Kezzie Knott, G. Hooks Talbert, and the former governor. All were surrounded by aimless doodles that appeared to have begun as question marks, as if Linsey had been trying to work out a connection. Luckily for me, he was missing the name that linked the three of us, that of Talbert's older son, the son whose crime furnished the material for Daddy to blackmail G. Hooks. "Help my daughter and I won't send your son to prison."

"What do you suppose that's about?" Will asked.

"I haven't a clue," I lied, "but these look like Linsey's personal files. Wonder why he had us in here?"

"Not just you and Daddy, kiddo. There's files on half the commissioners, on our DA —"

"But here's one with his birth certificate, his marriage license . . . hmm. Who's this, I wonder?"

It was a picture of a teenage boy in a Confederate uniform, complete with sword and rifle. On the back, spidery handwriting identified the boy as Cpl. Joshua Thomas.

"Some of this stuff probably needs to go to the historical society. I'll take my folder, but —"

"Oh, no, you won't," he said. "You want yours, you're going to have to take them all and let me know what's worth giving. And I want my name on it as the donor, okay?"

"Okay, but there's no way I can go through everything now. Give me a box and we'll stick them in my car."

Ten minutes later, we had emptied the hassock and stashed the files in the trunk of my car. By then I was more than ready for some lunch. A small refrigerator stood in Will's makeshift office and he brought out the chilled chicken salad sandwiches and soft drinks that he had picked up earlier.

As we ate, he finally got around to his real reason for getting me over there.

"Dwight says he and Cal are going up to Virginia and empty out Jonna's house when school's out. You think he'd like me to come help? I don't want to step on the boy's toes if there are things of his mother's y'all think he might want someday, but it sounds like there's gonna be a lot to get rid of."

"There is," I said, trying to remember the way the house was furnished. We had stayed there briefly after Jonna was killed. Because she had died intestate, Cal had inherited everything. "Dwight wants to sell the house and fatten up Cal's college fund."

"Many antiques?" he asked.

I shrugged. "I'm no expert. Her family founded the town and she had nice furniture, but only five or six pieces looked really old. There were some family portraits that Mrs. Shay wants back and Dwight says she can have them since Cal's her only grandchild and they'll probably come to him eventually anyhow. You'll have to ask Dwight, but you know something, Will? It might be easier on both of them to move it all down here to your warehouse if you've got room for it. Less emotional for Cal to think about it here than in that house, don't you reckon?"

We finished eating and he walked me out to my car. Dee Bradshaw pulled in beside us as we stood talking.

"Not late, am I?" she chirped as she got out of the car and pushed her sunglasses up on her hair.

Before Will could reply, her cell phone began to play a rap song. She checked the screen and made a face. "It's just my dad. He probably wants to know if you've fired me yet."

As the phone continued to boogie, Will said, "Give him a break and answer it. You've still got a few minutes on your lunch hour."

She shrugged and touched the talk button as she moved away from us. "Yeah?"

"So why don't you and Amy come for supper this weekend?" I said. "We'll grill some steaks and you can ask Dwight if —"

"*What?*" Dee Bradshaw shrieked. "No! When? Oh, Daddy, *why!*"

She was wailing like a child and we turned to see what the trouble was.

Tears streamed down her cheeks and her hands trembled so badly that the phone slipped to the ground. She stood there too shaken to pick it up.

"Mom's killed herself!"

CHAPTER 6

A scraping gentles an air of oak and mi-
mosa
and I hear sounds of boys playing basketball in the barnyard.
— *Middle Creek Poems,*
by Shelby Stephenson

When I got back from Will's, it was all over
the courthouse. As a prominent business
owner and chair of the county commissioners, Candace Bradshaw had enjoyed a
degree of power that affected a lot of lives,
so her death was major news. A cat's-paw
for the building trades and land developers,
she was less liked by those of us who wanted
to slow growth until a thoughtful plan was
in place; but both sides generally conceded
that however ill-equipped she might be to
run the county, she was thoroughly consci-
entious in her ownership of Bradshaw
Management. Not only did she provide

benefits and health insurance, she also paid her menial employees more than the minimum wages required by law — the result, it was said, of her own humble start.

In return, she expected to get full value for every dollar. The janitorial branch of Bradshaw Management had contracts to clean offices all around the county and it was well known that she could suddenly appear in the middle of the evening to be sure that her people were doing a satisfactory job and not simply going through the motions with their mops and buckets and dusting cloths. One uncleaned sink or toilet got a warning; two and the careless worker would be fired on the spot.

By the time I reconvened court, courthouse regulars agreed that Candace Bradshaw had died sometime after her daughter stormed out of the house and well before noon that day, when her cleaning woman let herself in. They also agreed that she had been found in her bedroom with a white plastic trash bag over her head. After that, the real truth was up for grabs.

"I hear she was in bed buck naked, so she'd probably been with a man."

"I heard she was made up to go out."

"Drunk as a skunk."

"Sober as an owl."

"Her face and arms were covered in bruises and somebody'd given her a black eye."

"No, there wasn't a mark on her."

"It was murder/suicide/an accident —"

"Bet you a nickel it was one of them . . . whadda-you-call-it? Something nasty. Autorotic something?"

"Autoerotic asphyxiation?"

"Yeah. She wasn't getting it from any man these days, was she? Well, there you go."

I suppose I could've slipped down to Dwight's office during my afternoon break and tried to wheedle the facts out of him, but we have a separation-of-powers agreement: I don't ask him about any of his cases that might come before me and he doesn't comment on any of mine until after I've ruled on them and signed off.

In truth, it's worked out better than you'd think, given my natural curiosity and his natural tendency to tell me what I ought to be doing, something he got in the habit of back when we were kids and he tried to boss me around like one of my brothers. Lucky for both of us, he doesn't have time to keep track of all the minor felonies that show up in my court these days, and as a district court judge, I'll never hear any of his homicide cases or major felonies. Too, he knows I'll be discreet if he does discuss a murder with me.

Even though this was a suicide, I put my curiosity on hold and despite all the speculations flying around, I managed to keep my mind on assault and forgery and the endless he-said/she-said that make up the bulk of a district court calendar. Between cases, my clerk kept me updated on each and every new assertion and by the end of the day, enough of the note Candace Bradshaw left had seeped out that people were starting to say she had seriously misused her office as chair of the board of commissioners and that she had killed herself rather than face the shame of exposure.

Not to mention the humiliation of probable jail time.

My clerk had an in with the dispatcher and whispered some of the details to me. It was a small trash bag, the kind with drawstrings, and Candace had snugged it around her neck and tied it off with a neat bow.

It appeared that she had made the bag airtight and then laid herself calmly down to die by gentle suffocation. Not the worst way to kill yourself, I suppose. I'm told that you pass out from asphyxia first and then you pass on.

Her body had been sent to Chapel Hill

for the automatic autopsy required by the circumstances, but there were no marks or bruises on her body, no broken fingernails or any signs of a struggle, so the autopsy would be pro forma with no expected surprises. Word came up that Deanna Bradshaw was pitching a fit all over the sheriff's department downstairs, insisting that never in a million years would her mother kill herself. "And she never wrote that note either. Okay, maybe Mom cut a few corners, did a few favors she maybe hadn't ought to've, but, hell, that's the way things work if you want to get anything done. No way would she have gone to jail for such little stuff. She knew where too many bodies are buried for anybody to try to prosecute her. Besides, Mom would never, *ever* kill herself without leaving *me* a note, too."

"Hmpf," my clerk sniffed. "I heard she and Candace had a huge fight yesterday. The kid's feeling guilty."

Normally Dwight leaves Dobbs at least an hour earlier than I do, but we had ridden in together that morning because his truck needed a new taillight where someone had backed into him in the parking lot, and our mechanic had said he'd work it in if Dwight could leave it there all day.

When I got downstairs Melanie Ashworth, the department's recently hired spokesperson, was patiently answering questions from the two reporters who were still there. One of them was Ruby Dixon herself, although she was slurring her questions and her pencil kept slipping off the lines of her reporter's tablet as she tried to record Melanie's comments.

I found myself remembering how Linsey Thomas would have handled this. He would've sent someone sober to question Melanie, while he himself would be on the phone, running down Candace Bradshaw's cleaning woman, questioning the other commissioners, interviewing staff members at Bradshaw Management, talking to Candace's daughter and maybe her former husband. By now, he might even have the contents of the note she'd left behind and a definite answer as to whether or not it was in her handwriting.

I found Dwight in his office, so absorbed in some reports that he wasn't immediately aware of me. He had loosened the knot on the tie that I'd bought him the week before and the cuffs of his blue shirt were turned back.

Dwight doesn't consider himself the least bit handsome and always says he looks like the Durham Bull in a pea jacket, muscle-bound and ungainly. Believe me. No.

He's taller than most of my brothers and okay, he's built a little more like a football player than the skinny basketball hotshot he was in high school, but there's nothing muscle-bound about him at all. Solid, yes, with big hands and feet, brown hair and eyes, and an honest, open face.

When he realized I was there in the door-way and looked up with that warm smile, my heart turned over. "Hey there," he said. "I was just about to go see how near done you were."

"You can leave now?" I asked.

"Sure. Why not? Oh, you mean because of Candace Bradshaw?" He shrugged. "I've got Richards and Dalton out going through the motions, taking statements."

"So what was in the note she left?"

"Now you know I'm not going to talk about that right now."

"But she really did break the law?"

He shook his head at me and buttoned the cuffs of his sleeves. "Give it up, shug."

"At least say whether it was suicide."

"That's what it looks like. Why? You hear something different?"

"No. Just that her daughter's refusing to believe it."

"Yeah, well, when we spoke to her this afternoon, she was blaming herself." He picked up his jacket and slung it over his shoulder.

"Because of their fight?"

"You heard about that?" He held the door for me, then switched off the lights.

"I heard Candace took her keys and threw her out of the house. True?"

"Appears to be."

He checked out with the dispatcher at the end of the hall and paused to leave some instructions for a couple of deputies, so I waited till we were outside in the mild spring air to ask what Candace and her daughter had fought about.

"The usual," Dwight said. He took my arm to keep me from stepping out into the street even though the nearest car was half a block away. "She said her mother was upset that she'd dropped out of college at Easter. Plus she didn't approve of the guy Miss Bradshaw's seeing. Did you know she's working for Will?"

"I was over there when she got the phone call."

"Since when does Will need a private secretary?"

"Is that what she told you? Will said she's just a temp that he hired last night to help

115

him take inventory for his spring sale, but I guess private secretary sounds better. Wonder who they'll appoint to take Candace's place on the board?"

"Nobody you'll take any comfort in," he assured me as we reached my car.

Even though judges no longer run on a political slate, everyone pretty much knows who's a liberal and who's a conservative and who's a yellow dog like me.

The head of the county's Republican party would get to appoint Candace Bradshaw's replacement. The best I could hope for was that they'd slip up and name someone who could think for himself.

Or herself.

Once again, I found myself thinking of Linsey Thomas, who would have had a lot to say on the subject of civic-minded commissioners as opposed to those who always seemed to think of personal profit first and public good last. As I turned the key in my ignition, I said, "I guess you and Bo have quit trying to find who ran down Linsey Thomas?"

Dwight frowned. "Ran him down? You think someone killed him deliberately?"

"Slip of the tongue," I said. "I meant find the car that hit him."

"By now that car could be in a slag heap.

You know well as I do that if we don't find it in the first couple of weeks, we almost never do. I'm not holding my breath till some drunk comes in and confesses. It's a damn shame, though. Thomas was a good man. And good for Colleton County even if he did hold our feet to the fire a few times."

I had been with someone else last spring so I hadn't followed the investigation as closely as I might now, although I did remember that the SBI lab had identified the make of the car by a piece of glass found by Linsey's body. "I guess you checked all the repair shops for a Toyota with a missing headlight?"

"We gave it everything we had, Deb'rah."

"No leads at all?"

But Dwight'd had enough of talking shop. "Haywood says the garden center's got a sale on dwarf apple trees. Maybe Cal and I'll run over and pick up a couple tomorrow afternoon. You care where we plant them?"

"Up to you," I said.

No use pointing out that we already had peaches, two varieties of pears, a line of blueberry bushes, figs, and a plum tree, and that there was no way in the world we'd ever eat that much fruit. In addition, we had five pecan trees to go with the countless dog-woods, hollies, oaks, and cedars he had dug up from the woods and set out all around the house. Planting trees and bushes seems to be Dwight's way of convincing himself that our marriage is as real and permanent as those roots reaching deep into the dirt beneath our feet, and I'm not about to discourage him.

Besides, there are still enough animals on the farm to take care of our excess fruit and Cal likes feeding apples and carrots to the horses.

After dropping Dwight off at Jimmy White's garage to retrieve his truck and settle up with Jimmy, I drove over to his brother Rob's house to pick up Cal. During the week, Rob's wife Kate keeps him after school. She's the guardian and adoptive mother of Mary Pat, who's in the same class as Cal. Kate swears that one child more is no trouble, especially since she and Rob have now hired a live-in nanny to help with four-year-old Jake and four-month-old R.W. so that Kate could get back to designing high-end fabrics in the remodeled pack house that now serves as her studio.

On this beautiful afternoon, the nanny, a nice young Australian with a delightful accent, had them out on the lawn playing red light while the baby slept in a net-covered carriage nearby.

I powered down my window to say hello as Cal grabbed up his books and got in beside me, flushed and sweaty. No plopping the kids down in front of a television for this young woman.

As I told Daddy, Cal and I have had a few bumps in the road since he came to live with us in January, but he had liked me before I married his dad and I was optimistic that he would eventually maybe even come to love me as much as my brothers came to love my mother. When he gave me one of his snaggletoothed grins, I wanted to hug him hard. Instead, I smiled back and said, "Good day?"

"Tomorrow afternoon, me and Mary Pat and Jake? We're going to go help Bobby and Jess and Emma set out tuberoses," he told me happily.

Oh, to be eight again and think it a treat to spend the afternoon setting out a flower crop.

CHAPTER 7

The tender days are gone.
Instinct cannot get you back.
    — *Paul's Hill,* by Shelby Stephenson

The sun rose Thursday in a cloudless blue sky. In a field bounded by Possum Creek on one side and a stand of trees on the other three, longleaf pines blazed greenly against the blue. With their curving branches and clusters of stiff needles, the tall straight trees looked like fantastic plants left over from *Jurassic Park.* Somewhere among the shorter hardwood trees, a downy woodpecker drummed on a dead, beetle-infested oak limb and a mockingbird marked his territory in long melodic trills that warned other male mockers that he held title to this particular plat of desirable nesting land and that only females need apply.

Kezzie Knott checked the time on a fat gold pocket watch that had once belonged to his father and slowed his rusty truck to a stop on the creek side of the field. As he opened the door and stretched his long legs, he paused to breathe in the smells of the cool morning. His brown, high-laced brogans were almost as scruffy as his pickup, and the cuffs of his blue shirt were as frayed as the hems of his chino pants. Both were so old and had been washed so often that they had faded to soft tones that blended with the light brown sand and pale blue sky. Two weeks ago, he had traded winter's felt Stetson for the straw panama he would wear until October.

These days, he had started leaving the tailgate down so that the older of his two hounds could jump out to join him without much effort. The dogs, too, paused to sniff the air as soon as their feet reached ground. This field had been plowed recently and the rows laid off, but nothing yet was planted. A faint scent of composted chicken manure wafted in on the breeze. It was not an unpleasant smell and it made Kezzie smile. He and Seth and Deborah had given this field to the grandchildren so that they could begin cleansing the land of commercial fertilizers and chemical pesticides. With the enthusiasm of youth, they intended to prove to their elders that a living could be made from the land that did not entail poisoning the environment. They were not naive enough to think that flowers would make the same profit as tobacco, but it was a first step toward a rotation of organically grown crops.

He did not take their desire for something different as a slam at him. Tobacco had been good to the state and to his family for years before farmers like him knew how bad it was. Yes, it took a lot of fertilizer to grow and it took herbicides to control the suckers and weeds and yeah, he reckoned it was unhealthy for most people, though he himself had smoked since he was twelve and was still going strong more than seventy years later despite the way most of the children nagged him to quit. Tobacco had fed and clothed his sons and it had paid the bills when Sue made him quit messing in white lightning.

He could not repress a rueful grin at that. 'Shine was about the only thing he had ever lied to her about. To please her, he did indeed cut back on his bootlegging activities, but he never quite gave it up entirely, and over the years, he continued to finance a few trusted men and a couple of enterprising women, too, who wanted to make their whiskey the old-fashioned way with corn mash, sugar, and pure well water that had never known a drop of chlorine.

Near to where Kezzie had stopped his truck, a narrow foot-path led off to the right and as soon as they left the open field for the cover of trees and vines, he could hear water rushing over the rocks along the creek bed. Blue jays jeered at them from the safety of their treetops and a nervous thrasher chirred a warning from the underbrush where a nest probably held her clutch of brown-spotted eggs. The path wound down around a two-hundred-year-old pin oak and they spooked a rabbit that went crashing off through the underbrush. Without waiting for permission, Ladybelle immediately streaked after it, but Kezzie could almost see Blue shrug at the impossibility of his arthritic old legs catching up to those younger ones.

The banks down here were considerably tidier since Grayson Village got built on the other side. The village's maintenance crew had trimmed back the wild grapevines. Poison oak had been eradicated, and greenbriers and blackberry brambles cleared away to make room for a path wide enough for two or three people to walk abreast and enjoy uninterrupted views of the creek. Discreetly placed black wire baskets encouraged hikers to toss their bottles and cans there and so far, it seemed to be working. No garbage in the water nor along the banks that he could see. Some of his sons still grumbled about establishing a greenbelt in common with Grayson Village, but Kezzie was pragmatist enough to know that if he had held Talbert's feet to the fire over the property line, the man might have put in a trailer park with trashy tenants just to spite him. Possum Creek could be a dirty, choked-up sewer instead of a clear stream that sparkled and gurgled in the morning sunlight.

He and Talbert might cooperate when necessary, "But we ain't never gonna be friends," he told himself.

Ladybelle waited for them at the bend of the creek, panting with exertion. She and Blue touched noses, then he followed her down to the water's edge.

Distracted by a bullfrog that had recently emerged from hibernation beneath the soft wet mud, neither dog immediately saw the man leaning motionless against a tall maple tree on the other side of the creek near a rustic wooden bridge. He wore tailored khaki pants pressed to blade-sharp creases, leather boots, and a tan windbreaker. Sunlight caught the gold of an expensive watch on his wrist.

The two men stared at each other across the water.

"Knott," the other man said evenly.

Kezzie gave a formal nod of recognition. "Talbert," he said.

"We're sure this is her writing?" Bo asked as he finished reading for the third time the letter found in Candace Bradshaw's bedroom.

"I faxed it over to the SBI lab along with known samples and they say everything was written by the same hand. No question," said Dwight.

The two sat in Sheriff Bo Poole's office with a copy of the letter on Bo's desk between them. The original pale pink sheet, monogrammed in a deeper rose, had been fingerprinted and was now preserved in an acid-free envelope under lock and key as part of the secured chain of evidence collected at the scene of every violent death, whether self-inflicted, accidental, or possible homicide.

"I've got a call in for Terry Wilson," Dwight said, referring to a supervisor in the State Bureau of Investigation who was as much a friend as a fellow lawman.

"Good," Bo said. "They've certainly got

more people than we do. I'll go upstairs and talk to Doug Woodall. If he's not too busy running for governor, maybe I can get him to remember he's still our DA and we need his full-time help on this."

He brushed back a strand of thinning broom-straw hair. A small trim man with an outsize reputation, the sheriff had won his last five elections and was likely to stay in office as long as he chose even though the allegations in this letter could be political dynamite. Granted, the alleged corruption probably would not reach beyond the county line and even if proved would not be worth more than a couple of paragraphs in *The News & Observer.* Nevertheless, thought Bo, a single small stick of dynamite can blow a damn big hole in any local power structure. They would need to move gingerly, and to do everything by the book. No point building a case — assuming there was a case to be built — only to watch the evidence get thrown out of court on a technicality. It was going to take the cooperation of the other agencies and his own best officers.

On the other hand, he knew as well as Dwight how tightly they were stretched these days. More people in the county meant more crime. In addition to the normal load of homegrown sin, gang activity had picked up down near Makely, crack and meth were pouring into the county, a clerk in the utilities office was accused of embezzling nearly a quarter-million dollars, and there was a hit-and-run on Old 48, only this time they had a witness and a detailed description of the car, which reminded Bo all over again that they still had an open hit-and-run on their books. "And damn, I hate that, Dwight."

"Me, too, Bo. Deb'rah was talking about it again just last night. She really liked Linsey. Something she said though's got me thinking. What if someone ran him down deliberately?"

"Murder?" Bo asked.

"Well, I look at this letter, I can't help wondering. Candace says she was greedy and that she enriched herself and some of her friends with her insider knowledge. You've heard the talk, Bo. Wasn't much said as openly last year as now, but what if it's not all partisan political grousing? Say she really was misusing the office more than usual — took kickbacks, tipped off friends so they could buy up land before the county expressed an interest in it. If Linsey got wind of it last year, you know what a snapping turtle he could be."

"He'd sure hold on till it thundered," Bo agreed. "So who was Candace Bradshaw balling these days, Dwight? Danny Creedmore?"

"That's what I've heard. Long as she was going to kill herself, it's too bad she didn't name names. It's almost like she wanted to slime as many people as she could."

The Humvee that drove into the farmyard that morning was black and menacing-looking, a behemoth that came nowhere close to matching the small bulldog of a man who swung himself down from behind the wheel. His jeans and his jean jacket were artfully faded, but their cut and fit did not come from Kmart and they were much newer than the authentically faded and stained pants of the big men who held their ground to watch the newcomer's approach.

"Mr. Knott?" he asked, stretching out his small pudgy hand with an ingratiating smile.

"I'm Robert Knott," said the elder of the two gray-haired farmers. After a slight hesitation, he put out a calloused hand that completely encased the other's. "This here's my brother Haywood."

"Glad to meet you both," the other said heartily in a broad Midwestern accent. "My name's Witkowski, Trevor Witkowski, and you're just the ones I was hoping to see."

"Oh?" said Haywood Knott from his perch atop a large green tractor hitched to a set of gang disks. A big friendly man who had never seen a stranger, he was less suspicious than Robert and always ready to be entertained. He pushed his porkpie hat to the back of his head and said, "How's that?"

"I moved into Grayson Village about three weeks ago and I've spent the past few days driving around this neck of the woods to get my bearings. One thing I noticed right off the bat. This looks like prime hunting land, but every square foot of it seems to be posted."

Haywood nodded while Robert kept a stolid silence.

"The signs say the land's leased by the Possum Creek Hunt Club. That right?"

Haywood grinned. "That's right, Mr. W'kowski."

"Witkowski," he said, emphasizing the *t*, "but call me Trevor. Please."

"So what can we do for you, Trevor?" Robert asked bluntly.

"Well, I couldn't find the club listed in the phone book and people tell me that you Knotts are the ones to see about joining. I went over to the Kezzie Knott house, but he wasn't there and his black servant gal sent me here."

The brothers glanced at each other and Trevor Witkowski was perceptive enough to catch it. "Did I say something wrong?"

"Naw," said Haywood. "It's just that we don't never think of Maidie Holt as a servant gal."

"Oh. Sorry. Anyhow, I was wondering what sort of game your club hunts here?"

"Deer, squirrel, rabbits," said Robert. "Sometimes possums."

"Any birds?"

"Bobwhites and doves in the fall."

"Pheasants?"

" 'Fraid not," said Haywood. "You more a bird hunter than a meat man, huh?"

"I wouldn't mind getting a nice big buck for my office," Witkowski said, "but mostly, I find the birds more challenging. Now can you tell me how I'd go about joining?"

"It's a thousand-dollar initiation fee," Haywood said promptly, "but we'd have to put you on the waiting list and they's about twenty-five ahead of you."

"I see. So how often do memberships open up?"

Both men shrugged and Robert said, "I gotta be honest with you, Trevor. That don't happen very often. Last one was more'n a year ago, back when — when was it Jap

Stancil died, Haywood?"

"Been at least two years ago, ain't it?"

"Tell you what," Witkowski said as he pulled out a wallet thick with credit cards and greenbacks. "How about I make it worth your while to jump me up to the front of your waiting list?"

Sitting high above him on the tractor, Haywood could see into the small man's wallet without really trying and he looked with interest at the hundred-dollar bills Witkowski was fingering.

"Well now, we couldn't put you at the *very* front," he said, but before he could decide how much it was safe to ask the man for, his brother stiffened and shook his head.

"Sorry, Trevor," Robert said. He glared at Haywood, who gave a sheepish grin. "Our club president knows every name on that list and he'd have our hides if we took money to jump up a stranger."

"Tell you what though," Haywood said to Witkowski. "They's a hunt club over in Johnston County that might have room for you."

"But —"

"We'd like to stay and talk, but we got right much plowing to do today," Robert said firmly.

Haywood pulled his hat back down to

shade his eyes and gave the stranger a cheerful wave. "Been real nice talking to you," he said and turned the key in the tractor's ignition.

At the house where Candace Bradshaw died, Deputy Detectives Mayleen Richards and Sam Dalton walked through the public rooms, giving them only cursory glances. Everything was coordinated around a color scheme of dark rose and white, with touches of green. Natural light flooded through the many windows and skylights, and the place looked like an illustration out of a magazine, not a home where real people lived and relaxed and littered every surface with newspapers and dirty dishes. Even the kitchen was immaculate.

"She must have dumped her old furniture," Dalton said. "All of this looks brand-new."

He was very much aware that his promotion to detective was provisional and he tried not to sound too much of an eager-beaver newbie.

Richards nodded. Sam Dalton was about five years younger than the deputy she had partnered most often before he signed up with a civilian company to work in Iraq — and every time a car bomb exploded in

Baghdad, she worried until Jack Jamison's wife dropped a casual mention of something he'd e-mailed her about. But Dalton had the same chunky build and the same willingness to carry his share of the load. Much as she missed Jamison, she had to admit that Dalton was shaping into a competent detective who could be trusted to do a thorough search.

At the master bedroom where the body had been found, she said, "You take this room. Maybe you'll get lucky and find a diary full of names."

He gave a lopsided grin. "You think?"

"Nope. But at least it cuts down on what we have to go through. Anything she kept must have significance to her, so keep an eye out for any personal papers."

At the other end of the house were two more bedrooms, one of which finally had a lived-in look. From the clothes strewn across the unmade bed and on the floor, this had to be the daughter's. A sloppy daughter's, thought Richards. Her own mother would never have let her leave her room like this.

Immediately, her mind shied away from thoughts of her mother. Things were so strained between them these days that they had not spoken in weeks. Her family could not accept that she loved a Latino and had given her a him-or-us ultimatum. Mike Diaz kept reassuring her that all would be fine once they were actually married and the babies started coming. "If the president of the USA can accept some 'little brown ones' in his family, your family will, too, *mi querida.* You'll see."

Reminding herself that Major Bryant had warned her about letting her personal life interfere with her work, she willed herself to stop thinking about the conflicting loyalties that were tearing her apart and to concentrate on the job at hand.

This third bedroom had been furnished as a home office. Or rather, thought Richards as she paused in the doorway to get an overall impression, it was furnished as someone's idea of what a home office should look like. Except for bathrooms and kitchen, the entire house was carpeted in an off-white wall-to-wall Berber. In this room, a pseudo-Oriental rug with a dusty rose background lay atop that. White enameled bookshelves bloomed with a collection of porcelain flowers. No books. In a niche below the shelves, a three-story dollhouse built to look like an antebellum plantation faced outward. Complete with white columns and tiny pots of artificial flowers on the porch, it sat on casters and rolled out smoothly when Richards touched it. Instead of having period furniture, though, the interior rooms were all modern.

She pushed it back into place and turned her attention to the adult toys. A thin laptop computer sat on the pullout counter of a cherry table desk beneath a window swathed in dark rose drapes and sheer white under-curtains. A flower-sprigged mug that held scissors, a silver letter opener, and an assortment of colorful pens sat next to the laptop between a bottle of rose-tinted nail polish and a porcelain angel with bowed head. A locked three-drawer file cabinet beside the desk was also made of cherry. A vanity wall above the cabinet had been hung with a few plaques and awards from local civic groups. Several silver-framed photographs of Candace Bradshaw with various elected men sat atop the cabinet itself. No other women in the pictures. No picture of her daughter or ex-husband.

A sturdily built five-foot-ten redhead with freckled face and arms and a slight unease whenever surrounded by so much blatant femininity, Richards doubted that much real work was done here. Nevertheless, it was a place to start collecting names. When the SBI reinforcements arrived, they would take a stethoscope and tongue depressor to this room and to the computer, but it wouldn't hurt for a CCSD deputy to check it out first.

She selected a likely candidate from the key ring found in Bradshaw's purse, unlocked the cabinet on her first try, and opened the top drawer. This seemed to be general storage for her supplies: extra printer paper, ink cartridges, and other odds and ends.

The middle drawer held neatly labeled hanging files and was apparently devoted to Bradshaw's work as a county commissioner. In addition to the minutes of the meetings and various reports, there seemed to be a file on each of her fellow commissioners, past and present. She picked one at random — Harvey Underwood. "VP at the bank. Approved B's loan w/o proper collateral. [fd] Wife, Leila. Two daughters in Raleigh. G'children. Drives late-model Lincolns. Doesn't drink or smoke. Sleeping with B, but I could prob. have him. Registered Repub, but can't be trusted to vote the right way."

There followed a list of issues that had come before the board and whether Underwood had voted with her or on the opposing side.

So she kept score, thought Richards and a

hasty flip through the other files confirmed it. There was a running tally on how each board member had voted since she became chair last year. The two Democrats on the board did not receive flattering comments. Jamie Jacobson seemed to be a particularly sharp burr under Bradshaw's saddle and the dead woman had quoted some of the other woman's comments with childish petulance, adding exclamation points and heavy underlining. The word *bitch* had been doodled in the margin.

She pulled a folder for Lee, Stephenson and Knott, the law firm where Major Bryant's wife had practiced before she became a judge. It held a few newspaper clippings of a case John Claude Lee had won in a civil suit that involved a farmer's defense of his land when the state tried to condemn it for an exit ramp to I-40. There was also a sheet of paper with Lee's name and that of Greg Turner, an attorney from Makely. That sheet bore the same *[fd]* notation she had spotted in Underwood's file.

[fd]? File drawer?

Maybe she meant a computer file, Richards decided, and switched on the laptop. While she waited for it to load, she looked through the bottom drawer, which was labeled PERSONAL. Here were Bradshaw's insurance policies, bank and medical records, tax returns, and a thick folder tabbed SEPARATION AGREEMENT.

Separation?

"I thought the Bradshaws were divorced," she told Dalton when he came to report that he'd found nothing of apparent interest in the rest of the house.

Dwight and SBI Special Agent Terry Wilson arrived at Bradshaw Management shortly after lunch to find Cameron Bradshaw seated behind the desk in Candace Bradshaw's office. He acknowledged them by holding up a finger to indicate that he would be with them in a minute.

According to the report, Candace had been forty-two and folks said her husband was nearly twenty-five years older. Dwight knew him by sight, although they had never interacted in the eight years he had been back in Colleton County. With that wrinkled face, white hair, and liver-splotched hands, Bradshaw did indeed look to be in his late sixties, but he seemed fit enough and his voice was vigorous as he said, ". . . taking it hard, but Dee's stronger than she looks . . . Thanks, Tom. And you be sure to tell Mary how much we appreciated that chicken salad she brought over last night, you hear?"

No sooner had he hung up than the phone rang again. "Sorry," he told them, then lifting his voice, called, "Gracie?"

The brightly dressed middle-aged office manager who had shown them in came to the door. "Yes?"

"I'm sorry, Gracie, but could you take all my calls? Tell people I appreciate their concern, but . . ."

"Sure thing, boss," she said with a solicitous smile.

"Boss," said Bradshaw. He pushed back from the desk and stood to shake their hands in old-fashioned courtesy. "I haven't been called that in a while. Smartest thing Candace did was keep Gracie Farmer on as office manager after I retired."

As the older man sat back down, Terry Wilson exchanged a quick glance with Dwight. A clerk at the courthouse had pulled the Bradshaw separation agreement and given them a quick overview. "Complete division of all the marital property and then at the last minute, they opted for a do-it-yourself separation instead of a divorce. Probably because of the business. It's in his name alone, but she got to do the day-to-day running while he bowed out."

So yeah, Dwight thought, Bradshaw might have wanted to retire at age what? Fifty-seven? Sixty? But today, he certainly looked like a farm boy who was happy to be back on the tractor again.

"I believe you read the letter your wife left?" Dwight asked when the formalities were out of the way.

Cameron Bradshaw sighed and nodded. "I saw it, but I was in such a state of shock. When her cleaning woman called me . . . I went right over — that horrible bag over her head. I tore it open, but it was too late, of course, and I guess I did read the letter while I was waiting for the rescue squad to come, but I was looking for a real reason for her to do this and —"

"Malfeasance as a county commissioner?" said Terry. "Kickbacks from special interests? Those didn't seem like sufficient reasons?"

"To you maybe." The older man seemed to brush them away like so many pesky gnats. "But for Candace to kill herself over that?" He shook his head. "I'd have thought it would take something more personal. Like cancer. Or maybe problems with someone she was seeing. You know. As for those other things, well —"

He broke off helplessly. "She wouldn't have come to me with personal problems, of course, and she didn't have any professional ones."

Dwight frowned. "Even though she says in her letter —"

"That's what I don't understand," he interrupted, leaning forward to make his point. "If she was in professional trouble, she would have asked for my help. She always came to me when she was in over her head with county business or our company here. Position papers she didn't quite understand. Reports and technical papers. That sort of thing. Statistics and projections were always hard for her. And nonlinear concepts. I was the only one she trusted to explain them."

"You told her how to vote on the issues?"

"Good heavens, no!" He drew himself up as if Dwight had suggested that he cheated at cards. "That's not what she wanted. She needed to grasp the main points so that she could discuss them without sounding dumb. And she wasn't dumb, although people like Jamie Jacobson thought she was ignorant because their literary allusions went right over her head. She only had a GED and she wasn't much of a reader, but common sense? About practical concrete issues? She was sharp as anybody. It was the esoteric and theoretical that she had trouble grasping. She was always giving me hypothetical scenarios. If A had this or did that, how would it impact on B or C? That sort of thing."

"And you explained it all to her?" Terry Wilson said doubtfully.

"When I was much younger, I wanted to be a teacher, Agent Wilson, but I needed to make money, to salvage what was left of the family fortune. I think I would have been a good teacher." His voice was wistful. "I wish she had told me what the real problems were. I could have helped her."

Dwight felt sorry for the man's grief. "You still loved her?"

Bradshaw gave a sad, hands-up gesture of resignation. "I never stopped. Oh, it was stupid of me to think she could be happy making love to someone so much older, but once we were living apart, we could be friends again and I liked knowing that she relied on me and on my discretion —"

"Your wife didn't name names in her letter, just general accusations. Do you know who she meant?"

"I'm sorry. I really don't remember any of the details. Do you have it with you?"

When Dwight shook his head, Bradshaw said, "Could I get a copy?"

"We'd rather not right now, sir. We're trying to keep her allegations confidential until we have a chance to investigate."

"Of course, of course. I understand. When will you —" He paused to find the right words. "When may we make arrangements for her funeral?"

"It shouldn't be too long," said Dwight. "I hope we can count on your cooperation and the cooperation of her staff here?"

As Bradshaw hesitated, Terry Wilson pulled out a court order he'd obtained to search the offices of Bradshaw Management for anything related to Candace Bradshaw's position as chair of the Colleton County board of commissioners.

Before her husband could put his glasses back on to read it, the office manager tapped at the door and opened it without waiting.

"Sorry, Mr. Bradshaw," she said formally, "but some people are here."

"They're with me," said Wilson of the two women behind her, special agents who specialized in documentary evidence.

Dwight grinned, recognizing the Ginsburg twins, which was how Tina Ginsburg and Sabrina Ginsburg were known around the Bureau. They were no relation but had somehow wound up in the same division. Mid-thirties, one was an attractive blonde with an easy laugh; the other an intense brunette. Both had stiletto-sharp minds and the hunting instinct of foxhounds for sniffing out white-collar wrongdoings.

"They have a warrant, Gracie," said Bradshaw. "I'll clear out of here for a couple of hours and you show these gentlemen where Candace kept her commissioner's files."

"You don't think you should stay?" A tall woman with a long plain face and a heavy jaw, the office manager was probably in her late fifties. Her clothes were a rainbow of primary colors: a bright blue jersey topped by a canary-yellow knitted vest that was edged in red wool and embellished on the back with multicolored 3-D yarn figures in a village market scene that suggested Central America. She did not seem happy with the situation. "All our confidential company records are here, too."

Bradshaw gave the newcomers a gentle smile. "They are officers of the court," he said trustingly. "I'm sure they won't take anything they shouldn't."

Gracie Farmer's raised eyebrow said, "Oh, yeah?" but she didn't argue with him.

"We'll give you a receipt for everything we do take," Wilson assured her.

Grudgingly, the woman moved to the computer and typed in the password that gave access to everything on the hard drive.

One of the agents sat down and began scanning the file names. "Which are the files connected to her work as a commissioner?"

"It's the one labeled CCBC."

When the agent clicked on it, all she found was a list of names and contact numbers for the current board and a calendar marked with meeting dates. "This is all there is?" she asked.

Gracie Farmer shrugged. "I think she kept all the other files on her home computer. She really only used this one for Bradshaw Management."

"What about hard files or CDs?"

"You're welcome to look, but I'm telling you — she kept the two totally separate."

While the two techie agents began to plunder both the electronic and the paper files, Dwight and Terry asked the office manager if there was someplace they could talk to her in private.

She led them to her own office, a space filled with ethnic crafts in bright colors. A small wooden oxcart painted with parrots and tropical flowers sat next to her computer and held the usual desk tools and pens. Several red-green-and-blue wooden parrots shared a perch suspended from the ceiling in a corner over pots of tropical plants in such lavish bloom that they had to

145

be artificial even though they looked real. The walls were lined with photographs and posters of Costa Rica. It was like stepping into a tropical travel agency.

"Wow!" said Terry. "You must really love it there. Do you get down often?"

"As often as I can," she said. "In fact, I'm hoping to retire there."

She gestured them to chairs and immediately got down to business. "Is it true then?"

"Is what true?" Dwight countered.

"I heard Candace left a letter saying she stole from the county and took kickbacks from people the board did business with."

"Does that fit with what you know of her?" Dwight asked.

Her plain face looked troubled and her eyes dropped before their gaze.

Trying a different tack, Terry said, "I guess you've known her a long time?"

Mrs. Farmer nodded and they noticed that her earrings were tiny enameled parrots that swayed when her head moved. "I was the one that first hired her to clean some rental property when the tenants moved out. In fact, I was the one encouraged her to get her GED out at the community college. She was a hard worker and didn't mind getting her hands dirty."

146

As if hearing how that sounded in this context, she shook her head. "Candace was ambitious. She wanted to be somebody. You know where she came from, right?"

"Tell us," said Dwight.

So Gracie Farmer told them of little Candy Wells's rocky childhood, her move to Dobbs, her struggle for a better life for herself. "I grew up dirt poor, too. My parents were sharecroppers, but they loved me and made sure I stayed in school. Candace had no one except an old sick grandmother and look how well she's done. Running Bradshaw Management, chair of the board of commissioners. I can't understand how she'd throw it all away for . . ."

She paused and looked at them. "If she did it, it wasn't for money."

"No?" asked Dwight.

"It would have been for power. Candace liked doing favors and having people beholden to her. She wouldn't have cared for the money. It was knowing that important people came to her for favors. It would be hard for her to say no if someone like that asked her to do something that wasn't strictly legal and didn't really do anybody any harm. If money was involved, I'm sure she would've thought of it as a sort of thank-you, not a bribe or anything."

Terry looked at Dwight with a wry shake of his head. "Kickbacks. When you care enough to send the very best."

CHAPTER 8

.... This is farm country and
You can see the enchantment and the
   hope that the characters will
Come and make the crops, but all they
   want to do is play.
     — *Paul's Hill,* by Shelby Stephenson

On Thursday, I went to the Democratic Women's luncheon. The speaker was Elaine Marshall, our secretary of state and the first woman ever elected to North Carolina's Council of State. We were trying to get her to run for the U.S. Senate, but she loved the job she had and seemed quite happy to stay in the area with her husband and friends.

"Hey, Deborah, look at me!" my longtime best friend Portland Brewer called as I crossed the parking lot to the restaurant. She did a happy pirouette on the gravel so that I could admire the fit of her favorite black sheath, which was topped with a lime-green linen jacket.

Ever since the birth of little Carolyn Deborah Brewer, about eighteen hours after she'd served as my matron of honor back in December, Portland had been struggling to get back to her pre-baby size.

"Way to go!" I applauded. "The carrot sticks are on me today."

Inside, we found seats at a table with Jamie Jacobson and Betty Ann Edgerton. Jamie's part of an ad agency here in Dobbs and is one of only two Democrats on the county board of commissioners, while Betty Ann is the builder who oversaw work on a WomenAid house I helped build a few years back when I was first appointed to the bench. She's a good ol' gal who, with the help of my mother, opened the all-male vo-tech classes at West Colleton up to females, too. She had no interest in the secretarial courses girls were supposed to take back then, but she made straight A's in woodworking and shop once she was allowed in.

It was a struggle for her the first few years until the building boom hit so hard that developers didn't care if their builders were male, female, or little green hermaphrodites from Alpha Centauri as long as the houses went up as fast as their profits. Since then, she's built a pile of them and gives a chunk of money to the Democratic party every year.

Candace Bradshaw's suicide was still on everyone's mind and like them, we also speculated on whom the Republicans would choose to succeed her.

"Danny Creedmore could pick himself," Portland said gloomily.

"No way," said Betty Ann, who is fifteen years older and wiser than we. "He'd have to recuse himself every time one of his projects came up. Much easier to put in another puppet he can keep claiming is disinterested."

"What I just can't get my mind around," said Jamie, "is why Candace killed herself. She *adored* chairing the board and playing Lady Bountiful. She acted as if the citizens who came to us with requests were asking her permission alone, as if she was doing them a favor with money out of her own pocket. Everybody knows whose pocket she was in —"

"Don't you mean whose bed?" Betty Ann said cynically.

"Same difference," Jamie agreed. "My point is, if she was doing something that could be proved to be illegal, then he'd be in it, too, and I've heard that Doug Woodall's cut a deal with Danny Creedmore. If the county Republicans promise not to give his opponent much support, then he won't rock any boats right now."

"That may not be a promise he can keep," I said. "Once her suicide note becomes public, there will have to be an investigation."

"You've read it?"

"You know what's in it?"

"Did she get specific?"

I held up my hands to block their questions. "Have I read it? No. Has Dwight told me one single word? No. But I've heard the same thing the rest of y'all have heard. That she misused her office and took kickbacks. If that's true, then Doug's obligated to do a pro forma investigation if nothing else."

Our food arrived, and talk turned to whether or not Kevin Foster could take Doug's place as our new DA, the number of turned ankles our friends had gotten from those high-heeled platform wedges ("Ugliest shoe of my lifetime," said Betty Ann), and did we think Cameron Bradshaw was going to keep the business going long enough for Dee to get her act together and take over?

"I hope so," said Jamie as she forked through her salad to extract the onions she normally liked. "Meeting with a client this afternoon," she explained parenthetically. "Much as I hated Candace's high-handed ways on the board, I have to say that she did give good value for the money when it came to cleaning our office. I once mentioned that I thought they were missing the floor behind the commode in the bathroom and she came in herself the next evening to make sure it was done right."

"I'll give her that," said Betty Ann. "We don't use Bradshaw Management ourselves, but the architects that rent in our complex do. I was working late one night last week and as I was leaving, here she came tripping across the parking lot in a fancy embroidered jacket and high heels to check up on one of her new cleaning gals. Tried to give me a sales talk right there in the parking lot about how she could probably give me a better deal than what I was paying."

"Could she?" asked Jamie.

Betty Ann shrugged. "I didn't get a quote. It helps out my crew if I hire some of their family members to clean for us. I give the crew chief a flat fee and they work it out between themselves. Don't you want your peach cobbler, Deborah?"

I virtuously handed it over. No way was I going to let Portland out-skinny me. "John

Claude still uses her service," I said, "but I never remember seeing her there after hours."

Portland dipped the edge of her napkin into her water glass and tried to sponge away a spot of salad dressing that had dripped on the front of her green jacket. I leaned over to help.

"Candace tried really hard to sell Avery and me on her services," she said when the worst was out, "but the woman who cleans our house is willing to go by a couple of times a week, so we didn't bother. Speaking of which, did y'all hear what happened out at that Church of Christ Eternal on Easter morning?"

"Is that the one split off from Jensen Memorial?" I asked.

"The one they built with no windows like they're barricading themselves against the world?" Betty Ann asked.

"I guess so," Portland said dubiously. "That's where my cleaning woman goes. Or rather, where she used to go up until Easter Sunday. Their preacher's one of those little pricks who think they're divinely appointed and that men are superior to women."

"Oh yeah, a guy named McKinney. I've heard about him," said Betty Ann. "The women can't wear slacks or sleeveless dresses. What's he done now?"

What she told us was almost unbelievable in this day and age. A man demanding so much obedience that he would order his wife to drink from his water glass after he'd spit in it?

"Don't tell me she did it?" I said.

Portland nodded. "Rena says she cried, but she drank it."

For a moment, I thought I was going to throw up and I saw my own horror and disgust mirrored on the faces of my friends.

"Dear Lord!" said Jamie. "Does he make her wear a veil and walk three paces behind him?"

"I don't know about that, but I do know it finished Rena with that church. She put her pride in her pocket and moved her membership back to Jensen Memorial."

"Good for her."

"But isn't it appalling?" said Portland. "Next thing you know he'll be telling her to drink the Kool-Aid."

"Been me," said Betty Ann, "I'd have put a little more spit in the glass and thrown it right back in his arrogant face."

Someone at the next table shushed us and we turned our attention to the podium as Elaine Marshall rose to speak. She was her usual witty and intelligent self and she wore a beautifully cut dark red pantsuit.

But then she was never going to get any votes from any Reverend Mr. McKinneys anyhow.

Judge Luther Parker, who was supposed to hold juvenile court that afternoon, had been called away at noon on a family emergency, and because my afternoon load was light enough to shift to the others, I volunteered to sit in for him. His calendar included the type of case that is becoming more and more common these days as town and country keep bumping up against each other. If we were totally suburban, there would be one set of problems with common perceptions, experiences, and assumptions. All country would present a different set, but again, most everyone would be on the same page.

But when you slap a closely built, hundred-house development down in the middle of farming country, neither side completely understands the other.

Today's case in point: trespass and malicious damage to real property.

Three twelve- and thirteen-year-old boys had been arrested after roaring over a farmer's field of young soybean plants on four-wheel ATVs, chasing one another in circles. They had torn up so many plants that the whole six acres would have to be disked under and replanted.

The farm was posted with NO TRESPASSING signs and yes, the kids could read and yes, it was thoughtless of them to do that much damage. No farm kid would have dreamed of wrecking a crop — *anybody's* crop — but these boys were from a nearby development and neither the kids nor their parents seemed to have a smidgen of knowledge of farming.

Several Christmases ago, I chipped in for a couple of ATVs for the nieces and nephews out on the farm. They've mostly graduated to cars, and the four-wheelers stay parked at our house these days for Cal and Mary Pat to use; but even at eight, they know to stick to the lanes or they'll lose their ticket to ride.

After lecturing the kids about respect for private property, I turned to their parents.

"Your houses sit on quarter-acre lots," I said. "When you bought your sons these four-wheelers, where did you think they were going to ride them? It's illegal for them to be on the road and you don't have any land. What were you thinking?"

All I got were indifferent shrugs.

"I see by their records that this is the

second time these three boys have been cited, which means that you had notice of their prior misuse of the ATVs."

Again, looks of indifference.

"In other words, Mom and Dad, your failure to supervise is negligence and makes you liable for all the damages and leaves you open to the possibility of being prosecuted for contributing to their delinquency."

Now I had their attention.

I leafed through their case folders and read over Luther Parker's notes. It took me a few minutes to process what he'd planned to do and when I next glanced up, two of the parents appeared distinctly worried.

"Last time, your sons got a very light slap on the wrist and there was no inconvenience to you. This time, I'm ordering that they be sent for a mental health evaluation, for which you will be billed."

I glanced over at the farmer whose beans had been destroyed. "Mr. Bell estimates the damage at fifteen hundred dollars, which is extremely reasonable, if not downright generous of him."

I then put the boys under the supervision of a juvenile court counselor, and ordered them to pay damages, to stay off Mr. Bell's property, and not to ride their ATVs anywhere that wasn't legally sanctioned.

Some of the parents were huffing by this time, but I warned them that if their sons came back to court again for misuse of their ATVs, they themselves would also face charges. "And penalties in adult courts are a lot tougher than here."

"Don't worry, Your Honor," said one of the mothers. "His four-wheeling days are over. There's going to be a FOR SALE sign on it this afternoon."

"Aw, Mo-om!" the twelve-year-old whined.

"You heard her," his father said sternly. "And your part of that fifteen hundred is coming out of *your* savings account, not ours."

Juvenile court can be a real downer at times and that afternoon, I dealt with a bully who's well on his way to spending his life in prison if someone doesn't shoot him first. I signed an order that would return a rebellious fourteen-year-old runaway to her family in Virginia, sent three repeat teenagers to a minimum security youth center, and arranged protective custody for two little girls whose foster dad was waiting trial for raping them.

At least I hoped I was giving them protection.

When Luther signed the papers that put those girls in that last foster home, he must surely have thought they would be safer there than where they were. I suppose you could say he was right if you call being raped safer than being beaten to a bloody pulp by their birth father, who's now serving life for killing their baby brother.

By the end of the session, I was totally drained. As I sat down at the defense table to read over a search warrant a Dobbs police officer wanted me to sign, a pair of familiar hands began to massage the muscles that had knotted in my neck. For once, the search warrant was properly filled out and I signed it without a murmur.

When we were alone in the courtroom, I looked up into Dwight's warm brown eyes. "Ummm. If I were a cat, I'd be purring about now."

"Rough day?" he asked as he kneaded the tension from my neck.

"Just this last half. How come you're still here? Where's Cal?"

"Kate called me. He's over at the farm with Jake and Mary Pat, helping to set out those tuberoses the kids are gonna grow."

Seth, Daddy, and I had given some of my

nieces and nephews a twenty-acre field to try to grow an economically feasible organic crop. They planned to put five acres in tuberoses and sunflowers, and the rest in soybeans.

I glanced at my watch. Almost five-thirty. "Will someone give them supper?"

"Supper and a sleepover at Seth and Minnie's. Tomorrow's a teacher work day, so the kids're gonna pick up a couple of pizzas and watch one of Jess's favorite horse movies."

His eyes twinkled and a bolt of happy anticipation shot through me. I do love Dwight's son, but hey! Dwight and I have been married only four months.

"You mean we have the whole evening to ourselves?"

"Want to drive into Raleigh? Drinks at Miss Molly's, then dinner or a movie?"

I shook my head. "Nope. I want to pick up something on our way home, then make popcorn and watch an old video the way we used to before I knew you loved me."

His smile turned into a mock leer. "*Exactly* the way we used to?"

I leered right back at him, remembering how chaste those evenings had been. "Only this time you can show me what was actually on your mind back then."

CHAPTER 9

... and if there is
a fly nearby, or dust, a blowing curtain,
the sun coming in through the glass, watch
   it:
that is yours to keep.
    — *Fiddledeedee,* by Shelby Stephenson

Friday morning

Walking down the hallway to his office next morning, Dwight eventually realized that all the smiles he was getting probably meant that he had a sappy one pasted on his face.

"Good morning, sir," one of the deputies said as he passed the squad room.

If he only knew, Dwight thought to himself, savoring the memory of Deborah when he had taken her a cup of coffee an hour or so earlier. No sooner had he handed her the mug than she had carefully placed it on the shelf of their headboard, then pulled him down next to her for a repeat of last night when she had disappeared into their bedroom, ostensibly to pick out a video.

"Need some help deciding which one?" he had called when she didn't return right away.

"That's okay. I've got it." A few minutes later, she appeared in the doorway. "*Men in Black,* or me in this?" she asked with a perfectly straight face.

As he felt himself begin to harden, he had laughed and said, "No contest. *Men in Black,* of course."

"You're in a good mood this morning," Bo Poole said. "You and Wilson come up with specifics on Candace Bradshaw yesterday?"

"Nothing worth talking about," he said. "If she wrote anything down, we haven't found it yet. Her assistant claims she kept her board membership pretty much separate from Bradshaw Management and says if she took money for her favors, she would've considered it more like a perfectly legitimate thank-you gift than a kickback. Richards came up empty on her home computer, too. The Ginsburg twins are going file by file on both computers just to see if she got cute and hid something under an innocuous label, and I've asked Danny Creedmore to come in this morning, but I don't expect to

163

get much out of him until we have something to pry him open with."

They were still talking when Dwight's phone rang and a doctor in the medical examiner's office over in Chapel Hill handed him a crowbar. Because Candace Bradshaw's death had been tagged a probable suicide, there had been no huge rush to do the postmortem.

"Good thing that whoever found her tore that bag open without disturbing the drawstrings," the doctor told him. "Soon as I cut the bag away from her neck, it was clear that it didn't line up with the original marks on her neck. She didn't die from asphyxia, Bryant. She was strangled first with a thin ligament and then the bag put on."

"Yeah? Wait a minute while I let Sheriff Poole know." He pressed the speaker button on the phone base so that Bo could hear. "They're calling it a homicide, Bo."

"You sure about that, Doc?" asked Bo. "She didn't do it herself?"

"Excuse me?" The doctor sounded offended. "I won't have the full report for another day or two, but I can tell you now that the force was such that one of the rings in her trachea was broken. There's no way she could have garroted herself from behind and then tied on that bag."

"What about scratch marks on her neck? Or fingernail scrapings?"

"Sorry. Nothing like that. If she fought her attacker, it's not evident and her wrists don't seem to have been tied, although there's some faint bruising on both arms that could indicate she struggled to get out of some sort of soft restraint — maybe a blanket or a sheet? — and there was a fresh bruise on her right knee for whatever that's worth."

"What about a TOD?" Dwight asked.

"Find somebody who can say when she ate a spinach salad with hard-boiled eggs," the doctor said crisply. "She died about two and a half hours after eating it. Lacking that and only judging by the rigor, time of death could be anywhere from mid-afternoon to midnight."

"Thanks, Doc," said Bo and leaned over to switch off the speakerphone. "I better go let Doug Woodall know."

"I'll call Terry," said Dwight. "And I'll get some people to nail down when she ate that salad."

"Don't forget you've got Creedmore coming in."

"I haven't. You want to sit in on it?"

"I might should," said Bo. "I always feel better myself when I have a witness to any

165

conversations with ol' Danny."

Barefooted, Daniel Creedmore probably stood five-seven, the same as Bo Poole. His tooled leather cowboy boots added an extra inch, though, and his waistline looked to be about four inches bigger. On this mild spring day, he wore a black poplin windbreaker and a maroon shirt that was unbuttoned at the top and tucked inside charcoal-gray slacks. Like Bo, he was midfifties and had a friendly open face, shrewd blue eyes, and thinning brown hair. Unlike Bo, he was not someone who immediately commanded attention and he did not possess Bo's innate easygoing nature, despite telling everyone to call him Danny. It was as if his mama had told him he could catch more flies with honey and he had spent his adult life trying to hide the astringent vinegar that lay just beneath a surface of assumed warmth and friendliness.

"Good to see you, Bo," he said as he entered Bo's office and took a chair across from him. "Hey, Bryant. How's it going?"

"Thanks for coming in," the sheriff said, "and let me offer my condolences on Candace Bradshaw's death."

"Thanks," Creedmore said blandly, pretending to misunderstand. "The county and

166

the party both have suffered a great loss. We were hoping to put her up for a state office this next cycle."

"Like you did last time?" asked Dwight.

"That's right," Bo said, leaning back in his big padded chair. His blue eyes twinkled. "I did hear that Woody Galloway's throwing his hat in the governor's ring."

Woodrow Galloway was a state senator who would have a tough primary fight for the party's nomination. Unfortunately, his seat in the General Assembly was up for election this time, too. Two years ago, one of the representatives from the county was in the same position. That's when it was decided to get Candace Bradshaw to file for his seat. After he lost the nomination he had sought, Candace gallantly withdrew her name in his favor, which was how she became chair of the board.

It was an open secret that they hoped to do the same with Galloway's slot — that Candace would keep his chair warm in case he lost the primary, which most assumed he would.

Creedmore shrugged. "Would've been a little harder this time around. Candace didn't have much name recognition outside the county, but with enough backing, we thought she was up to it."

"As you say, a real loss," said Dwight.

"On a personal level as well, right?" Bo added.

Danny Creedmore's eyes narrowed. "You want to explain that, Sheriff?"

"I think you know where this is headed," the sheriff said mildly. "Her name's been linked to yours ever since you and your friends first ran her for the board. It seems to be fairly common knowledge and I suppose we could document times and places if you make us."

They locked eyes for a long moment, then Creedmore caved with a rueful laugh and a hands-up what-the-hell gesture of locker-room camaraderie. "Shit, Bo, she was a good-looking woman and who doesn't like a little strange nookie on the side when you've been married long as I have?"

Bo gave an encouraging grin and Creedmore obliged with colorful details on just what a hot little number Candy Bradshaw could be. No man ever knows another man completely, thought Dwight, but he'd be willing to bet everything he owned that Bo had never been with another woman while Marnie was alive.

"Why'd she kill herself?" Bo asked as the other man wound down.

"Now that I couldn't tell you. Surprised

the hell out of me. It was like getting a sucker punch in the gut when they told it yesterday. I hear she left a letter? Don't suppose you can tell me what was in it?"

"Sorry. Any truth to it?"

Creedmore thrust his hands in the pocket of his black jacket and stretched back in his chair with a smile and a shake of his head. "Good try, Bo."

"When did you last see her?" Dwight asked.

"It'd been at least a week. To be honest with you, it was sorta cooling off between us. Sexually, I mean. I think she was seeing somebody else and —"

"Who?" said Bo.

"Could be almost anybody, I suppose. Thad Hamilton. One of our representatives. Hell, maybe even Woody Galloway himself."

Dwight frowned. "But you yourself had no contact with her the week before she died?"

"Didn't say that, Bryant. I said I hadn't seen her. We talked almost every day. There was a public hearing on the planning board's recommendations Tuesday night and she was opposed to them. Wanted to game it with me."

I'll just bet she did, thought Dwight. He glanced inquiringly at Bo and got an almost

169

imperceptible nod. "Who wanted her dead, Creedmore?"

"Huh?" No one ever said that Creedmore made his fortune through dumb luck alone. "You telling me she was killed? She didn't do it herself?"

"We'd appreciate it if you'd keep that under your hat for a few hours," Bo said. "But yeah. Someone strangled her."

"Well, damn!" said Danny Creedmore. They could see the wheels turning behind those shrewd blue eyes. "You talk to her good-for-nothing daughter yet?"

"What do you mean I can't move back in here?" Dee asked indignantly.

She had appeared at the door of Candace Bradshaw's new house with her duffle bag, and Special Agent Sabrina Ginsburg and Deputy Mayleen Richards had immediately blocked her entrance.

"This is my mother's house. I live here and I'm her only child so I probably own it now." She glared at the two law officers and all but stamped her foot in indignation.

"Unless she left a will, I rather doubt that," said the blond Ginsburg "twin." "It's our understanding that she and your dad were still legally married, so he would be one of her heirs if she died intestate."

"Whatever. So call him. I'm sure he'd rather I stay here than keep sleeping on his couch, and besides, I need fresh clothes."

"You really can't move back in," Richards told her, thinking that Deanna Bradshaw was acting more like twelve than twenty-two. "You can pick up some of your clothes, but you can't stay till we finish our investigation."

While Sabrina Ginsburg went back to checking the files on Candace Bradshaw's laptop, Mayleen Richards followed the daughter into her messy bedroom next door to the office.

The girl stopped at the doorway and gave a look of distaste at the state of her room. "Oh crap! I guess you're not letting Sancha in to clean either."

"That's right," Richards said. "While you're here, though, I need to ask you some questions. You may have been the last one to see your mother alive. Did she give any indication that —"

"— that she was going to put a bag over her head and end it all? No! Okay, we had a fight. She was still pissed that I let a guy stay over last week and we got into it again."

"What guy?"

"Doesn't matter. I've dumped him. He

can't hold his liquor. Puked all over her new couch."

"I need his name."

Rolling her eyes, Dee muttered the boy-friend's full name and that of his dorm over at Chapel Hill.

"Thanks," Richards said, writing it on the yellow legal pad she carried. "Was your mother depressed? In some kind of trouble?"

"My dad told me what she wrote." Dee upended her duffle bag on the bed and began to pull clean lingerie from an open drawer. "But he didn't believe it and I don't either. Mom liked her life. She was kicking ass and having fun."

"Whose ass, Dee?"

"Anybody's who needed it, I guess. How should I know? I was at school till Easter most of the time."

"That when she moved in here?"

"No, it was Christmas. She was real big on giving herself presents. New Toyota for her birthday last spring, this house for Christmas. First new house she'd ever lived in. You'd've thought it was Buckingham Palace," she said with all the scorn of someone born to the privilege and status her father's family had possessed.

"Our old house had been in the Bradshaw

family for a hundred years," Dee said, "and she just walked away from everything there. Sold it all or sent it to the landfill. Even my stuff. The only thing she kept was her dollhouse and her clothes."

"*Her* dollhouse?"

"You don't think she ever let me play with it, do you? Mom didn't like to share. When she was little, I guess her people didn't have much. She used to talk about the dollhouse she'd seen in a shop window and how she used to wish on the new moon for one, so Dad gave it to her for their tenth wedding anniversary. She was always fiddling with it and buying new stuff for it."

There was a sudden catch in her voice and Richards realized she was not quite as indifferent to her mother's death as she would have everyone believe.

"So when did you see her last?" Richards asked gently.

"I don't know. Tuesday? Around two, maybe? We fought. She said I could go back to school or I could go live with Dad. She made me give her my key as I was leaving, but she was already starting to cool off."

"Oh?"

"Yeah, she was eating a late lunch and watching a history program at the kitchen counter — some guy jumped out of an

173

airplane twenty-five years ago with a bag of diamonds or something."

"Eating what?" Richards asked.

"One of those grocery deli salads."

"What kind?"

"Spinach."

"With hard-boiled eggs?"

"Yeah. Why?"

"Depending on how far along digestion was, it helps us establish a time of death."

"Oh gross!" the girl said, making a face.

"And you're sure that program was on?"

"Yeah, they were showing pictures of the jewelry and Mom was like drooling over the diamond necklaces."

After Dee Bradshaw had departed with extra makeup and clean clothes, leaving her dirty ones still piled in a heap on her bed, Richards called to Ginsburg, "You hear that?"

"Already on it," the SBI agent said, busily searching the Internet. "Here we go. *Unsolved Mysteries: The Nicholas Radzinsky Case.* You remember him?"

"Sorry, I was too young, but I read the article in the *N&O* a couple of weeks back about it. Guy stole his employer's plane one night, along with a gym bag full of jewelry worth millions, put the plane on automatic, and parachuted out somewhere between

Washington and the Great Smokies, right?"

"Yeah. I was eleven at the time. My friends and I figured he must have flown right over us up there in Lynchburg. We spent that whole damn spring hiking the woods, absolutely convinced he must have dropped the bag and we were going to find it and get that big reward. All we got were chiggers and poison oak."

Richards laughed. "So what time did the program air in this area?"

Sabrina Ginsburg ran a beautifully manicured, pink-tipped finger down the screen. "According to this, it was a half-hour segment that ran from one-thirty to two."

"So if she finished eating by two, that would put our TOD somewhere around four-thirty to five o'clock, give or take a half-hour."

Ginsburg nodded. "Rush hour. Wouldn't you know it?"

"Between four and five-thirty, hm?" Dwight said when Richards called him to report. "Good work, Mayleen. Denning should be there any minute now with the van to take another look at her bedroom. I can't believe he'll find anything, but we have to jump through the hoops. Any progress with her laptop?"

"No, sir. Ginsburg's going to take it back to Garner with her and put some of her techies to work scanning every file, but it turns out that she had a CD that's a digital shredder, so she's not very optimistic."

"Yeah. I'm over at Bradshaw Management and our twin's downloading everything to flash drives for a page-by-page examination, too."

"What about the house, sir? The daughter's pushing to move back in."

"You've done a thorough search for any papers?"

"And for CDs and flash drives. Ginsburg and I talked about those 'fd' notations on her paper files. Could stand for flash drive. I'm not gonna say she doesn't have a secret hidey-hole somewhere in the house, but if she does, we haven't found it and we've sure looked."

"Clothes pockets in her closet? Plastic bags in her refrigerator? Books?"

"No books, almost nothing in the refrigerator. No flour or sugar canisters. Cupboards almost bare except for a couple of cereal boxes that only hold cereal. I guess she didn't cook much either."

At that slip of her tongue, Mayleen Richards felt herself flushing a bright red. When Mike didn't cook, they usually ate take-out, but she had tried to make a rice dish last night and had wound up cooking it to mush. She was mortified, but he had laughed and called in an order for Chinese. "They say it will be twenty minutes," he had said, pulling her to him.

She flushed again at the memory. If Major Bryant picked up on that "either," though, he didn't mention it.

"It helps that the house is so new," she said hastily. "Her daughter says she was pretty ruthless about throwing out the old and starting fresh, so there's not a ton of stuff to go through. Here's Denning now." She gave the department's crime scene specialist a come-on-in wave of her hand. "I'll search again while he's working, but if she used a flash drive, we're talking something about the size of a lipstick."

"I know," her boss said with an audible sigh. "But we can't hold things up forever. Did you tell the daughter that Candace was murdered?"

"No, sir."

"Good. Wilson and I'll go speak with her and her dad and tell them we're finished with the house."

"Hey, Percy," Agent Sabrina Ginsburg said, automatically fluffing her shoulder-length blond hair.

"Blondie! My lucky day," the department's crime scene specialist said with a big grin. "I'd've gotten here quicker if I'd known *you* were working the house."

As if, thought Mayleen, sliding her cell phone back into the holder on her belt. Percy Denning was nice, but nerdy. Ginsburg was sweet, though. She talked enough flirty trash with him to send him on down to the master bedroom with a silly grin on his face.

"Damn flash drives," Agent Sabrina Ginsburg said when Richards said she was going to make another search. "If she used one for the illegal stuff and never saved anything to hard drive, we may never find anything if she ran her digital shredder periodically. You look in all her purses? In her lipstick cases? What about drugstore magnifying glasses that come in those pretty little metal cases?"

She pulled a bright yellow plastic flash drive from her own purse. "I keep all my picture albums on this one. I could hide it anywhere."

"Tell me about it," Richards said wearily. She had a purple one in her shoulder bag that she could use on any computer to jot quick notes to herself for writing up fuller reports. "I wonder if her daughter knows?"

She pulled out her cell phone, located the number Dee Bradshaw had given her, and put the question to her directly.

"A flash drive?" asked Dee. "Sure. I gave her one last fall."

She didn't know where her mother kept it, "But if you find it and she hasn't changed it, the password's *hotwater.*"

"Hot water? All one word?"

"Right."

"The thing is," said Ginsburg when Richards relayed that information, "it's been my experience that white-collar criminals usually keep their data handy so they can get at it easily."

She had already powered down the laptop and stashed it in the black carrying case, a case that had first been thoroughly searched, and she had pulled several paper files as well.

Together, she and Richards examined every inch of the cherry desk, taking out the drawers and looking for evidence of tape on the backs or undersides. They ran their fingers into the crevices of Bradshaw's padded swivel executive's chair in case she'd slipped a thin DVD case or flash drive there. The only other places within easy reach were her wastebasket and file cabinet.

Again, nothing.

"The drapes?" asked Ginsburg.

The desk did sit in front of the heavy rose-colored damask drapes, so that the chair faced the door in the opposite wall. Easy to swivel around to a pocket on the backside of the drapes.

Nada.

"The chair's on casters," Mayleen pointed out, and there was enough space between the desk and wall to roll out while still seated, so they widened the range. Unfortunately, the only other items in the room were the dollhouse, a half-empty chest of drawers, a white velvet love seat that made into a single bed for overnight guests, and a small closet that held four winter coats and jackets.

Ginsburg swung the dollhouse around on its casters. She hadn't paid it much attention before and she was charmed by the detailed nursery on the third floor. Not so charmed, however, that she didn't look under the embroidered white crib blanket or the white satin coverlet on the bed in an adjoining room.

The chest received the same thorough examination as the desk. Ditto the love seat when they opened it. Ditto the closet. In the end, they even lifted the area rug that sat atop the white Berber carpet. No papers.

"Maybe Tina's having more luck at the office," Ginsburg said when they finally called it quits.

"Hey, look what my metal detector turned up in her bedroom floor," Denning said from the doorway. He held out a clear plastic evidence bag and they saw a bullet slug. "The pile's so thick on that carpet, I missed it completely the first time around."

At Bradshaw Management, the interviews with Candace Bradshaw's office staff had elicited the information that their boss did occasionally use a flash drive when she worked on the computer.

"Oh, yes," one of the billing clerks nodded when specifically asked. "You see how her desk faces the door? She said it was feng shui, but I think it was because she didn't want anybody to ever see what was on her screen. And if you went around her desk to show her a paper or something without being asked, she'd jump down your throat. Sometimes she'd make me wait till she closed whatever was on her screen and she'd unplug her memory stick and put it in her purse or her pocket. She never left it plugged in. *Never.*"

"You know something?" said Gracie Farmer when Dwight Bryant and Agent

Terry Wilson questioned her again amid the lush tropical decor of her office. "Mindy's right. I'd forgotten about it."

The opening and closing of her door when they entered had set the wooden parrots behind her gently swaying on their perches until Terry almost expected to hear them squawk. As he sat down in a chair near one of the large flowering plants, a leaf brushed his neck and he could not repress an instinctive swat of his hand, as if it had been a tarantula or some sort of equatorial pest.

"You know how you get so used to seeing somebody do the same thing over and over till you just don't notice? Candace and I had a lunch meeting with a new client last winter, a twenty-unit rental apartment on North Street. We set it up for one o'clock, but he called us at twelve-twenty, wanting to know where the heck we were because he thought we'd agreed on twelve. We went rushing out and were halfway to the restaurant when she remembered she'd forgotten to pull the flash drive. I couldn't talk her into waiting. She dropped me at the restaurant and went right back for it. So yeah, whatever she used it for, she sure didn't want anybody else getting their hands on it."

As she spoke, Farmer automatically tidied

her desk, squaring the corners of the file folders in front of her, placing paper clips and stray pens in the brightly decorated miniature oxcart that served as the desk's catchall.

"She even bought one of those digital shredders on a CD and ran it on her computer a couple of times a week. I just assumed she was being extra careful with confidential board business because there's no need for anything like that with the business."

As she talked, both men were sizing her up. There was nothing she could do about her Jay Leno–size jaw, but she seemed to take pains with her hair and makeup. Although she was a few pounds overweight, today's colorful outfit consisted of a rainbow-banded peasant skirt, an orange tunic, and a necklace of small wooden multihued flowers. She could have stepped out of one of the Costa Rica travel posters on her wall. Her hands showed her age, though, and her closely trimmed nails gave mute testimony that she could still push a mop or scrub a toilet bowl if need be.

"What time does the office here close?" Dwight asked.

The office manager smiled and shook her head. "Technically, it doesn't. We lock the front door at five and put the regular office phones on automatic answering, but there's a twenty-four-hour emergency number that tenants can call if a sink backs up or a fuse blows. And our cleaning crews work until nine or so, depending on how many show up on any given evening, which means we have someone here to lock up after they check their vans and equipment back in."

"What about you?" said Terry. "What time do you leave?"

"Depends. Usually around five. Sometimes it's later, sometimes it's earlier. If I have to check on a job in Cotton Grove or Makely, I don't bother to come back here before going home."

"And Mrs. Bradshaw?"

"Again, it depended. We have good people, independent workers. Candace loved to quote Eisenhower: 'Trust 'em or bust 'em,' she'd say. I've never found it necessary to hold a stopwatch on anybody more than once. Candace pretty much kept the same hours as the rest of us. Once the commissioners made her chairman of the board, though, that did take up a lot of her time. On meeting nights, she usually left at noon to go home and change and read over the agenda items."

"That what happened Tuesday?" asked Terry.

Gracie Farmer nodded. "And if you're asking me again why she'd leave here perfectly normal and then go home and kill herself, I have to say again I honestly don't know."

She fingered the wooden flowers of her hand-carved necklace and her troubled blue eyes met Dwight's. "Have you learned anything at all?"

"Nothing definite." He shifted in his chair and said, "Who were her friends?"

The woman knitted her brows. "Close friends? I don't know if she had any. Not women friends anyhow. There were some women in her party that she would have lunch with once in a while, but someone to sit around and dish the dirt with?" She shook her head. "I told you about her childhood and upbringing. I think she felt inferior because she didn't come from money and she didn't have much of an education."

She removed a loose thread from the sleeve of her orange tunic. "Poor Candace. I don't think she really fit in anywhere once she left home and moved to Dobbs. The caste system's everywhere, isn't it? The women here in the office tend to look down on the janitorial staff, but once she married

Cameron and started working here in the office, she was their boss. She joined the Republican Women and went to all the meetings but if she ever got close to anyone in particular, I never heard her say. Most of them have college degrees and can talk about art and music and things that went over her head.

"Cameron — Mr. Bradshaw, he tried to educate her taste, but she wasn't much interested. I think that's one of the reasons they broke up. She got tired of trying to meet his expectations. I remember once she slammed down the phone on him because she wanted to go to a Willie Nelson concert and he wanted to go to Raleigh to hear some 'effing harpsichords.' Those were her very words. I don't know what she had against harpsichords, but it was about a month later that she filed for divorce."

"Which was never finalized," said Terry Wilson.

"No. Actually, Cameron's probably the closest thing to the kind of friend you're asking about. He really is a nice man and once he was out of the house and not trying to improve her mind, she liked him again. It was like he was her favorite uncle."

"What about her daughter?"

"Dee?" Gracie gave a sour laugh. "Dee

might have been her ticket to becoming Mrs. Cameron Bradshaw, but Candace was no touchy-feely mommy. Not really her fault though, was it? I don't know how she could've been anything else, coming from the home she did."

"What about you, Mrs. Farmer?"

"Me?" She seemed a bit surprised by that question. "I suppose so. I mean we liked each other, and I guess she talked to me as freely as to anyone else, but . . ." She shrugged. "Again, it's boss and employee, isn't it?"

"You hired her," Dwight said. "Did you resent it when she became your boss?"

"No. Not really." She heard the doubt in her voice and gave a rueful laugh. "Okay, it was a little awkward in the beginning, but I knew way more about this job than she did and she knew it. Once I realized she was here to work and that she would be capable of running it profitably herself, I quit worrying about it. I'm not ambitious, Major Bryant. I live alone. I make a good salary. I've had good luck with some of my investments and I don't care about power. She didn't have to watch her back with me."

"Who *did* she have to watch?" asked Terry.

"Nobody, so far as I know. Well, maybe Roger Flackman at first. He's the accountant Cameron hired to go over the books twice a year. But we keep accurate books and he's never found that she was holding back so much as a dime. Cameron told me about her letter, though. Is that what you mean? You think someone was going to blow the whistle on her?"

"Was there a whistle to blow?" asked Dwight.

She shook her head. "But isn't that what politics is all about these days? On every level? Both sides playing one long game of gotcha?"

CHAPTER 10

No one knows what's going on. A sense of
　drama
Seems inviting, but nothing happens.
　　— *Paul's Hill,* by Shelby Stephenson

Friday noon

When Dwight and I remodeled the house
to add a new bedroom, bath, and two
walk-in closets, he'd had the usual male reaction while helping me switch closets.

"I didn't know I was marrying Imelda
Marcos," he said. "Who needs twenty-three
boxes of shoes?"

I laughed. "This from a guy who has
about three dozen old ties hanging in his
own closet?" I took the boxes from him and
stacked them on the shelves, happy that he
hadn't noticed that at least four of those
twenty-three boxes held two pairs of summer sandals.

Fancy Footwork is the moderately priced

189

shoe store that used to get a big chunk of my income till I became an old married lady. I haven't dared step foot in it since I ordered satin slippers to match my wedding dress back before Christmas, but they were having their big semiannual sale, so I decided to skip lunch that day and feed my shoe appetite instead. Besides, I rationalized, hadn't I broken the heel on my favorite pair of boots? This was the time to replace them. And I hadn't spent a penny on the blue plaid summer dress Aunt Zell made me, so surely I'd still be ahead if I accidentally came across shoes that matched the scrap of blue cloth in my purse?

As I drove through town, headed for the mall on the outskirts of Dobbs, I saw in the lane far ahead of me a beat-up old red pickup. Trucks like that are by no means unique to the area, which is why Daddy likes his so much. Goes with the I'm-just-a-poor-ol'-farmer image that he likes to hide behind. More than once, I've overtaken similarly battered trucks only to see a complete stranger at the wheel, so I didn't bother to try to catch up to this one, especially when it continued on past the first entrance to the mall parking lot.

While I waited in the left turn lane for the green light, I saw that pickup signal for a left turn at the far end of the parking lot and when I had parked and glanced down that way, I saw my father's tall figure, topped by his trademark straw panama. For a brief moment, I hesitated between shopping for shoes and seeing if he wanted to grab a bite of lunch together.

Shoes won.

The store was crowded and yes, there were bargains, but none I could justify and nothing that really called out to me. I did find a pair of boots that were exactly what I wanted. Unfortunately, they didn't have any left in my size. I put my scrap of blue cloth next to several pairs of sandals and was amused to see Jamie Jacobson on the other side of the rack trying to match the same sandals to a blue silk scarf. We agreed on the difficulty of finding the right shade of blue and that we ought to get together for lunch again soon.

"Have a good weekend," she said as she held her scarf next to a pair of aqua flats.

"You, too," I said.

Ten minutes after entering the store, I was back outside and in my car. Two minutes after that, I was parking it alongside Daddy's truck.

I hadn't watched to see which store he'd gone into. It was a fairly safe bet though that he wasn't there for maternity clothes or computers. That left the pawnshop in the middle and before you start thinking cheap guitars and zircon rings, think again. This one was more like a consignment shop for expensive jewelry and tabletop accessories such as silver boxes and leaded crystal candlesticks.

As I entered the store, several women were browsing the front display cases and a clerk was helping a white-haired woman select from a tray of antique cameo pins. I saw Daddy in consultation with someone at the rear. They were so absorbed in the object on the counter between them that they were not immediately aware of my presence and I heard the other man say, "— estate jewelry in New York. Maybe thirty thousand retail, but down here in this market, I could only get twenty for the pair."

"Hey, Daddy," I said and the object disappeared into his pocket, but not before I caught the flash of a glittery earring.

The other man immediately dropped his jeweler's loupe into the breast pocket of his jacket.

I felt suddenly awkward, as if I'd crashed a party to which I was definitely not invited.

"I saw you come in and thought I'd see if you wanted to come have a sandwich with me," I said.

"Naw," he said brusquely. "I ate 'fore I come. You go on ahead though. I reckon you need to get back to the courthouse."

I knew from that tone of voice that there was no use asking any questions and at that point, I was too confused to know what to ask.

Instead, I stood on tiptoe to kiss his leathery cheek and said maybe Dwight and I would see him that weekend.

Then I went back outside and drove my car out the nearest exit onto the highway where I merged with traffic, circled the block, and reentered the parking lot a fair distance from that store. I slid into a space amid a bunch of similar cars and scrunched down in the seat to watch. It was another seventeen minutes before Daddy came out and got in his truck.

What the hell was he up to? And where did he get a pair of diamond earrings worth twenty thousand retail? The only jewelry he had ever given my mother were modest tokens of his love — a gold bracelet, earrings set with tiny sapphires, a silver necklace. So far as I knew, her only diamonds had been a band of small ones on their twenty-fifth anniversary, a ring that could not have cost more than a couple of thousand tops.

When he pulled out onto the highway, I was six or seven cars behind him. I stayed way back and followed him through town until it seemed apparent that he was headed back toward Cotton Grove and home.

By then it was ten minutes till I was due to resume court, so I did a U-turn in front of a service station.

No shoes, no sandwich, no notion as to what my daddy was up to.

CHAPTER 11

The mouse traps are set.
   — *Paul's Hill,* by Shelby Stephenson

Once he was absolutely certain that Deborah was no longer following him, Kezzie Knott left the main road and turned onto a lesser one that would eventually get him back home in a more roundabout way.

Bad luck that she'd caught him like that, he thought, but he had to make sure them diamonds was real. Who was it said "Trust, but verify"?

Now that he was sure that he was not the one being played for a fool, he could get on with his fishing.

He seldom bothered to lock the truck but the collapsible fishing rod that Dwight and Terry had given him a few years back was still there on the seat beside him. They liked to fish nearly as much as he did and they each kept rods like this in their own trucks

195

so they could wet a line whenever they got near an unexpected body of water. He had been polite about it at the time, but a bit dubious about the need for such a thing. Still and all, it had proved handy more than once and he had wound up thanking them more sincerely a few months later when he caught a four-pound catfish out of a creek he hadn't planned on fishing when he left home that evening. But the man he was there to meet was late coming and Kezzie had killed time by throwing his hook in the water, a hook baited with a scrap of a fried chicken wing left over from his fast-food supper.

To his way of thinking, fishing was one part luck to two parts skill. You had to know where the fish were and you had to know what bait they'd bite on. Put the right bait on your hook, he thought, and even the wiliest ol' catfish in the creek can't help but rise to it. Once you set the hook, it was only a matter of playing him easy, giving him enough slack to let him think it was his idea to come swimming toward you. Jerk too hard and you'd tear the hook out of his mouth or else he'd put up such a fight that he'd break the line before you could get him in your net.

And thinking about bait . . .

Kezzie swung into the dirt parking area of a small country store. The ground was hard with sixty years of metal bottle caps stomped into the dirt. Once this had been a thriving one-pump gas station. Now the only fuel sold was kerosene. The air hose still worked though and the drink box still held chunks of ice to chill the glass bottles. You could buy ice and hoop cheese, tinned meats and crackers, and you could buy live crickets and red wigglers by the cupful. You could also buy a jar of 'shine if the proprietor knew you or you were vouched for by someone utterly trustworthy.

When they had nothing else to do the ATF agents would occasionally swoop down for a bust, but so far they had never been able to find the owner's stash of untaxed white liquor, which is how it is referred to when agents testify in court.

Even though he had not supplied this store in several years, Kezzie knew who the current supplier was and he knew where the stash was hidden.

"Hey, Mr. Kezzie," the proprietor said. "Ain't seen you in a coon's age. How you been?"

"Real good, Jimmy." He pushed his hat to the back of his head. "How 'bout you?"

"Just fair. Got a little arthuritis in my

hands these days, but not nothing else to complain about."

A couple of the men seated at the front of the store stood up to give him a chair.

"Naw, now, y'all keep your seats," he said genially. "I ain't staying long enough to set. Just stopped in to get a little bait. Anybody know what the perch're biting on over in Hinton's pond these days?"

There was a moment of silence while they digested his question. None of them would point out that he had two well-stocked ponds and a creek on his own property less than a half-hour away. If Kezzie Knott wanted to fish Millard Hinton's pond, that was his business and none of theirs.

"Ain't heared nobody say," the store owner said, already reaching into the cricket cage with a small cardboard cup. "How 'bout I give you some of both?"

"That'll work." Kezzie pulled out his wallet, but the other waved it away.

"Now you know your money ain't no good here, Mr. Kezzie."

The older man shook his head and laid two dollars on the counter. "I 'preciate that, Jimmy, but you got a living to make, too, and them crickets must eat a lot of mash."

Millard Hinton was an upright pillar of the

community, a farmer who had never been known to use tobacco in any form nor to take a drink of anything alcoholic. As soon as the tobacco buy-out began, he sold his poundage and began raising cotton, sweet potatoes, and soybeans.

"Ain't nobody ever found Jesus in a cigarette," he said. "It's Satan that wants to get you in his fire."

Nevertheless, he had told Kezzie Knott years earlier that he would be proud to have him fish in his pond anytime he wanted. A couple of elderly men who knew about the arrangement also knew what that old bootlegger had done to merit the lasting gratitude of such a man of God, but neither of them ever spoke about it.

The man-made pond lay about a half-mile off the road and had been scooped out of three acres of soggy bottomland that had never been much good for anything except pigs and maybe holding the world together.

When Kezzie and his truck topped the rise and headed down the lane to the water's edge, he saw another vehicle there before him. A lone man watched him approach. He was fishing with a cane pole, and a red plastic float out on the surface of the pond showed where his hook and line were.

"Evening," said Kezzie, stepping down

from the truck and taking out his own rod.

The man gave him a friendly nod.

"It ain't gonna bother you, is it, if I do a little fishing myself?"

"Not a bit, Mr. Knott. This place is big enough for both of us."

"I'm afraid you've got the better of me," Kezzie said, giving the man a closer look. "I don't believe we've met?"

"My name's McKinney," the man said, stretching out his hand to shake. "Faison McKinney. I'm the preacher at the Church of Jesus Christ Eternal over near you."

CHAPTER 12

. . . the cotton's tied up in burlap
sheets waiting to be weighed: my mother
  picked
385 pounds in one day!
How, I said, could you do that . . .
  — *Fiddledeedee,* by Shelby Stephenson

Friday afternoon
The doorbell pealed through the condo unit and the two lawmen heard Dee Bradshaw call from inside, "I'll get it, Dad."

Even though Terry was now in a serious long-term relationship himself, Dwight heard his friend's sharply indrawn breath when the young woman opened the door and they were confronted by a mass of reddish brown hair, bright green eyes, black skintight biker pants, and a black bandeau top that left almost nothing to the imagination.

Mourning attire for the next generation,

thought Dwight, trying not to admit to himself that he was looking, too, and wondering if that top ever slipped all the way down.

"Oh," she said, obviously disappointed that they weren't someone else. "I guess you want to see my father?"

"And you, too, Miss Bradshaw," Dwight said, as she stood back to let them in.

Inside, the place was larger than they expected. The hall was fairly wide. One side opened into the living room, the other into a small formal dining room with an oval table that would seat six. Farther down the hall, they glimpsed the edge of a kitchen and a spacious family room. Bookcases lined several of the walls and the shelves were filled with books that looked worn and well-read.

"If you'll wait in there," Dee Bradshaw said, gesturing to the living room, "I'll tell him you're here."

They moved into that room as directed and were surprised by the portrait over the couch.

"Is that the mother or the daughter?" Terry asked.

"The mother," Dwight said when a closer look made it clear that this vibrant woman had more steel in her face. She was not as beautiful as her daughter, but she radiated a purposefulness that the younger woman lacked. Where Dee looked petulant, Candace was clearly more determined. And yet there was something provocative and sexy in that half-smile and the tilt of her head, almost as if she were saying "Damn straight you'd like to have me, but how much are you willing to pay?"

"Beautiful, isn't it?"

Dwight and Terry turned to see Cameron Bradshaw smiling at them from the doorway with proprietary pride.

"Candace was twenty-five when that was painted. At the separation, this was the only thing she really wanted that I wouldn't let her have. It's a Gillian Greber. I paid the artist fifteen hundred to paint it; I turned down fifteen thousand from her gallery last year. Candace thought I kept it only because it was a portrait of her. She had no idea how good it was."

"Mom's portrait's worth fifteen thousand?" Dee Bradshaw was incredulous. "Really?"

"I said that's how much the gallery offered," he said. "I imagine they would sell it for at least twenty-five."

"Whoa!"

"Forget it, honey," he said.

She started to protest, but then laughed. "That obvious, huh, Dad?"

He turned to his visitors. "Major Bryant, Agent Wilson. Please be seated. What can I do for you?"

"I'm afraid we have more questions," Dwight said.

"Don't be afraid," Bradshaw said with a wry smile for his mild joke. He gestured for Dwight to sit in a tall wingback chair upholstered in deep blue leather and he lowered himself into its nearby twin. The chairs echoed the blue leaves and flowers of the couch and also the blue of the dress in the portrait. His daughter took one end of the couch and smiled at Terry, who sat down at the other end. "We want to help however we can. Have you learned why Candace felt she had to do what she did?"

"I'm sorry, sir, but it wasn't suicide after all. Your wife was murdered."

Dee's mouth dropped open and Bradshaw looked bewildered. "Murdered?"

"It was meant to look like suicide but the medical examiner is positive that she was strangled from behind and the bag put over her head after her death."

"Strangled? Who?"

"That's what we're looking into."

"But that note. It was her handwriting."

Terry nodded. "She was probably forced to write it."

Dwight said, "Miss Bradshaw —"

"Oh for heaven's sake, call me Dee."

"Very well, Dee. You told Deputy Richards today that your mother moved into her new house at Christmas and you were at Carolina from Christmas to Easter. Is that right?"

She nodded and slid to the floor, where she could lean back against the couch and tuck her legs beneath her.

"Were you and your mother close?"

She shrugged. "I guess."

"Did you come home often? Talk on the phone?"

"Not really. She had her life. I had mine. Anyhow, she was pretty busy. Every time I called, she was usually rushing off to a meeting or heading out to check up on one of the cleaning crews." Her tone was light but her eyes betrayed her. "She thought the only reason I called was because I wanted something. Money or clothes."

"Be fair, Dee," Bradshaw said softly.

"You know it's true, Dad." Her voice was sulky, but she dropped her eyes and stretched out the top of her bandeau to tug it up, inadvertently giving Terry a view of her firm young breasts.

"So she never mentioned that a gun had been fired into her bedroom floor?"

"Huh?"

"A gun?" asked Bradshaw.

"One of my deputies dug a bullet out of the floor just now," Dwight told them. "Did she own a gun?"

"Absolutely not! She was completely opposed to handguns, even though she's never said it in public. Her constituents, you see."

"Then that might be how she was forced to write that note," said Terry. "Her killer could have fired into the floor as a warning threat that he'd shoot her if she didn't do as she was told."

Dee looked up at him. "So the letter was a lie? She wasn't doing anything wrong after all?"

"Hard to say. We might still learn that something illegal was going on and the killer wanted to set her up as the fall guy. We haven't talked to any of the commissioners and she seems to have kept files on them. On some of the more prominent business leaders in the county as well, but we can't find them."

"Files?" asked Bradshaw. "What sort of files?"

"We don't know, but we get the impression that some things were too personal —

and maybe too candid — to leave lying around for anyone to read. We don't know if it's papers or a CD or a flash drive."

"What's a flash drive?" he asked.

"Thinner than a Bic lighter but about the same shape," Dee explained to him. "Plugs into your computer and has a ton of memory."

"I'm sorry," he said. "I'm pretty much a Luddite when it comes to computers. I read *The London Times* and *The New York Review of Books* online, and I can do e-mail or look up information, but as far as understanding the mechanical side of it?" He gave a hands-up gesture of ignorance.

"What about you, Dee?"

"Yeah, she used flash drives for her personal sh—" She caught herself. "Her personal *stuff.* See, there was this story on the news. About some crooked politician or one of those sleazy corporations? And how they got nailed by their computers because even if you delete or erase, it's still there on your hard drive? For some reason, that really freaked Mom, so I told her that if she'd get herself a memory stick and work from that and never save anything to the hard drive, she ought to be safe from most snoopers. That's when she bought her laptop. I showed her how to download to the flash drive and then transfer the files to her new computer. I even told her how to disable the automatic backup on her word processing program. She bought an extra stick, so I know she used at least one for her private stuff.

"Next time I came home, I told her about digital shredders that even get rid of cache files. She said she wished she'd known about that before she took apart her old computer and smashed the insides with a hammer. I thought that was a little over the top. I mean, what did she have that was so damn secret? A formula to blow up the world? She laughed and said I was closer to the truth than I knew."

"And how did you interpret that?"

Dee gave a dismissive shrug of her bare shoulder. "I thought she was just trying to sound important."

"When was this?"

"Last fall. Before she moved into the new place."

"It's an expensive house," Dwight observed. "She must have been doing very well with the business."

Cameron Bradshaw looked uncomfortable at that, and Dwight made a mental note to look into the financing of that house.

"I'm sorry, Officers," Bradshaw said,

clearly trying to cover his lapse. "I never offered you anything to drink. Tea? Or I could make coffee?"

"Would you, Dad?" Dee asked, deliberately widening her clear green eyes to coax him. "Dad grinds his own beans and I'm absolutely addicted to his coffee."

"Flatterer," Bradshaw said with an indulgent smile, but he was already rising from his chair. "Officers?"

"Yes, please," Terry said before Dwight could decline. "Let me help you, sir. I know how Major Bryant likes his." He gave Dwight a significant wink as he followed Bradshaw.

As soon as they were clear of the room, Dee turned to Dwight and in a low and urgent voice said, "You're right, Major Bryant. Dad's in denial, but Mom was doing *very* well. She bought a new car last spring even though her old one was only two years old. She just gave it away to her cousin in Georgia, a cousin she didn't even like all that much." Unforgotten resentment darkened her pretty face. "He came through with a load of peaches and a hard-luck story and she just handed him the damn keys. Paid cash for a new one the very next day. Same with the house. She paid cash for it, too. I mean, I guess when she sold our old house, she must've got a nice chunk of money, but the new house probably cost half a million and she just wrote a check."

"Where do you think the extra money came from?" Dwight asked her.

"I'm sure she was skimming from the company. Dad thinks because he hired his own accountant that the books are straight, but I know Mom. There was never a man she couldn't get around once she set her mind to it and Roger Flackman's a real weenie."

"Any other man in particular?"

She shrugged. "Look, you asked if Mom and I were close? We used to be. Not maybe when I was a little kid because she was working so hard and I got left with day care or babysitters, but once I hit ten or twelve and didn't need a sitter any more, she'd take me along on some of the jobs, especially after she and Dad split. We'd go shopping and eat out a lot. I was proud of her and in her way, I think she was proud of me. Little things. Like, she took me to one of those Chamber of Commerce banquets one year when I was eleven and it totally cracked her up that I knew which was the salad fork and which was my bread-and-butter plate. She told me later that she'd never even seen a salad fork till after she married Dad.

"And that thing about guns? She wouldn't talk about her parents very often except to say that they were trailer trash and that she used to pretend they had stolen her away from her real parents. But she did let slip once that her father used to get drunk and shoot up the trailer they lived in. Scared the hell out of her."

She looked up at Dwight in sudden wonder. "I guess I never thought about it before, but she really did come a long way, didn't she?"

"Sounds like it," Dwight said.

"I mean, no money, no family connections, no education except a GED. Yeah, marrying Dad helped, but she took advantage of all her opportunities, didn't she? Making enough of a name for herself to run for the board of commissioners? She was always saying she wanted to be somebody, but it was like nothing was ever enough. Important people could praise her to the skies, but if the *Ledger* ran a critical letter from some nobody out in the country, it cut her to the quick.

"You want to know what was probably on her flash drive? I guarantee you it had everybody who ever said something ugly about her. She had the memory of an elephant. I'm not saying she used her position to hurt that person, but she certainly wouldn't have gone out of her way to do him any favors."

"So who did she do favors for, Dee?"

The girl looked back at him and Dwight saw her jaw tighten.

"You said you weren't close to her when she died. What happened?"

But the time of confidences seemed to be over. It was as if suddenly realizing why her mother had been so driven to succeed had made her no longer willing to speak of any failings Candace might have had.

"You do know that whoever killed her might have been one of those she did favors for?" he said gently.

"I'd better go help Dad bring in the coffee," she said, unfolding herself up from the floor just as Bradshaw and Wilson returned.

The coffee was every bit as delicious as promised and Bradshaw seemed as willing as ever to help, but a distinct chill radiated from his daughter.

"When can we have the house back?" she asked as she handed Dwight a cup of fragrant brew.

"My deputies are finishing up there now." He looked at his watch. "I guess they're probably done. But if you come across that flash drive, I hope you'll call us right away."

She gave an indifferent shrug that promised nothing.

"Of course she will," said Bradshaw. "Cream or sugar, Bryant?"

"No, thank you. Just a couple of further questions. Can you suggest anyone at all that might want your wife out of the way?"

The older man shook his head. Dee sat motionless, as if her mind were elsewhere and she wished they were gone so that she could go wherever that was.

"Would you tell us, sir, where were you Tuesday evening between four-thirty and six?"

"Is that when it happened?" The man shook his head sadly. "I realize you must ask that question, Bryant, but I could never hurt my wife. I was here at home then."

"Alone?"

Bradshaw nodded. "Dee dropped her things off earlier, but she was gone by then."

"There's no one to corroborate that?"

He placed his spoon precisely on the saucer and set them back on the tray. "Sorry. I sat on my patio with a drink and a dictionary of quotations until dark, but I saw no one until a neighbor came out to walk his dog on the commons. That would have been around seven or seven-thirty."

"Dee?"

"I was at a friend's house till four." She gave the friend's name and address. "Then I drove back into Dobbs for a five o'clock job interview. After that I went out to supper with more friends and didn't get back to Dad's till almost ten."

"Job interview?" asked Dwight.

"I believe he's your brother-in-law," she said with a mocking smile. "Mr. Will Knott?"

CHAPTER 13

Hope is forgetting that one's
Father will be in the deep, running cur-
rents
Forever.

— The Persimmon Tree Carol,
by Shelby Stephenson

Shortly before the Friday afternoon break, my clerk leaned over between cases and whispered, "Someone down in the office says Danny Creedmore told his secretary that Candace Bradshaw was murdered."

"Really?" It had been difficult to think of Candace killing herself, but somehow less surprising to hear that she'd been murdered. "Any details?"

"Not yet. I'll IM Faye Myers. See if she knows anything."

Faye Myers is a plump and gossipy dispatcher who's married to an EMS tech. Between them they know most of what's going on in the county before anyone else does. Bo Poole keeps threatening to fire her, but somehow he never has, probably because she seldom reveals anything sensitive to an investigation before it becomes common knowledge. It might also be that he regards her as a barometer of public opinion and likes the feedback she gives him. Grapevines do tend to run in both directions and there's a reason Bo barely has to break a sweat out on the campaign trail every four years.

If Faye knew more than the bare facts though, she wasn't responding to my clerk's instant message, so I wandered around to Luther Parker's office during the break. As soon as I walked in, he said, "I hear Candace Bradshaw didn't kill herself. That true? What does Dwight say?"

"Sorry, friend. I buzzed his office but he's not there and I don't like to bother him on his cell phone during working hours."

"Yeah?" He lifted an eyebrow and grinned. "Since when?"

Roger Longmire, our chief district court judge, stuck his head in. "Y'all hear that Candace was murdered?"

We batted it around for a few minutes, wondering if the motive was personal, a love affair gone wrong, something connected

216

with her business or with her position as a county commissioner.

"I'm guessing it was something to do with kickbacks for approving some of those iffy housing developments," Longmire said.

"I don't know," said Luther. "I heard she and Creedmore had a falling out over a clerk down in Ellis Glover's office."

Ellis Glover is our clerk of court and gives a lot of young women their first jobs. Like us, he has to run for office every four years, too, so he always seems to have an opening for the sister or daughter of constituents. Many important men — and yes, dammit, men still hold most of the power in our county — are grateful to him for looking after their female relatives. He makes sure that his "girls" are the first to hear of any opening in other county departments so that he can cycle them out and cycle in a new group to keep widening his circle of supporters. Democrats or Republicans, it doesn't much matter to Ellis. He knows that men are daddies and brothers and uncles and grandfathers first, party members second.

I didn't recognize the name of the young woman that Danny Creedmore was supposed to be lusting after, but it wasn't important. Most courthouse affairs have a sell-by date from the get-go and they usually end with no hard feelings on either side.

"From all I've heard, it wouldn't really matter if Danny and Candace weren't lovers any longer. They were still in bed together, weren't they?" I asked.

Convoluted but Luther and Roger knew what I meant.

"Yeah," said Roger. "She was still saying 'How high?' when Danny said 'Jump.' Although I did hear that she wanted to be taken seriously if she filed for Woody's seat. She really thought she could be a state senator."

"Hey, if Dubya could be president," said Luther.

We laughed and returned to our separate courtrooms.

Dwight is normally finished by four and I had no compunctions about calling his cell number then. Now that Cal is part of our lives, one of us has to pick him up every afternoon.

He answered on the first ring. "On my way. What about you?"

"I may be a little late," I told him, virtuously refraining from asking about Candace. "I need to swing past Seth's for a few minutes."

■ ■ ■ ■

That encounter with Daddy at lunchtime was still bothering me. When I got to Seth's house, though, no one was home and I decided the hell with it. Go to the source. Ask Daddy flat out what was going on. Yes, he can be touchy as a hornet when questioned about his private business, but you don't deserve any honey if you're not willing to get stung. And don't bother telling me that hornets don't make honey. You know what I mean.

There was no sign of his truck at the homeplace, and Maidie was putting his supper in the oven so the pilot light would keep it warm.

"I never know when he's gonna be home these days," she said. "Walk on down to the house with me, honey, so I can start Cletus's supper. And you're welcome to eat with us."

"Thanks, Maidie," I said, "but Dwight and Cal are probably waiting for me."

Maidie was my mother's right arm after Aunt Essie married a policeman up in Philadelphia when I was a little girl. Cletus was working for Daddy back then, too, and it got to the point that they couldn't keep him away from the kitchen. He was eight or nine years older than Maidie, yet way too shy to pop the question.

Exasperated because he could never find Cletus when he was needed, Daddy stormed into the kitchen one day and said, "Now look here, Maidie. This man's acting like a moonstruck calf and it's got to quit."

That's when Mother and Maidie started laughing.

Daddy was too wound up to stop and Cletus had turned ashen beneath his brown color. Daddy gave him a sour look and said, "I don't know why on earth you'd want to marry him, but if you do, for God's sake and mine, tell him so I can get some work out of him. All right?"

Still laughing, Maidie said, "All right."

"Huh?" Daddy and Cletus were both dumbfounded.

"She said yes," Mother told them. "Now will you two please get out of my kitchen? We've got a wedding to plan."

The little clapboard house that Maidie and Cletus have shared for thirty-odd years is just past the barn and down the lane from the main house. The garden that he and Daddy had planted was growing vigorously. Peas and potatoes were blooming and the first planting of sweet corn was almost knee-high. No stakes yet for the tomatoes because they were still too short, but the cabbage plants had begun to head up and butter beans had their first true leaves.

"I hear Dwight's planted y'all a garden, too," Maidie said.

"Oh yes. I've told him that I don't can and I don't freeze, but that hasn't stopped him."

Maidie laughed. "And how's that Rhonda working out?"

"You were right," I admitted ruefully, having resisted hiring someone to help me with the housework for as long as I could. "I don't know how I ever got along without her."

"I know exactly how you were getting along," she said tartly. "I saw the dust and dirt in that house."

"Dirt?" I protested. "It wasn't dirty. Not really."

"Them windows? Those baseboards? Them dust bunnies under the beds? I was pure ashamed of you, Deborah."

Which was why she had bestirred herself to find someone to clean for me when it became clear that Dwight and Cal and I weren't keeping to her standards. She no longer has a pool of nieces and cousins to draw from. The Research Triangle and state government departments have siphoned them off. But through her own grapevine, she found an energetic young white woman willing to work mornings so she could be home with her children in the afternoons, and Rhonda Banks comes once a week now. She dusts, mops, scrubs, changes the beds, and does the laundry. I pay her more than twice the minimum wage and she's worth every penny.

But it was soon apparent that Rhonda wasn't what Maidie wanted to talk to me about. Cletus wasn't back yet either and we went out to the kitchen, a kitchen warm and cheerful with red-checked curtains, tablecloth, and dish towels. I picked up her big black cat and stroked it under its chin while she sautéed three thick pork chops in her iron skillet.

"Is everything okay with Daddy?" I asked, plunging into it.

"Well, now, that's what I wanted to ask you," she said, a worried look on her warm brown face. "You know well as me, Mr. Kezzie ain't never been religious."

I nodded, wondering where this was going.

"I've prayed on it, your mama used to pray on it, and I think Miss Zell still does, but I figure the Lord knows he's a good

222

man deep down even if he might not've always been right with the law."

That was putting it mildly.

"But?" I asked.

"But right lately he's been asking me a lot about what it means to be saved. And what somebody needs to do to get right with the Lord. Now I know he's getting old and starting to slow down a bit, but getting right with the Lord's never been something he cared one lick about, now is it?"

I had to admit she was right about that. I don't have a clue about Daddy's religious beliefs, but I do know he never goes to church except for weddings and funerals. He adored Mother, but I've never heard him speak of being reunited with her in heaven and, if asked, would have to say that he probably doesn't believe in a heaven.

Or hell.

"You don't reckon he's sick, do you?"

"Does he act sick?"

"Well . . . no, not really. And he still eats good."

I waited while she seemed to concentrate on cooking. The chops had nicely browned in the hot grease, so she put them in a bowl, poured off most of the grease, and began to brown some diced onions and a little flour with the pan scrapings.

Even though I had skipped lunch, I didn't think I was hungry, but those sizzling onions gave off an aroma that made my mouth water. I tried to ignore the rumble in my stomach.

"He's just not hisself these days," Maidie said, cocking her head at me. She's only fifteen years older, but her hair had passed the tipping point and was now more gray than black. (Of course, mine may be gray, too. Only my hairdresser knows for sure.)

"Has he been to a doctor?"

"No."

"Well, if he's eating good and staying active, what's got you worried, Maidie?"

She shook her head and didn't answer. I watched as she poured water in the pan and a cloud of steam boiled up. After stirring until the water and the flour and onions had turned to a smooth gravy, she put the pork chops back in the pan, covered them with a lid and turned the flame to low.

Her face was troubled as she sat down at the table across from me and the cat slid off my lap in one graceful, fluid motion to go sit in hers.

"I don't want you laughing at me," she said at last, smoothing an almost non-existent wrinkle from the red-and-white cloth on the table between us.

I was indignant. "When did I ever laugh at you?"

"Just don't you be starting now." She stroked the cat, who began to purr so loudly I could hear him clearly from my side of the table. "All his talk about getting right with the Lord? I've seen it before, Deborah. Sometimes old people seem to know when it's their time. They can be up and doing one day and then tell you they'll be gone by that time next week. It's like they feel His hand on their shoulder saying 'Come on along now, child. Time to go home,' and they just lean back in their rocking chair or lay down on their bed and they're gone. Gone home to Jesus."

Her words chilled me on two levels. One, because she was right. At least twice I've seen elderly relatives who had never talked of death suddenly say quite matter-of-factly that their time was up. They said it without drama. No sadness, no anger. They spoke of their imminent death as casually as if they were discussing the weather. Except that in a day or two, they died.

(Of course, I've also heard even older relatives claim they were ready to go and then linger on for another five or six years in increasing impatience. As if they'd missed a celestial bus and had to wait till the next one swung past them again.)

But Maidie's forebodings touched an even deeper, more primal level that my brothers and I won't even discuss. We know Daddy's getting old and he's not as strong as he used to be. But his spine is still straight as a flagpole and his mind is as sharp as it ever was, so we tell ourselves that he's going to live forever.

Intellectually, we know it isn't so.

Emotionally?

Once when I was little, I woke up crying in the night because I had suddenly realized that everyone dies — my cats, my chicken, my brothers, my parents — everyone, and it was breaking my heart to think I might be left alone. He had picked me up and carried me out to the porch swing. As I sat on his lap with my head against his chest and we gently swung back and forth in the moonlight, he had solemnly promised me that he would not die till I was an old, old woman.

I remind myself that he's never yet broken a promise to me.

And thirty-nine isn't old, old.

"Maidie, are you sure he was asking questions about religion for himself and not so's he could pass it on to someone else?"

"Now why would he do that? He wants to

know about God, all he's got to do is talk to Herman's wife. Nadine's his own daughter-in-law. She'd tell him all about it."

"Yeah, and then she'd try to haul him off to her church, wouldn't she?"

Nadine's one of those straitlaced bornagain Blalocks from Black Creek and she's always trying to get us to go visit her home church. Their preacher's a male chauvinist whose bark is worse than his bite. I once sat through a sermon that was basically a reminder that a woman's place is in the home, yet immediately afterward he told me quite sincerely how proud they all were that I was now a judge.

I grinned at Maidie. "Daddy probably feels it's safe to ask you. He knows you won't try to get him to Mt. Olive."

Like it or not, our churches are the last bastion of self-segregation. No white would ever be turned away from a black church; no white church would ever bar its doors to blacks. We're tolerant as hell and on Sunday morning, we smile when the nursery class sings

Red and yellow, black and white,
They are precious in His sight.
Jesus loves the little children of the world.

All the same, our churches still split along racial lines for the most part.

"Daddy may want to get right with the Lord, Maidie, but he also might be up to something. You say you never know when he's going to be home these days. What's he doing?"

"Oh, honey. You asking me where he rambles? That's like asking me where this cat goes when I put him out for the night."

"Then tell me this. Did Mother ever have any fancy jewelry?"

"Why sure she did. You remember that pretty ring Mr. Kezzie give her for their anniversary and them sapphire earrings? Didn't he give them earrings to you? I know he gave the ring to Will when he married Amy. And —"

"No, I'm talking diamond earrings worth thousands."

Maidie shook her head. "Your mama had some diamond earrings from her mama. You don't mean them, do you?"

"No."

Those went to Aunt Zell at Mother's death, but again, they were simple teardrops, nothing like the glittery splash I had seen Daddy snatch up before I could get a good look.

"Why you asking about her stuff?"

"Just wondering," I said.

She cut her eyes at me, but Cletus came in then and I quickly stood up to go.

"I thought I saw your car up at the house," he said. "You ain't staying for supper?"

"And leave you with only one pork chop?" I teased.

"That what smells so good?"

He insisted on giving me a dozen eggs and some fresh tendergreen for a salad and then went into the bathroom to wash up. I hugged Maidie and told her not to worry. "Daddy's going to be just fine, but you call me if it looks like he's up to something, okay?"

"If you say so, honey. But you know how he don't like nobody hound-dogging him, so you can't tell him I told you."

"I won't," I promised.

I could have checked back by Seth's again, but it was getting on for dark and besides, I was starting to have second thoughts. What if I'd totally misunderstood? What if that earring had been nice rhinestones instead of diamonds? Good period costume jewelry can fetch decent prices these days and the best seems to come from estate sales.

Instead of "thirty thousand retail," maybe that jeweler had really said "thirty now at retail," meaning he could sell it for thirty dollars and would therefore offer Daddy twenty.

So it wasn't Seth I should talk to. It was Will.

CHAPTER 14

The house is part of the whole
Cohesive world we live in.
 — *Paul's Hill,* by Shelby Stephenson

Saturday morning is usually the beginning of a peaceful family weekend. Or so we always hope.

Cal rides his bike down to the mailboxes at the end of the lane to pick up the paper for us while Dwight and I take our time with second and third cups of coffee. Reading *The News & Observer* is a communal activity for us. Cal gives us the long-range weather report and shares the comic strips that make him giggle. I read aloud the human interest stories or the latest outrageous thing our politicians have done. Dwight does the scores of selected sports events and lets us know about any local happenings that might affect us. One of us will explain Dwayne Powell's political cartoon for Cal if he doesn't get it, and whoever gets to that page first scans the obituaries for any visitations we might be obligated to attend. (If you have to run for office, you try not to miss too many funerals for your dearly departed constituents.)

After breakfast, Cal stacks the dishwasher and shakes out the blanket in Bandit's crate while I straighten up the beds and tidy the house, and Dwight gives the bathrooms the lick and a promise that keep things halfway decent till Rhonda comes.

Dwight and I usually mind Kate and Rob's older two on Saturdays because the Aussie nursemaid has the weekends off. As we were leaving to go pick them up, Cal asked if we could open one of the bluebird boxes scattered around the property.

"Sure," I said.

He chose one out by the drive and lightly tapped on the side of the box so any adult birds would fly out, then pulled out the long nail that holds the front in place and tilted up the hinged board. Inside was a shallow plastic box that let him gently slide out the whole nest. There, huddled together in the center, were four tiny bluebirds, so young that we could still see their skin through the downy fuzz. Their eyes were not yet open and their yellow bills looked rubbery and way too big for their marble-sized heads.

"Awwww," said Cal, and I smiled, too, as he slid them back inside, lowered the board, and put the nail back in its hole.

At Kate's, I warned her that I might be a little late bringing the children back.

"Will and Amy are coming over and I thought we'd grill some steaks outside since it's so warm and then let the kids roast marshmallows, if that's okay?"

"Great," she said. "Miss Emily's going to sit with R.W. this afternoon so that Rob and I can go to a kiln opening at Jugtown."

"Say hey to the Owenses for me," I told her, turning the key in the ignition.

At home, as we drove back into the yard, Dwight was in front of the garage with a hose, washing his truck, with Bandit supervising. The little terrier danced toward us as we got near. Suddenly, Cal started yelling and opened the door before I'd come to a full stop.

"Dad! Dad!"

"Cal, wait!" I cried, but he was already out of his seat belt and there was no stopping him.

"Snake!" he screamed, pointing to a birdhouse out in the middle of an azalea bed.

At that instant, a slender black snake no thicker than my thumb gained the top of the box and inserted its head into the hole. The adult birds were dive-bombing it in a brave, if hopeless, frenzy.

Dwight instantly realized what was happening and almost without thinking, he jumped over the low stone wall and in two strides reached the box, yanked on the snake's tail, and sent it flying across the yard.

Bandit rushed back and forth between Dwight and Cal, but he hadn't seen the snake and didn't seem to understand what all the ruckus was about. Unfortunately, the rest of us saw a baby bird lodged in the snake's mouth as it disappeared under a pink azalea bush.

Cal and Mary Pat were almost crying. Jake, who was still too young to comprehend the finality of death, was in awe that Dwight had actually grabbed a snake barehanded.

Truth be told, I was, too, even though I know that black snakes are harmless to humans. I was never one of those kids who stroked a snake at petting zoos.

Still don't.

"Sorry," Dwight told me. "I knew I should have put collars around the poles before now."

"Can't you just kill that mean ol' snake?" Mary Pat asked, tears streaking down her pretty little face.

"Yeah, Dad," said Cal, who stood on the wall and looked fearfully over at the bushes where the snake had gone to earth.

"He's not mean, honey," he told Mary Pat. "Black snakes eat a lot of mice and rats and other pests so we can't blame them if they get a bird now and then. That's just their nature. What we *can* do is fix it so they can't get at any more nests. I think I saw some tin under Uncle Robert's shelter the other day. Y'all help me finish washing the truck and we'll go borrow some."

After Cal came to live with us, all three of the kids began to call my brothers and their wives *Uncle* and *Aunt*. From the way they immediately tackled the dirty rims on Dwight's pickup, I'm sure they were imagining dozens of snakes slithering around, just waiting for a chance to snack on baby bluebirds.

I drove my car into the garage and remembered the boxes Will had put in the trunk on Wednesday. I suddenly itched to dive into Linsey Thomas's files and learn just how much he'd known about my appointment, but there were steaks to marinade, potatoes to scrub, the fixings of a salad to assemble, so I carried them into the house and stuck them in the third bedroom, which we use as an office.

By the time I had finished in the kitchen, the others were back with the tin and it was time for lunch. Afterward, I helped cut and shape collars to go around the cedar poles of the half-dozen bluebird houses. The downward slope of the tin, plus its wide circumference, would baffle any snake that next tried to climb up. Naturally, the children wanted to see every nest as Dwight nailed the collars in place. One box had a clutch of unhatched eggs, one was empty, the other four had young birds that ranged from just hatched to nearly fledged.

"There," Dwight said as we adjusted the last collar, "that should do it."

We showered and changed into fresh jeans, then I put the potatoes in the oven to bake and he started the charcoal.

Will and Amy got there as he was taking a steak off the grill and I let the children go ahead and eat early at the table on the back porch while the adults had drinks out on the grass overlooking grill and pond. I had also invited my nephew Stevie and his girlfriend to join us. They were seniors over at Carolina, but Gayle had a major paper due, so she had stayed in Chapel Hill and

Stevie brought his sister instead. Jane Ann was finishing up her first year at UNC-G in Greensboro and they had both come home for a friend's wedding this morning.

Stevie was now almost twenty-two and of legal drinking age, yet, out of deference to Jane Ann, he opted for iced tea, too. Just as I try not to let on that Seth is maybe my favorite brother, I try not to dote on Haywood's son, but he really is a nice kid.

"Dad tell you about the guy who wanted to join the hunt club day before yesterday?" he asked, a broad smile on his face.

Will laughed out loud and Amy said, "They still doing that?"

The Possum Creek Hunt Club is nothing but a figment of Daddy's imagination. He learned long ago that simply posting the land won't keep hunters off. But if the woods are posted with signs that say NO TRESPASSING. LEASED BY THE POSSUM CREEK HUNT CLUB, most people will respect them. They get three or four inquiries a year from newcomers.

"The guy was driving a Humvee and didn't blink when they told him the initiation fee was a thousand dollars. He even wanted to bribe Dad and Uncle Robert to put him at the top of the waiting list. Dad said his wallet was full of hundred-dollar bills and he was really tempted, but Uncle Robert wouldn't let him."

"Hmmm," said Will, with a faraway speculative look in his eye.

"No," Amy told him firmly and I added, "It would embarrass Dwight to death to have to arrest you for fraud, wouldn't it, Dwight?"

"Oh, I don't know about that," he said, reaching for Will's beer mug. They've been friends since grade school and he has no illusions about my brother. "Top anybody else's glass off?"

It wasn't long before the children began to clamor for the marshmallows they'd been promised and Jane Ann hopped up to help supervise. The smell of burned sugar was soon rife in the land.

"Toast one for me," Amy called. She's Will's third wife, with short dark hair and dark eyes that she claims come from some Latino blood somewhere in her ancestry. She has a bawdy sense of humor and a fuse as short as Will's. They blow up at each other at least once a month and we used to hold our collective breaths, fearful that their marriage was going to blow up, too. Over the years, we've come to realize that Amy loves drama and Will must as well, because he seems intent on not messing up this time.

Jane Ann brought them both a marshmallow. Dwight, too. I passed. They don't really go with bourbon. The men licked their fingers and Will said, "Reminds me of Daddy's bonfires."

I smiled as he and Dwight began to reminisce about roasting marshmallows when we were kids.

Daddy never burned his brushpiles in daylight. He always waited until dark, and a moonless night was his favorite time. He would poke the fire and send geysers of sparks shooting up fifteen or twenty feet into the night sky.

"A poor man's fireworks," he'd say.

And Mother would often walk down from the house with a bag of marshmallows for a perfect ending to the day.

Eventually Dwight decreed that the children had eaten enough sugar and shooed them away so he could replenish the bed of coals with more from a starter can.

While Jane Ann and Amy cleared the porch table and reset it with china and tableware, I sent the kids to the showers to get rid of the stickiness that clung to their hands and mouths — Cal and Jake to his bathroom, Mary Pat to the master bath. Kate and I keep changes of clothing in both houses, so I laid out fresh pajamas for them and popped a DVD into the television in our bedroom.

"Mary Pat's in charge of the remote and no bouncing on the bed," I warned them as they settled back against the pillows to watch a movie they'd seen at least a dozen times.

It was full dark and the steaks were just coming off the grill when I got back out to the porch. Conversation had turned to Candace Bradshaw's murder and the names of various prominent builders were being tossed around as suspects. Not her husband though. Dwight had told me that various neighbors had seen him from their windows throughout Tuesday afternoon.

"Her daughter says you're her alibi," Dwight said as he split his potato and added a large dollop of butter to the steaming interior.

"She does?" Will cut into one of the steaks on the platter to make sure it was rare enough before transferring it to his plate.

"She says you interviewed her for a job Tuesday evening. You remember the time?"

Will's eyes narrowed as he visualized the scene. "Yeah. She was the only one who answered my ad. She got there at five on the dot and by five-thirty I had hired her.

All I need is someone who can spell and use a computer for a few hours a week. Of course, she was only there for one morning and then Cam Bradshaw called her with the bad news. Guess I'll have to find someone else now."

Stevie paused in the middle of slathering A.1. sauce on his steak. "Dee really did get a job?"

"That surprises you?" I asked at the same time that Dwight said, "You know her?"

"Sure. We graduated from high school together. And yeah, I'm surprised that she got a job."

"Why? She's not in school any more," said Dwight.

Jane Ann made a face. "She was just yanking her mother's chain."

"By getting a job?"

"She told us that nobody in her mom's family had ever gone to college. In fact, Mrs. Bradshaw was the first to finish high school even if it was with a GED, so it was real important to her for Dee to graduate." Jane Ann served herself some salad made with the greens Cletus had given me and passed the bowl along to Amy. "But Dee wanted a new car, and when Mrs. Bradshaw wouldn't buy her one, she threatened to quit school and get a job so she could have some decent wheels."

"She's a spoiled slacker," Stevie said flatly. "She's never had to do a lick of work, she got a big allowance, and she had a car of her own that ran just fine. Remember last spring, when my car was in the shop? She gave me a ride home to pick it up and all she could do was bitch about how her mother gave a worthless, good-for-nothing cousin her practically new Toyota and then bought herself another new one while Dee had to keep driving the Audi she'd had in high school."

"She thought her mother would come around with a new car to keep her in school. But Dee'll go back. You'll see," Jane Ann said cynically. She shook her head at the offer of garlic bread. "In fact, she'll probably stay on for two masters and a PhD so that she doesn't have to punch a time clock for another five years."

After supper, Stevie and Jane Ann had other plans for the evening. They offered to drop off a pair of sleepy children on the way. Cal's eyelids were drooping, too, and he only offered a pro forma objection when Dwight scooped him up and carried him to his own bed. He was probably already asleep by the time Dwight came back to join us.

Amy poured coffee and I spooned warm peach cobbler into dessert dishes, then topped each with a dab of vanilla ice cream. Dwight and Will dug in as enthusiastically as if I had peeled the peaches myself and made the flaky crust from scratch.

Amy enjoyed hers, too, but couldn't resist asking me what brand of piecrust I bought.

"Sh-hhh," I told her. "Don't spoil the illusion."

Will grinned. "She just wants to know because this crust tastes better than what she buys."

"Bastard," Amy said amiably.

"If you can't tell it from the real thing —" I hesitated one second too long.

"What?" said Dwight. He really does know me way too well at times.

"When you go in to appraise an estate, Will, do you ever do jewelry?"

He took another bite of cobbler and shook his head. "Not usually. Most people either want to keep it or else get a jeweler to do the appraisal. And more likely than not, they have an inflated sense of what it's worth. Why?"

"Just wondering. What about costume jewelry?"

He laughed. "There it's just the opposite. Most people think it's worth less than it is because it's fake. They see Bakelite and think 'plastic.' Well let me tell you something, honey. An authentic vintage Bakelite bracelet can fetch anything from two hundred to two thousand dollars depending on its condition and rarity."

"You're kidding!"

"Don't believe me, go check out eBay."

"What about rhinestones?"

"Again, it depends on the quality and whether the piece is signed by a collectible name."

He looked at me speculatively over the rim of his coffee cup. "C'mon, Deb'rah. You're not just wondering. You happen onto a nice find of old costume stuff?"

I shook my head.

The three of them were now too curious to let it drop.

"All right," I said finally, "but you've got to promise not to say anything to the rest of the family about this. I'm probably making mountains out of what's nothing more than an anthill and I want y'all's word on it, okay?"

They all promised, so then I told them about my encounter with Daddy in that consignment shop yesterday, about the flash and sparkle of an earring, about the words I thought I'd heard that clerk with the jeweler's magnifying eyepiece say, and how Daddy had sent me on my way so brusquely.

Will frowned. "You're sure he used a loupe?"

"And put it in his pocket as soon as I walked up — the instant that Daddy palmed the earring."

"Tall thin guy? Had his glasses pushed up on his forehead? Starting to go bald in front?"

I nodded.

"Then he had to be looking at something really interesting if he was using his loupe. I know him. Dave Carter. Good guy. Why don't I drop by and see him Monday?"

"Only if you think he won't call Daddy the minute you're out of the store," I said. "You know how mad he can get if he thinks we're checking up on him."

Dwight looked at me quizzically. "You don't really think he has diamond earrings worth thirty thousand dollars, do you?"

"Makes about as much sense as rhinestones worth twenty," I told him.

We batted it around for a few minutes more till Will said, "I'll talk to Dave on Monday," and the talk turned to other subjects.

I briefly considered telling them what Maidie had confided about Daddy's sudden interest in getting right with the Lord, but decided I'd already been disloyal enough for one evening.

"You have a chance to go through Linsey's papers yet?" Will asked as he and Amy were leaving.

"Tomorrow," I promised.

CHAPTER 15

Back when I came along, everybody used
   to wrestle, jump —
see who could do the most work.
Now we study money.
                    — *Middle Creek Poems,*
                       by Shelby Stephenson

Next morning, I slept in while Dwight
dropped Cal off for Sunday school at the
church he and I grew up in. Cal's not crazy
about putting on Sunday clothes, but his
Uncle Rob teaches the Junior Class and he's
made friends with some of the boys, so he
seems to enjoy it once he's there.

Preaching services begin at eleven, which
meant that Dwight and I had a little time
alone for this and that.

Mostly that.

We were a few minutes late getting there,
but everyone was standing for the first
hymn, so it wasn't noticeable when we

247

slipped into a back pew.

Because the minister is new and we don't make it to church every week, I haven't quite taken his measure, but with Rob on the pulpit committee, he can't be too far right. Not as intellectual as Carlyle Yelvington at First Baptist in Dobbs, but nowhere near as opaque as the preacher at Nadine and Herman's New Deliverance down in Black Creek. And nothing — thank you, Jesus! — like that demagogue at the Church of Christ Eternal.

Every time I think about the way that arrogant bastard humiliated his wife, I want to throw up and then go slap him across the face with a dead trout.

No, Sweetwater's Quincy Bridges is young and earnest and doesn't seem to have an arrogant bone in his body. He doesn't threaten with hellfire and brimstone; he entreats with the promise of a well-lived life for those who follow the Golden Rule.

After lunch, Dwight and Cal went off to the woods to see if they could find a couple of redbuds small enough to move up to the house, and I started going through Linsey Thomas's files that Will had found.

Last night, Dwight had told me about Candace Bradshaw's missing flash drive and how it might hold something about me on it.

"Me?"

"Well, not you per se," he'd said. "More likely John Claude or Mr. Kezzie. Richards found a file folder with the firm's name and a sheet of paper with yours and Mr. Kezzie's names and a note to herself referencing that damn flash drive."

That sent a chill down my spine. Dwight doesn't know about Daddy and Talbert. We've never sat down and exchanged lists and details of people we've been in bed with and I figure G. Hooks Talbert falls in that category.

Once I got into Linsey's files, I breathed a lot easier. It was clear that he suspected something fishy about Hooks Talbert speaking up for me with the Republican governor in office back then, but he had never connected all the dots and there was nothing new or incriminating in those files. The news clippings and references to Daddy and me were all in the public domain. I transferred the more flattering notices into a folder I'd started in my own file cabinet, and shredded the rest. One of these years, I really might get around to putting together a scrapbook.

"Yeah," said the voice of the pragmatist

who lives in the back of my head. *"Right after you label all those digital pictures and transfer them to a CD."*

Another of the folders could have been Linsey's own scrapbook. Here were clippings from the *N&O* and the *Ledger* of milestones in his life. His high school report cards, a picture of his class in front of the UN building in NY, his diploma from Carolina, his marriage certificate and passport, the obituary of his wife, and a notarized living will that directed his doctors not to prolong his life were he to fall into a persistent vegetative state.

Poor Linsey, I thought. Instantly killed by a hit-and-run driver as he walked home from the newspaper on a warm spring evening. No old age, no long descent into peaceful death. I hoped he didn't know or care what had happened to his beloved paper. Too bad he died without a will. And yet, who would he have left it to? No siblings, no close cousins. Maybe that was why he'd never gotten around to writing one.

Which only served to remind me that Dwight and I hadn't updated our own wills since the wedding, something we really needed to do for Cal's sake if not our own.

The next folder that came to hand was

the one with the Civil War picture of an ancestor. It held more family pictures, each identified on the back by name and date. Here was a copy of the affidavit each white adult Confederate male had been required to sign after the war, swearing allegiance to the Union, before his citizenship and voting rights were restored. And here was an envelope addressed to Linsey's grandfather that carried a 1923 postmark. Inside was a lock of light brown hair, tied with a faded blue string. Unlabeled. Whose?

If I knew that, I'd know why he'd kept it.

I put all those aside in a pile to take to the Colleton County Historical Center and made a note that they were being donated by William Richard Knott.

The files that remained seemed to be news stories or editorials in the making. The tabs carried the names of many prominent people in the county with a heavy concentration on our county commissioners.

I opened the one on Harvey Underwood. He's a banker and a nominal Republican, but as Linsey's notes showed, he wasn't a hard-liner and he didn't always vote with Candace. And *whoa!* He was involved with Barbara Laughlin at the time Linsey died? Barbara's a VP in an insurance company, attractive, bright, divorced, with a son who's been in front of me a couple of times for possession of marijuana and later a couple of rocks of crack. So far as I know, he's been clean the past two years, but between his attorneys and his rehab, it must have cost Barbara a pile of money. Harvey's a married grandfather and an advocate for the sanctity of marriage. I'd never heard a whisper of this. Either Linsey had been mistaken or they had been — still were? — pretty damn discreet.

The next folder was that of an upscale developer. Shortly after leaving the board, he had gotten board approval for a set of plans in which the houses were to be built on half-acre lots with a certain amount of land left for a playground area. According to Linsey's notes, the lot sizes were actually four-tenths of an acre so that more houses had been built than were formally approved, and the playground area was less than specified as well. Somehow or other, this had gone unnoticed till it was too late.

Cute.

From his notes, it was clear that Linsey had intended this to be part of a larger story he planned to do on board cronyism. I guess Ruby Dixon decided not to bother when she became editor. Too much potential flak.

And just to prove that greed and chicanery

crossed party lines freely, here was Greg Turner, a Democratic attorney from Black Creek. Someone had told Linsey that Turner had dipped into an elderly client's bank account and made unauthorized withdrawals to the tune of some sixty thousand dollars. When the client's son asked for an accounting, Turner had managed to stall it off until he could replace the money. According to Linsey's notes, it appeared that he narrowly missed being accused of embezzlement with the real possibility of jail time and subsequent disbarment.

My internal preacher sadly shook his head. *"I thought Greg Turner was as ethical as they come."*

"Yeah, but look how they're coming these days," said the cynical pragmatist who shares the same head space.

All the same, Greg Turner's name resonated for some reason I couldn't quite remember.

Oh well.

I picked up Jamie Jacobson's file with trepidation. She was a friend. I liked her and I really didn't want to know it if she had done anything shabby. But in for a penny . . .

To my relief, the papers inside mostly had to do with professional consultations between the two of them. Jamie's ad agency generated a lot of the *Ledger*'s custom-designed advertising. The only thing puzzling was another sheet of Linsey's doodling on a page torn from a yellow tablet, which seems to have been his way when trying to figure something out.

This time, the heavily circled center was GRAYSON VILLAGE, G. (as in Grayson) Hooks Talbert's foray into the Colleton housing market. One arrow pointed to ADAMS ADVERTISING. Another to SASSY SOLUTIONS. An arrow from Sassy Solutions pointed to Danny Creedmore's name, and a line of question marks led from Creedmore to Candace Bradshaw.

Huh?

Impulsively, I reached for the phone and dialed Jamie's home number. A sleepy voice answered on the fourth ring.

"Did I wake you?" I asked.

"Deborah? No. Well, maybe. I thought I was watching a cooking show, but maybe I did drift off."

I heard her yawn and said, "Sorry to bother you, but I was wondering. Did you do the ads for Grayson Village last spring?"

"No," she said promptly. "We did a presentation, but a Raleigh agency got the job. Why?"

"How come you didn't get it?"

I could almost hear the shrug in her voice. "Who knows? The client liked their presentation better. Especially since they went first and by coincidence, they had thought of some of the same angles I had, so I guess it looked like I was copying them."

"Sassy Solutions?"

"Yes. Why?"

"What's Danny Creedmore's connection to them?"

"None that I know of. Are you going to tell me what this is about?"

"Nothing really. Danny's got his fingers stuck in so many pies, I just wondered if that was another of them."

"Sorry. Did you find any blue shoes Friday?"

"Not yet. The hunt is part of the fun though. How about you?"

"I found some online that look like a good match."

We discussed the pitfalls and conveniences of shopping online and agreed to have lunch together on Tuesday, then I went back to Linsey's files.

So far, I had avoided the one marked BRADSHAW/CREEDMORE. The very label confirmed that Linsey had thought of the two as one. Puppet and puppeteer.

"Should you be reading that?" the preacher asked sternly. *"Isn't this Dwight's province?"*

"Oh, one little look can't hurt," said the pragmatist. *"You'll be doing him a favor, saving him some time by seeing if there's real evidence of wrongdoing or just pure speculation."*

Linsey had kept news clippings and public tax records and scraps of notes to himself. There was also a very rough chart that appeared to list cause and effect. It would seem that Danny Creedmore had given Candace Bradshaw specific directions on how to vote on certain issues. Okay, that was generally known. What I couldn't immediately understand was that Candace seemed to have given him information on deals that hadn't actually come before the board, deals that allowed him to get in early and either buy up land before it had been offered at a public sale or put in bids for jobs that weren't yet formulated.

It looked as if Candace had a network of spies all over the county. Maybe we'd underestimated her. Maybe she was a lot more savvy than we'd thought. Linsey had felt the same way, because scribbled after one of those deals was his frustrated "How the sandpaper did she know?" and it was circled in heavy black lead.

Seeing that gave me a bittersweet smile. One of Linsey's more endearing traits was his refusal to use regular cusswords.

If Linsey's facts and figures were right though, Candace must have been doing very well from her liaison with Danny. For sure, he had gotten rich off of her information. What's weird is that the partnership began long before she ran for the board.

Was her board seat a reward for services already rendered instead of a positioning for services to come?

No matter which, if Terry Wilson's Ginsburg twins could substantiate these charges, Candace could well have been looking at jail time.

Danny, too.

How lucky for them that Linsey had died and Ruby Dixon had taken over the paper.

"Yeah, wasn't it?" said the pragmatist.

Dwight and Cal came back to the house about a half-hour later. They had found and tagged three young redbuds that Dwight planned to move the next time rain was predicted. I thought he was running out of places to put trees, but he seemed to think that because they don't make heavy shade they could go in one of the azalea beds.

He was ready to stretch out on the couch

and watch a ball game, but Cal asked if he could ride his bike over to Andrew's. One of the rabbit dogs had a new litter of puppies and he was anxious to see them.

"Finished your homework?" Dwight asked.

"Yessir."

"Okay with you, Deborah?"

"Sure," I said. "Just don't try to talk Uncle Andrew out of one. Bandit might get jealous."

"Okay," he said and promised to be home before dark.

Dwight wandered out to the kitchen, where I was pouring myself a glass of wine. "Any of that peach cobbler left?"

"One serving. With your name on it."

Dwight sat down at the table to eat it and I gave him Linsey's file on Candace Bradshaw. "You may think this is crazy, darling, but what if Candace found out that Linsey had all this material and was getting ready to write about it in the paper? What if she was out in her car the night he was killed?"

"Huh?"

"Well, you heard Stevie. Dee's still sulking because Candace gave away a practically new Toyota last spring and then immediately bought another one. And y'all never found the Toyota that hit him."

He paused with his fork in midair. "She griped about it to Terry and me Friday, too. And you know what else? Dee even said it galled Candace every time Linsey wrote something negative about her. A no-good cousin from Georgia, huh? Be a real convenient way to get it out of the area."

He put down his fork, picked up his phone, and punched in some numbers. When he reached the detective on duty, he said, "See if you can run down Dee Bradshaw or her dad and find out when Candace Bradshaw got rid of her old car last spring. And while you're at it, get the name and address of the cousin she gave it to."

CHAPTER 16

... charged with exit
routes wrongturned.
— *Paul's Hill,* by Shelby Stephenson

On Monday morning, we learned that Candace's body had been released and that there had been a private cremation the afternoon before. Only Cameron Bradshaw, her daughter Dee, her office manager Gracie Farmer, and the minister of her church were present. There was mention of a future memorial service once her killer was found and locked away. In the meantime, it was said that Cameron wanted to buy space in a columbarium for the two of them, but that Dee thought she should be scattered over Colleton County from a helicopter. No one seemed to know exactly where her ashes were at the moment, only that Cameron had bought a very expensive and very tasteful urn for their eventual repose.

I was callous enough not to care about the whereabouts of her ashes so much as the whereabouts of her previous car.

"Sorry, hon," Dwight said when we passed in the back halls sometime in mid-morning. He was upstairs to testify in a superior court trial; I was on a break while the attorney tried to bargain down the charges on his client with Julie Walsh, today's prosecutor. "Bradshaw says he doesn't remember a cousin and the daughter's not answering her phone. Richards has gone to talk with the office manager, see if there are any personal records. And Terry's got Sabrina Ginsburg looking on her computer for an address book."

"What about Georgia's DMV?" I asked.

"Down, tiger," he said with a grin. "We'll get there. It'll just be easier all around if we have a name for them."

I conscientiously put the matter on a back burner of my mind and concentrated on the cases before me. In addition to the usual roll call of simple assaults, property damages, and break-ins, we had Elton Lee back in court again.

Less than a year ago, Mr. Lee had stood in front of me and pled guilty to a Class H felony, obtaining property by false pretenses. I had given him a suspended eight-month prison sentence on the condition he pay restitution and remain on probation for three years. Yet here he was again on the same charges: two more real estate scams.

Somehow or other, the man manages to get access to empty houses. Either they are houses that have been on the market a while or else they are model homes in half-built, modestly priced developments. Preying on the hopes and dreams of his low-income victims, he poses as a sympathetic real estate agent, takes their five- or six-hundred-dollar down payments, and then quits taking their calls. When one of his victims recognized him at a local grocery store, he told her that there was something wrong with her credit and that he was still trying to get her loan approved. She was trusting enough to give him another three hundred dollars to help hurry things along.

After taking his guilty plea to these new charges and hearing a summary of the facts, I found him guilty again.

"Mr. Lee, what's it going to take to make you stop doing this?" I asked him.

He gave me a sheepish shrug. He really does have a warm and charming smile and he's articulate as well. I can readily understand how his victims could trust him, especially when they so want to believe that he's helping them buy a home of their very own. This was a man who could sell snake oil to doctors.

"You realize this new offense means you have violated your probation and that some judges would send you to jail for eight months right this minute?"

"No, ma'am, Your Honor, I didn't, but I surely hope you won't have to do that," he said earnestly.

Frankly, I did, too. If I gave him active time, his victims would get no restitution.

"I see that you paid restitution for your first conviction?"

"Yes, ma'am."

"Well, that's one thing in your favor." I sat back in my chair and considered all the possibilities. At last I leaned forward and said, "Here's what we're going to do, Mr. Lee. I'm going to sentence you to another eight months, to run consecutively with the first eight, and contingent upon several conditions. That means when you've served the first, you get to serve the second if you break probation again. Do you understand, sir?"

"Yes, ma'am, I do."

"This time, I'm ordering house arrest. You'll wear an ankle monitor for the duration so that your probation officer can keep track of you and the only place you can go is to church and a legitimate job. And you will pay restitution to these new people even if you have to sell your own house. Do you understand that?"

"Yes, ma'am."

"You're a bright man, Mr. Lee. There's no reason why you couldn't be a very successful salesman somewhere in the business world."

"Even with this against me?" he asked.

"Even with this against you."

"Ma'am, you reckon you could write me a letter of recommendation?"

I couldn't help returning his smile. "You apply for a job and I'll consider it," I told him.

What the hell? He'd be a natural for a boss willing to keep him on a short leash.

Dwight and I met for lunch at the Bright Leaf Restaurant and he reported that Dee was still not answering her phone, but that a likely Georgia name had been found among Candace's records: Manfred "Manny" Wells of Peach Blossom Mobile Estates in a suburb of Augusta, Georgia. Just over the South Carolina border off I-95.

"Wells was Candace's maiden name," Dwight told me.

I was ready to send the cavalry down I-95

to circle Manny's double-wide until he gave up the car, but I reined in my impatience and reminded myself that I had leaped to groundless conclusions before. It could still be a total coincidence that Candace, in an act of unprecedented generosity, had given away a practically new Toyota at around the same time that Linsey Thomas was killed by one.

"Thanks for not telling me it's none of my business," I said as the waitress departed after bringing me a small spinach salad and Dwight a grilled chicken sandwich.

"So long as you remember it really isn't," he warned me. "What did Portland say when you told her?"

"I didn't."

"No?"

"No."

Dwight knows that Portland Brewer used to be the first person I hashed out all my concerns and speculations with. She's Uncle Ash's niece and we bonded as children over a mutual hatred of an angelic little prisspot who used to tell on us and get us into trouble. She will always be my best friend, someone with whom I can bitch and moan about life's big and little irritations. We've been too close for too long for that to change in a major way. Her marriage to

Avery didn't change things and neither has mine to Dwight. Shortly before we married, I had admitted that yes, Portland knew he was good in bed. "Just as I know that Avery is. But if he's ever had performance anxieties, Por never mentioned it. That would be off-limits. Same for anything to do with your job, okay?"

For some reason, though, he finds it hard to believe that we really don't tell each other every single thing.

We were sitting adjacent to each other at the table and I put my hand on his knee under the table. "Performance anxieties?"

"Okay, okay." He covered my hand with his. "I get it."

I smiled and took another bite of my salad. The spinach leaves were young and tender and so flavorful that they could have come out of Cletus and Daddy's garden. The croutons had a homemade herb-and-onion flavor and offered a crunchy contrast to the greens and sliced hard-boiled eggs. "Have the Ginsburgs come up with anything solid against Danny Creedmore?"

Dwight swallowed a bite of chicken and shook his head. "If Candace kept any records, she's covered her tracks well. There's nothing incriminating on her hard drive and they still can't find the flash drive she's supposed to have used. By the way, they told Terry to tell you thanks for Linsey Thomas's files. They seem to think they're going to find pure gold there."

As we ate, several people had stopped by the table to speak to us — attorneys, various county department heads, and Jamie Jacobson, who leaned in close to murmur, "You were asking if Danny Creedmore had a connection to Sassy Solutions? I mentioned it to my husband and he told me that Sassy is owned by Danny's brother-in-law. We definitely need to talk tomorrow."

"What was that about?" Dwight asked as she moved toward the door.

"She and a Raleigh advertising agency were asked to submit proposals for the ads for Grayson Village last year. The other company got the job."

"So?"

"So one of Linsey's diagrams linked that agency to Grayson Village through Danny and Candace. You might want to point that out to the Ginsburgs."

He made a note of it and signaled our waitress that he was ready to pay. As we walked back to the courthouse, he offered to pick up a pizza for our supper. "I suppose you'll want a side of those disgusting anchovies?"

"Yes, but I always keep a jar on hand, so don't bother getting more." One quick kiss in the momentarily deserted atrium, then we parted at the stairs, I to the courtroom upstairs, he to his office down below.

"I'll try not to be late," I promised.

In the end though, it was Dwight who was late. Cal and I had to settle for scrambled eggs instead of pizza.

The reason Dee Bradshaw wasn't answering her phone today was because someone had shot her the night before.

Once in the back, once in the head.

Chapter 17

Then it was gone . . .
The world takes back its toys, my mama
used to say.
      — *Paul's Hill,* by Shelby Stephenson

Mid-afternoon on Monday and Deputy Percy Denning turned to Major Bryant. "You remember that slug I dug out of the rug here on Friday?" He had photographed the crime scene from one end of the room to the other. Now he gingerly pried a new slug from the wall. "This looks like the same size. A .22, I'd say. What do you want to bet that when I get them under a microscope they'll both match the two in her?"

"No bet," Dwight said, as he tried to reconstruct the shooting. Dee's body lay facedown in the living room, on a line with the hole in the wall, a hole that was almost chest-high to Denning.

"She was running away from the shooter,"

he theorized. "The first bullet missed, the other got her square in the back. Or the first bullet took her down before the second one arrived."

From behind him, Deputy Richards said, "Then to make sure she was dead, he stood over her and fired again through the side of her head."

Three days ago, she had been vibrant and sexy and looking forward to her inheritance, thought Dwight. A spoiled slacker, Stevie had called her. The daughter of a woman who didn't know how to be a mother, according to Gracie Farmer. From his own observation, she had been a conflicted young woman who had not finished growing up.

Now she never would.

"Did she surprise an intruder or was the shooter someone she let in herself?" Dwight wondered aloud.

"I think she let him in." Richards pointed to the dead girl's bare feet. "Looks like she kicked off her shoes there by the couch. There's her wineglass, the cork, and the opener. Her glass is still half full, but the bottle's almost empty. She might have drunk it all herself, but someone else could have had a glass with her."

"Make a note of it for the ME," Dwight

told Denning. "You check the kitchen, Richards?"

"Yessir, and there are dirty dishes and fast-food cartons but no used wineglass. Either he washed it clean and put it back on the shelf or else took it with him. Seems like everybody's heard of DNA these days."

Her rueful tone reminded him of something Bo Poole had said about one of the county's high sheriffs. "I heard that a sheriff back in the nineteen-twenties tried to keep Linsey Thomas's granddaddy from describing fingerprint technology in the *Ledger.* He thought it was telling the criminals how not to get caught."

"Yeah," said Denning as he bagged and tagged the slug. "Even if we had the time and equipment to process this house like one of those CSI shows on television, so many people have tromped through here the last few days, there's no way you could separate out what's relevant from what isn't."

From his aggrieved tone, Dwight knew he was still smarting over having to admit in court last week that no, he had not lifted fingerprints off the digital camera that a thief, the meth-addicted son of a local businessman, had walked out of the store with.

"He had it inside his jacket," Denning would say to anyone who would listen. "Why the hell would we bother to match his fingerprints to it? He was holding the fricking thing when he was arrested!" Nevertheless, until someone with a little common sense finally spoke up, the jury had almost declared the shoplifter not guilty because of that lack.

"Anything else disturbed or different from when you were here last?" Dwight asked them as two more deputies returned from canvassing the neighbors, who, predictably, had seen nothing.

Richards shrugged. "Denning and I think that her room is messier than it was before. But then she moved back in on Saturday, so she had at least a day and a half to trash it some more. Drawers and cabinet doors are open all over the house, and there're some cardboard boxes in her bedroom and in the kitchen, like she was starting to pack up whatever she planned to keep."

"Can't say for sure if she tossed the house or someone else did," said Denning. "Looking at the kitchen, I've got her pegged as a natural slob. Most of the drawer knobs are too textured to show prints. I got a couple of smears off the smooth knobs in the kitchen, but that's it."

272

One of the EMS techs pointedly tapped his watch. "How 'bout it, Major Bryant? Can we transport her now?"

"Yeah, okay," Dwight said, and watched as they zipped Dee Bradshaw's small stiff body into a body bag, lifted her onto the gurney, and wheeled her through the doorway.

Outside, beyond the yellow tape that bounded the yard, a knot of uneasy neighbors had gathered to watch. More deputies were keeping them back, but he saw cell phones raised to record the scene. No doubt it would soon be on someone's website. The local TV crew left when the door of the EMS truck swung shut.

The days were steadily getting longer. Four o'clock and the sun was only now starting to settle into the trees. A shaft of sunlight through the leaves caught Richards's auburn hair and turned it bright as a new copper penny.

The EMS truck pulled away just as Terry Wilson's car coasted to a stop on the circular drive.

"Sorry," the SBI agent said as he opened the door and got out and slipped on his jacket to cover his shoulder holster. "Got held up on another case. What the hell's going on here, Dwight? Why was she killed?

You reckon she found that flash drive?"

"Who knows?" Dwight turned back to his deputy. "Where's Bradshaw?"

"In the sunroom with his office manager," Richards said. "McLamb's babysitting them."

"Show me," he said.

The east-facing sunroom was at the back of the house and looked out onto a grassy berm that was topped with a thick mixture of evergreens — cedars, hollies, camellia bushes, and boxwood — that disguised the highway beyond and effectively screened the house from both passing motorists and nearby neighbors. The far wall consisted of wide arched windows with French doors that opened onto a flagstone terrace, where a set of white wrought-iron patio furniture waited invitingly.

The room was furnished in the colors that Candace Bradshaw apparently favored: white carpets, rose-patterned fabrics on the chairs and couches, deep rose accent cushions, and crisp white shades on the table lamps. A wet bar had been discreetly hidden in a cherry armoire, but the doors were folded back at the moment and a bottle of bourbon sat on the counter.

Deputy Raeford McLamb stood up when

they entered the room, and Mrs. Farmer gave them a sad smile, but Cameron Bradshaw remained huddled at one end of a couch and seemed oblivious of their presence. He cradled a highball glass in his hands and looked closer to eighty than sixty.

If ever a man had a right to look shattered, though, it was this man, thought Dwight. First the wife that he had continued to love, and now his only child. And he had been the one to find her.

"We were supposed to have lunch together," he told them in disjointed sentence fragments, as if it was an effort to think in logical sequence. "We were going to go over Candace's will again — she left the house to Dee. Talk about selling it, decide what to do with the furniture. She wanted to get your brother-in-law to come over and give us an appraisal. He was nice to her, giving her a job like that. She liked him. But she was going to go back to school. Make up the work she missed. Get her life on track. But she didn't meet us and she didn't answer her phone, so Gracie and I came over. Her car was here, and — and —"

"You have a key?" Richards asked gently.

He nodded. "I opened the front door and called and there she was. On the floor. Soon as I saw her, I knew it was no use. Blood all over Candace's white carpet. So much blood for such a little thing. My beautiful little girl. All that blood."

He lifted the glass to his lips with both hands and drank deeply. It was clear that this was not his first nor even third drink.

Tears puddled in Mrs. Farmer's eyes as she watched, but she didn't try to stop him.

"Who would do this, Bryant?" Bradshaw asked in a voice that was rough with grief. "What did Dee ever do to make a monster shoot her down in her own house? She was just a girl still."

"When did you last see her?" Dwight asked.

"Yesterday. After the service for Candace. Gracie made us come home with her for supper so that we wouldn't have to go to a restaurant. Not that any of us were very hungry, but Dee left before dark. She wanted to get started packing up her clothes and the things she wanted to keep."

"Did you talk to her later that evening?"

"I didn't, but Gracie — ?"

Gracie Farmer nodded. "We talked a couple of times on the phone. I asked her to look for an umbrella of mine that Candace had borrowed last week. It cost more than I usually pay, but it has parrots and tropical flowers, so . . . Silly to even think of such a thing when Candace . . ." Her voice trailed off and they could see her try to recover control.

Unlike the cacophony of clashing colors they had seen her in before, today's outfit was almost somber: dark red linen slacks and white silk shirt, a zip-up white cotton sweater randomly striped in thick and thin red lines. Black patent shoes with low Cuban heels, a black leather purse. Her short fingernails were painted the exact same shade as her lipstick and slacks.

"You said you talked a couple of times?"

Mrs. Farmer nodded. "Around six, I think. She called me about the dollhouse. Wanted to know if she could store it in my attic till she had a place for it. I told her of course she could."

Bradshaw turned to her in wonderment. "She was going to keep it?"

"That surprises you, sir?" asked Mayleen Richards.

"She always made fun of Candace for playing with it and buying new furniture and things for it. She didn't care much for dolls even when she was a little girl, but Candace? Candace never had the toys and pretty things that Dee had, and the dollhouse was important to her in ways I'll probably never understand without talking to a psychiatrist. Wish fulfillment? Restructuring her childhood? Candace seldom talked about her family and home life to me. I think it embarrassed her. But I gather it was most" — he hesitated, searching for the discreet term — "chaotic and thoroughly unpleasant and —"

He lapsed into silence.

Gracie Farmer patted his arm consolingly and said, "When she came to me for a job, she was sixteen and pretty much on her own. She had left home and moved in with her grandmother, who died two or three years later. But Cam's right. Dee did make fun of the dollhouse. But when she called to ask if I'd keep it for her, she was crying and blaming herself for not understanding Candace better."

"And that was the last time you spoke to her?"

"No, she called back around eight and said she'd found the umbrella. She was going to give it to me today when —" Her voice broke and she reached for her handbag and some tissues to wipe away the tears that were freely coursing down her cheeks.

"The night she was born, I was there. Remember, Cam?"

He nodded without looking up from the empty glass in his hands.

"Little blond ringlets all over her tiny little head."

Dwight stood up and said, "Mrs. Farmer, may we speak with you privately somewhere?"

She nodded, wiped her eyes, and suggested they go into the dining room next door.

As she stood, Bradshaw handed her his glass and nodded toward the bar. "Don't fuss, Gracie. Please?"

Without comment, she poured him another stiff one, then led Dwight, Richards, and the SBI agent through the double doors into a formal dining room. The long polished table had seating for twelve. The centerpiece was an arrangement of silk roses and baby's breath so realistic that Richards had to touch one to convince herself that they were not real. At least five dollars a stem, she thought, and not from any local discount house.

"This is an awfully big house for one person," Terry Wilson said as they sat down at the table.

Gracie Farmer looked around the room, almost as if seeing it for the first time. "Candace thought she might start entertaining if she ran for the state senate. This would have been a great place for a dinner party, the way the double doors open into the sun-room."

"How did she pay for it?" Dwight asked bluntly.

"Pay for it?" The older woman's voice faltered for a moment. "She owned half of Bradshaw Management, Major, and she had just sold her old house. She could afford it."

"Afford to pay cash?"

She looked at them in bewilderment. "Is that what she did? I assumed she took out a mortgage. I mean, this is one of the smaller houses in this development, but I'm sure it must have cost her close to half a million by the time she added on the extras and the landscaping. She wasn't taking that much money out of the business and the old house was in such bad shape that — are you *sure* she paid cash?"

"That's what they told us at the bank."

"Dee thought she was skimming from the business," Richards told her.

"Never!" Mrs. Farmer said indignantly.

But then a shadow crossed her face and Dwight glanced at Wilson, wondering if his old friend was thinking the same thing he was — that here was a woman who should never play poker for money. She sat silently for a moment, pleating the fabric of her red slacks as she thought about what they had said.

"Okay, look. I told y'all that she sometimes probably took money for some of the favors she did a few developers and real estate people? She really did care more about power and having people think she was very important than about money, but I guess she probably liked the money, too. If she was skimming though, Roger Flackman had to know about it."

"Mr. Bradshaw's auditor?" Wilson asked.

The office manager nodded. "I hate speaking ill of the dead, but it's not as if Candace was really married. And you know how beautiful she was. Looked more like thirty than forty. I don't know if he would have cooked the books for her, but she could be very persuasive when she was trying to sell something."

"And sometimes she paid with sex?"

Gracie Farmer had quit meeting his eyes. "You'll have to ask Flackman about that. I truly don't know."

"Tell us about her cousin down in Georgia," Dwight said.

"Cousin? Oh, yes, the one with the peaches. Someone from your office called me about that this morning, asking about her car. All I know is that he showed up at the office last spring and said his name was Manny and that Candace had called him, asked him to bring some peaches up for the office staff. There were like five bushels. Even the cleaning crews got a few. Candace said his truck broke down and she was going to lend him her car to get back."

"Lend it to him?"

"But then she decided to just give it to him because the peach orchard wasn't doing so good and she felt sorry for him. I told you she liked doing people favors."

"And that's all you know?"

"He was scamming her with that hard-luck story about the orchard," the woman said, as if remembering an old grievance. "He didn't own any orchard. Those peaches came from north Florida, not north Georgia. When I went out to the truck to take a look at them, one of the baskets had a label. I said something about was that the name of his orchard and he immediately shifted it around. I'd already seen the Florida address though. By the time those baskets came inside, every label had been torn off. And something else. That wasn't his truck either. It was one of those rent-a-wrecks."

"Did you tell her that?"

"I tried, but she got mad and said it was none of my business, so I backed off."

"Do you remember the date, Mrs. Farmer?"

"The week after her birthday," she said and told them the date.

Exactly one day after Linsey Thomas was killed.

They allowed Mrs. Farmer to rejoin Bradshaw and were discussing the implications of what she had told them when Denning appeared in the hall doorway. "Major Bryant? You might want to see this."

They followed him back to the front of the house. In the foyer, opposite a large coat closet, was a small powder room. When Denning opened the door, a strong odor of a chlorine-based toilet bowl cleanser hit their noses. He had removed the lid of the tank and left it propped against the wall. The three crowded into the room and peered inside the tank, where a wineglass lay completely submerged in the cleanser.

"Cute, huh?" said Denning from behind them. "Try getting DNA off *that* glass."

CHAPTER 18

Quiet lies the body under the limb . . .
The ground's a harp strung with shadows.
— *Middle Creek Poems,*
by Shelby Stephenson

Monday afternoon

Sweat poured from Faison McKinney's face, gnats whined in his unprotected ears, and the pace that old man had set was giving him a painful stitch in his side. How in the dickens could a man who was at least forty years older and six inches taller eel his way through briars and vines and low-hanging limbs without once tripping or banging his head? He himself had already fallen twice and he knew he had a nasty scrape on his forehead where he had misjudged a pine limb.

" 'Fraid I'm gonna have to ask you to slow down a little, Brother Kezzie," he called, embarrassed that the man ahead should be in such better shape. Maybe it was time to cut back on the cakes and pies the ladies of the church insisted on sharing with him and Marian. Cut back on the barbecue, too. Marian didn't seem to gain an ounce, he thought irritably, but he'd had to let out his belt another notch recently and the gold band with the nice diamond inset that he used to wear on his ring finger when it was new only fit his pinky now. He was going to have to talk to her, make her — no, not *make,* he corrected himself — *ask* her to quit serving the rich foods he liked and learn how to prepare healthy low-calorie meals that still tasted just as good and rich.

"Sorry, Preacher," Kezzie Knott said when McKinney caught up with him, huffing like a steam engine. "It ain't much further now. Just on the other side of that big oak yonder."

A few yards on and he came to a stop by a large tree that must have fallen in the last hurricane. He sat down on the trunk and a grateful McKinney sank down beside him, trying not to breathe too strenuously. Kezzie Knott seemed to be breathing normally and if the man had broken a sweat, McKinney couldn't see it.

"It was right here," the old man said. "Twenty-five years ago. I had me a still down the slope there on the creek bank and I come along this way that day. Never went to any of my stills the same way twice. You don't want to make a path, see? Laziness'll give you away quicker'n the smoke or the smell."

He paused as if remembering old secrets of his craft. "It was just a little still. I'd purty much got out of making it myself by then. My wife didn't like me messing with it and you know how women are. You got to promise them things, don't you?"

"Well . . ." said McKinney, mopping his sweaty face with his handkerchief. "I believe it's a woman's place to abide by her husband's wishes, but moonshining? She was probably trying to save your soul."

"And my hide, too," the old man said with a chuckle. "Them ATF men was plumb aching to catch me out and stick me in jail. That's why I put my still down here on Sid Pritchard's land so that —"

"Pritchard's land?" McKinney exclaimed. "This is part of Frances Pritchard's land?"

"Yeah. I wouldn't never do stuff like that on my own land. Ain't safe. Didn't I tell you?"

"No, Brother Kezzie, you did *not* tell me. Isn't there a road right over there? Why did we have to walk a mile through the woods when we could've driven almost right to the spot?"

"And park my truck on the road out yonder for every passing busybody to wonder what I was doing in here?" asked Kezzie. "No, sir. That ain't my way. Iffen you don't want people asking questions, then you don't give 'em nothing to ask questions about."

He stood up and pointed up into the limbs of the tall oak. "Right here's where I found him hanging, all tangled up in them parachute lines. He was dangling just a few feet off the ground, and every time the wind blew, the branches make it look like he was still alive, but he won't. His neck was broke. I cut him down and after I seen what was in his backpack, I buried him right here. Him and his parachute and everything on him except that backpack."

"I see," said the preacher.

"It's been a-eating on me for twenty-five years," the old man said, "and I just can't go to meet my maker knowing he didn't have a Christian burial and I didn't take the opportunity to make things right when I got the chance. That was pure-out providence meeting you Friday."

"The Lord still works in mysterious ways," McKinney agreed solemnly. He waved away the gnats that were buzzing around his eyes. "I think He led us both to that fishpond for his own reasons."

"I reckon you're right, Preacher. Anyhow, his people never knowed what happened to him and that man he stole from never got his stuff back. So I'd really appreciate it, if you'd do what you can and say a few words over him for me."

"Of course," said the other man. He came to his feet and pulled out a small Bible. "How exactly did you bury him?"

"Right here," said Kezzie, sketching a narrow rectangle with his hands. "Head up there, facing east, his feet right about down here."

He sat back on the tree trunk again and listened respectfully as McKinney read from the Bible and then prayed for the repose of "thy servant, Nicholas Radzinsky. And, Father, we ask that You forgive his sins and let him enter into the paradise of Your blessed radiance, for we ask it in the name of our Lord and Savior, Jesus Christ. Amen."

"Amen," said Kezzie. "Thank you, Preacher. I surely do appreciate it and I believe he does, too."

They sat in silence on the tree trunk for several long minutes as the sun sank lower in the west. McKinney was thinking of the long walk back to Kezzie Knott's truck, but there was something even more important on his mind. When the other man remained silent, he said at last, "When you told me about this and asked my advice, it sounded so fantastic that if you hadn't shown me that earring —"

"Oh. Yeah. I almost forgot about it," said Kezzie. He held out his hand and the preacher pulled it from his pocket and held it up in the sunlight. The diamonds flashed and glittered.

"I took it to a jeweler I know," he said as he reluctantly dropped it in the old man's calloused hand.

"Yeah?"

"He said it was at least sixty years old and that the pair of them would be worth about two or three thousand dollars."

"That all?" Kezzie Knott's blue eyes looked disappointed. "I thought they'd be more'n that."

"He looked at the diamonds under a magnifying glass and they're not flawless."

"They ain't?" He held them up to the sun again and squinted. "They surely do sparkle."

"The flaws aren't visible to the naked eye," the preacher explained in a kindly tone. "It's what they call occlusions. Little cloudy spots no bigger than a speck of dust. They don't hurt the way they look to you and me, but they can bring the price down real quick."

"You sure your man knowed what he was talking about? The newspapers back then said he jumped out'n that plane with jewelry worth four million dollars. And that was twenty-five years ago. I was thinking that'd come out to be six or seven million these days what with inflation and all."

"Oh, I imagine the owner might have exaggerated the value a little bit, don't you? To get what he could from the insurance company? People aren't always truthful, Brother Kezzie."

Kezzie Knott nodded. "You ain't never said a truer word, Preacher."

He tucked the earring into his shirt pocket and buttoned it securely. "Still and all, every time me and mine's ever insured anything, the man wants to see it. Wants to see the bill of sale, too, if it's something that's worth right much. Don't you reckon the man these was stole from had to show receipts, too?"

"Hard to know, Brother Kezzie. I went and looked it up online. The owner was a fancy jeweler in Miami. Dealt in what they call estate jewelry."

"Yeah, I've heared my boy Will talk about that stuff."

"He's dead now himself. Died about eight years ago, but he did collect on the insurance. If his family were to get these back, they'd have to turn around and come up with the four million he got paid."

"That could work a real hardship on 'em, couldn't it?"

"It could, Brother Kezzie. It really could. That man might've paid four million for 'em, but that doesn't mean his people could sell them for that today. My jeweler says there's auction value and then there's insurance value and sometimes the two are miles apart."

Kezzie Knott nodded sagely. "When it comes time to sell something, don't matter how much you paid for it. You got to find somebody willing to buy what you're selling."

"That's the way of the world, I'm afraid."

"The thing is, I ain't never stole nothing in my life, but this ain't really stealing, is it? I got land, but I ain't got money. I was hoping maybe them earrings would be enough to buy the Pritchard land so no bulldozer could ever turn up them bones, but if they ain't worth more'n a couple of thousand, don't look like that's gonna happen."

McKinney swept the gnats away again with his handkerchief. "Tell you what, Brother Kezzie. Why don't you go get the truck and drive it around here and let me take it to the Lord in prayer? He's led us together and I'm sure He has a purpose in mind."

"That's real kindly of you, Preacher. I ain't never been much for praying, but I'm feeling easier about this now that I've got you to help me do the right thing."

As he walked away into the underbrush, Kezzie Knott glanced back and saw the preacher on his knees with his handkerchief draped over his head.

CHAPTER 19

The top of my head, Mister Paul, grows
  bald.
I mean the Old South is gone, ain't it?
  — *Paul's Hill,* by Shelby Stephenson

With the death of Dee Bradshaw, the investigation took on a new urgency. Richards and McLamb spent Tuesday morning tracking down the county commissioners and getting statements as to their whereabouts on the previous Tuesday afternoon when Candace Bradshaw was killed and for Sunday evening between six-thirty and midnight, the assumed time of her daughter's death until the ME told them differently.

Other deputies interviewed her office staff and any janitorial workers with whom Candace might have had words.

Predictably, most could not substantiate their movements. Several claimed to have been on their way home between four and five-thirty on Tuesday, or in church on Sunday evening.

Harvey Underwood, a commissioner and the banker who had handled the sale of Candace's house, was the only one with solid alibis for both times. On Sunday, he and his wife had made the three-hour drive to Charlotte for their granddaughter's birthday and had spent the night there. During the relevant time on Tuesday, he had been in consultation with his wife, a plumber, and a handyman about adding a closet for a second washer and dryer next to an upstairs bathroom.

"Damn foolishness, if you ask me," he'd grumbled to Richards. "The cleaning woman does all the laundry and she's never complained about having to take the sheets and towels downstairs."

When pressed to elaborate on the source of Candace's cash payment in full for the house, he looked uncomfortable, but claimed to know nothing about it. "She deposited a cashier's check for a hundred thousand dollars ten days earlier, Deputy Richards, and she sold the old Bradshaw house for $140,000. That's all I know."

And no, he was not inclined to speculate on who had given her the cashier's check.

It was duly noted that Candace was the

only commissioner who had missed the meeting Tuesday night and none of them had noticed anything odd or constrained about any of their colleagues.

Or so they said.

Cameron Bradshaw would also appear to be in the clear on his wife's murder. When his neighbors were canvassed, several confirmed that they had seen him sitting outside on his terrace that afternoon. One or another placed him there from around three o'clock till after five. As for Sunday evening, some old friends had called by to offer their condolences and the last did not leave until after nine.

Gracie Farmer had spent Tuesday afternoon inspecting a couple of offices in the area in preparation for drawing up cleaning contracts; and Dee's cell phone records confirmed the calls between them, although Farmer lived alone and could not prove that she had stayed in all evening. "Too bad my two cats can't talk," she had said wryly.

Dee had kept her phone busy throughout the evening. Among the calls was one at 6:47 to Chapel Hill, to the dorm where her boyfriend lived, and an earlier one at 6:32 to Will Knott.

"Yeah," he said when Dwight stopped by his warehouse. "She wanted to apologize for not showing back up for work. Hell's bells, Dwight. Her mama'd been killed and she was worried about that? She said she was going to go back to school and wanted me to come over and take a look at the house, give her an appraisal of what the furnishings were worth. Maybe handle a sale for her. I agreed to drop by yesterday afternoon, but —" He shrugged. "Hell of a note, idn't it? Pretty young thing like that? Why you reckon she was shot?"

"Beats me, Will. We're starting to think maybe she found some records that her mother kept that might put somebody in jail."

"And she let 'em know?"

"Wouldn't be the first time somebody played with dynamite and had it blow up in their face."

As for the boyfriend, his roommates confirmed that he'd been drunk and semi-comatose by late afternoon on Sunday. No way could he have driven from Chapel Hill to Dobbs. Last Tuesday evening? "Hey, man, who can remember that far back?"

The Honorable Woodrow Galloway, North Carolina state senator for their district, was unavailable for questioning about the deaths. Or so said his office. The senator, they said piously, was personally saddened by Mrs. Bradshaw's death. The county and the state had lost a dedicated public servant who had worked tirelessly to further the growth and prosperity of her county and her state, but he himself could add nothing substantive to the investigation. They were friends and colleagues, nothing more, and any attempts to paint them as lovers were merely the usual smear tactics of the Democratic party. If Sheriff Poole insisted, Senator Galloway would try to make time in his busy schedule, which was posted on the senator's website.

A few phone calls to disinterested parties confirmed that Galloway had indeed been in a committee meeting in Raleigh last Tuesday afternoon until after six and at a church function on Sunday evening that broke up around ten o'clock.

Dwight himself questioned Danny Creedmore, another man with no confirmed alibis. To Dwight's complete and utter lack of surprise, Creedmore was indignant that he would be asked to account for his movements and insisted that all his dealings with Candace Bradshaw had been open and aboveboard. "Yeah, okay, so we got it on for a couple of years, but that part was ending with no hard feelings on either side." He sat back in his chair with the air of a man who thought the world was his for the taking. "We were still working together to help the county grow and prosper."

That cashier's check for a hundred thousand dollars?

"Maybe somebody gave it to her as a housewarming present."

"For services rendered?" Dwight asked.

Creedmore shrugged and again denied any knowledge.

"According to her phone records, Dee Bradshaw called you a little after eight."

"Yeah."

"What was that about?"

"To be honest with you, Bryant, I'm not real sure. She didn't make a whole lot of sense. I couldn't tell if she was drunk or just mad."

"Mad about what?"

"Who knows? She accused me of using Candace and said she could prove it. Before I could ask her what the hell she was talking about, she said the doorbell was ringing and just hung up on me."

Dwight did not find it needful to warn Creedmore that the SBI would soon be asking permission to subpoena his financial records. Triple C had poured all the concrete for the development where Candace lived and they had picked up hints that he had negotiated a lower price for her with the developer, who was a former board member.

One hand scratching the back of somebody who was scratching someone else's. So what else was new? They'd have to wait for the Ginsburg twins to sort it all out. In the meantime, their own DA was trying to stay out of it.

"You bring me some solid evidence, and I'll indict," Doug Woodall told Bo when the sheriff caught him heading out to give a speech in Raleigh, "but this is a tricky time for me."

"You saying we should lay off Danny Creedmore?"

"No, I'm saying I can't afford to go on any fishing expeditions right now. You can understand that, right?"

"Right," said Bo and tried to keep the distaste from his face.

"Don't get so high and mighty with me, Bo Poole. You don't know what it takes to run for statewide office. Yeah, you may think Creedmore's crooked as a snake. Hell, I'm not all that crazy about him myself, but he's got a lot of clout in this part of the state."

"And how'd he get that clout, Doug?"

"At the moment, that's not my concern. The reality is that here and now, he's got it and he's willing to swing some votes my way. We may not need the open endorsement of Republicans, but we sure as hell don't need their active opposition. Now if you'll excuse me, I've got to go make a speech."

"On law and order and the need for clean local government?" Bo asked sardonically.

"Fuck you and the mule you rode in on," said the Colleton County district attorney.

Roger Flackman was not only a CPA, he was also on the board of commissioners. When asked to come to Dwight's office, he initially resisted.

"Or we can come to your office," Dwight said mildly. "My colleagues from the State Bureau of Investigation are looking into Mrs. Bradshaw's financial dealings and they have some questions, too."

At the thought of the gossip that could ensue from a visit by state agents and sheriff's deputies, Flackman decided he could, after all, make time to come to Dwight's office that afternoon. A thin man with large ears and a prominent Adam's apple, he nervously smoothed his thick brown hair with his long bony fingers and straightened his tie and glasses upon his taking a seat across from the desk between them. He seemed rattled by their questions and twirled a white ballpoint pen around and around between his thumb, index, and middle fingers as they thanked him for coming in and questions got under way.

"Who paid you to audit the books at Bradshaw Management?"

"Mr. Bradshaw. It was purely a formality though. Part of their original divorce agreement."

"Only they weren't divorced," Terry Wilson observed.

"True, true," said Flackman, as that pen turned faster, "but he decided it would be to his advantage to keep the arrangement in place. It's not at all unusual in these circumstances."

"So he didn't really suspect his wife of holding back on him?" asked Dwight.

"Not really. There may have been a little distrust in the beginning. I mean he *did* hire me, didn't he? But they've actually been quite friendly these last few years."

"The business was doing well?"

"Extremely well. All the growth in the county has given rise to new apartments to rent and new businesses that need cleaning, but the company was stagnating under Mr.

Bradshaw's leadership. Mrs. Bradshaw grew their business a good thirty percent after she took over. I've heard that you suspect her of wrongdoing, of using her position on the board to benefit herself, but I assure you, it was not the case." The pen was almost a blur now as it spun around and under those long thin fingers. "She was a smart businesswoman and it was not unethical to avail herself of opportunities for more work when new businesses expressed a desire to locate here."

"That how she could pay for her new house with cash?" asked Dwight.

"*And* buy a new car?" Terry Wilson added.

"I had no access to her private accounts," Flackman said primly. "If she saved and invested prudently —"

He shrugged and let the suggestion die on its own. The pen slowed to a leisurely twirl and it did not quicken when Dwight said, "Dee Bradshaw told us she thought Candace was skimming from the company."

"Certainly not. The company books balance out to the penny. Sorry, Bryant, Agent Wilson. If Candace Bradshaw had more money in her bank account than she could account for, it didn't come out of the company. You can bring in your own auditors, if you want."

"You sleeping with her, Mr. Flackman?" Terry asked politely.

"That something else Dee told you?"

When they didn't answer, he shook his head. "No. I'm not going to say I didn't want to — my wife left me eight years ago — but it never happened. Sorry."

With his eyes on that pen, now almost motionless in Flackman's fingers, Dwight said, "What about your own position on the board? She throw some of those extra opportunities your way, too?"

Roger Flackman's Adam's apple bobbled as he denied it, but his pen was suddenly twirling so fast that it flew out of his fingers and clattered across the table.

"Oops! Sorry." He retrieved the pen and slid it into an inner jacket pocket. With his hands planted firmly on his legs under the table, he told them that he had gone home early on Tuesday with a migraine headache and that he stayed home watching television alone on Sunday.

Greg Turner had the blond good looks of an All-American lacrosse player, as indeed he had been when he played for Duke twenty years earlier. With straight hair so blond that it was almost silver, extremely fair skin, keen blue eyes, a neck almost as wide as his head, and a lightly muscled body that stood two hairs over six feet, there was a prosperous sleekness about him when he poked his head in Dwight's door in mid-afternoon and said, "You left a message with my office that you wanted to speak to me?"

Mayleen Richards was there to report on the morning's findings and she rose to go, but Dwight motioned for her to stay, so she sat back down and nodded politely as introductions were made. She knew who this attorney was. Greg Turner was gaining a reputation for infallibility and clever arguments, especially in the big-money civil cases. Courthouse gossip had him divorced and currently unattached. He was certainly handsome, but did not appear conceited, and he was pleasant to everyone, even sheriff's deputies with a high school education, while he himself was a graduate of the Duke school of law.

This was the man of her mother's dreams — a super-white, Anglo-Saxon Protestant professional. There were some whispered speculations about his sexual orientation, but as long as they were only whispers, her mother could easily ignore them.

What she couldn't ignore was Mayleen's involvement with a dark-skinned Latino who owned a landscaping business and probably burned candles and incense to obscure saints no right-thinking Baptist had ever heard of.

Mayleen sighed and tried to concentrate on the interview.

"Yes," Turner was saying with an easy smile. "I did get a phone call from Dee Bradshaw Sunday night. She left a message on my answering machine. Said she wanted to talk to me about her mother."

"What about?"

"I have no idea."

"The time of her call was around seven-fifteen, right?"

He nodded.

"You were out?"

"No, I was there, but I was in the middle of cooking myself an omelet for supper and I didn't want to turn it off. I figured if it was anything important, they could leave a message and I'd call back."

"It was quite a long message," Dwight said. "Almost three minutes."

"Yeah. She was talking about how Candace took her position on the board of commissioners very seriously and knew I did, too."

"Do you mind if we listen to that message?" Richards asked.

Turner glanced at her as if surprised to

find her still there and allowed to speak, but he gave her one of his high-wattage smiles meant to convey amused regret. "Sorry. I always erase my messages as soon as I've finished listening to them."

"And you didn't call her back?"

He shrugged. "Callous of me, I suppose, and now that she's dead, I wish I had. But it had been a hard week and I just didn't feel like dealing with a bereaved daughter at that moment."

"Is there anyone who can vouch for your being at home alone all evening?"

He gave a small ironic smile. "Sorry. *Alone* means just that, Major Bryant."

CHAPTER 20

> . . . started out with a mule. Now
> he's got sixteen big John Deere tractors:
> $100,000 a piece.
> — *Paul's Hill,* by Shelby Stephenson

I recessed for lunch a few minutes early on Tuesday at the request of the two attorneys who had not yet reached an agreement over damages incurred when a tree service dropped a huge dead oak tree on a neighbor's in-ground swimming pool late last fall, smashing one corner and flattening the fence. The neighbor wanted an all-new pool, and he wanted it filled with water he didn't have to pay for. He was also asking damages for the mental trauma caused by a tree falling near the sandbox where his two young sons were playing.

The tree service's insurance company wanted to repair the corner and replace the fence, but they were not willing to pay for more than half the water as the pool had already been winterized and was a little low at the time. (With so many extra straws sipping water out of our rivers and treatment plants these days, water's getting to be real pricey.) Because both parents had been at work while the boys played under the watchful eyes of a babysitter, the insurance company disputed how much trauma the neighbor had actually suffered.

If anyone had suffered trauma, it was probably the sitter. Unfortunately for her, she wasn't a party to the suit. Testifying for the insurance company, she described how terrified she had been when she saw that tree come crashing down, but that the boys were delighted by the whole incident. Too young to realize how close they had come to serious harm, they thought it great fun to clamber up onto the tree trunk and walk along its length. They had even begged to keep it and cried when it was removed from their yard.

I left the attorneys to it and joined Portland Brewer and Jamie Jacobson for lunch at a Tex-Mex place three blocks from the courthouse. The food is cheap and good and there are booths along the back wall where we could talk without being interrupted. Even though I was early, they already had frozen margaritas in front of them. I knew that Portland was still nursing the baby, so hers would be a virgin and I told the waitress to bring me one about half the strength of whatever Jamie was drinking.

Jamie laughed. "And just what makes you think mine's not a virgin, too?"

"I'm psychic."

We caught up on each other's doings over the weekend, but soon shifted to Jamie's curiosity about Sassy Solutions and Danny Creedmore's brother-in-law.

"It's not a big deal," I said, and explained how Will had come into possession of Linsey Thomas's files and how some of them were clearly meant to be the basis for future *Ledger* stories. "For some reason he linked Grayson Village to you and Sassy Solutions both."

"So? We both submitted proposals," Jamie said, sipping from the salt-rimmed glass before her. "Wonder why he thought that would make a story?"

"You tell me. There was an arrow from your agency to Grayson Village, but the arrows to Sassy came from Danny and Candace."

"I still don't see why Linsey would care that we were competing for the same client. Happens all the time. They've got some sharp people working for them and we've come up with almost the same identical ideas at times, darn 'em! That's how I missed landing Grayson Village. I thought I had a unique angle on a marketing approach and darned if they didn't have the same angle, but with a slightly different spin."

"Why'd he have a file on you and Mr. Kezzie?" Portland asked.

"Oh, you know how people always think it's funny that a reformed bootlegger has a judge for a daughter. He probably thought it might make an amusing sidebar to another story."

"So who else did he have files on?" asked Jamie as she delicately licked a grain of salt from her fingertip.

I lifted my own margarita for a first taste of its sour sweetness to give myself time to think about the affair Barbara Laughlin was supposedly having with Harvey Underwood, about Greg Turner's flirtation with embezzlement, and a couple of implied acts of malfeasance on the part of the commissioners. Although it's always fun to dish, I could wait until Terry's people decided if there was anything that could be prosecuted. Portland and Jamie would be discreet if I asked them, but if I couldn't hold my own tongue when it was part of Dwight's investigation, how could I expect them to hold theirs?

So I shrugged and said, "I didn't see anything except largely unsubstantiated allegations and Dwight's turned it all over to the SBI."

"Not to Doug Woodall's office?"

"Doug's too busy running for governor," I said and talk turned to county politics until the waitress brought our food. I keep thinking I'm going to order fajitas or the quesadilla of the day because I like them when Dwight lets me put my fork in his, but somehow I always wind up ordering the taco salad. I'm hooked on guacamole and sour cream.

"We got the word that the Republican party's voted to have Barry Dupree replace Candace," Jamie said.

"Who's Barry Dupree?" Portland asked.

"A go-along, get-along farmer from down near Makely, who'll no doubt vote with the majority."

"So now you're our only woman commissioner."

Jamie nodded. "It really bugged Candace when I came on the board. She was a Susie Sharpe clone."

Susie Sharpe was our first female supreme

court judge. She broke many of the gender barriers during her long career, but she was no feminist — in fact, she actively opposed ERA and swayed our then-senators to oppose it, too — and she certainly wasn't interested in welcoming other members of her sex to the state's highest bench. She was one of those pull-the-ladder-up-behind-me types. She liked being unique and thought she did it all on her own merits. Like Candace.

"We also got the word that the question of slowing growth is going to go to the voters this fall," said Jamie. "For all the good that'll do. The other commissioners didn't like the recommendations of the planning board, so they're going to put it to the public as to whether we get a transfer tax or a higher property tax."

"No choice about an impact tax that the developers would have to pay?"

"Bite your tongue," Jamie told Portland. "Not that it matters. Candace was already saying that it didn't matter what the electorate said, they weren't going to implement it."

"Unless the electorate voted against the taxes, right?" I asked.

"You got it, kid. Then and only then will they say they're bowing to the wishes of the people."

Our food arrived and the guacamole came the way I like it with little lumps of avocado. As I began to mix up the salad inside its taco shell, a woman passed our table and Portland nudged us both with a significant cut of her eyes.

"What?" we asked when she joined three women at a far table.

"Don't stare!" Portland said under her breath.

So we glanced aimlessly around the room as if looking for our waitress and let our eyes slide over that table without pausing.

Three of the four women wore print dresses with modestly cut sleeves, high necklines, and hems that stopped at the calf, not the knee. The woman Portland had pointed out wore a loose white tee under a shapeless beige cotton jumper that buttoned down the front. Her brown hair was shoulder-length and held away from her face with a mock tortoiseshell headband. No apparent makeup. No jewelry that we could see from where we sat.

"That's Marian McKinney."

"Who's Marian McKinney?" I asked.

"The wife of the preacher at Christ Eternal. The one who drank her husband's spit water."

I almost gagged on my margarita and Jamie was looking vaguely nauseated, too.

"Did she leave him yet?"

"No, and she doesn't plan to. She told her prayer group that she was proud to serve as an example of selflessness for the other women who might question God's commandments. Even though my cleaning woman quit that church, she still hears what's going on there. Y'all know Nancy Wolfe?"

We both shook our heads.

"She's the office nurse for Dr. Linda Maloof over in Cotton Grove."

I know Dr. Maloof by hearsay. She's Minnie's GP in the medical group that she and Seth go to, but I'd never heard Minnie mention a Nancy Wolfe.

"And her husband works at the farmer's market."

At that far table, the waitress had brought four glasses of iced tea — "Lips that touch wine shall never touch mine"? — and we watched as the women joined hands and bowed their heads.

"Which one is Nancy Wolfe?" asked Jamie.

"She's not there. Besides, Nancy wears slacks," Portland said with a grin. "And makeup."

"I thought that wasn't allowed," I protested.

"It isn't *encouraged*," Portland corrected me. "According to Rena, Nancy wasn't all that thrilled to leave the old church and follow McKinney, but it was what her husband wanted. And their teenage daughter was the only one in the breakaway congregation that could play the piano, so that was another reason to come. But Rena says that Nancy walked out of that church Easter morning before the service ended and she's told her husband he's welcome to stay there if he wants to but she's never going back and neither is their daughter."

"Good for her," said Jamie.

I was in complete agreement. "Why on earth would any woman stay in such a church?" I wondered. But then I thought of Nadine, brought up in a patriarchal family where the husband is God's chosen head of the household. Her father had been a kindly man and my brother Herman is easy enough to manipulate, so any self-imposed gender yoke must rest lightly on her shoulders.

And Daddy certainly considered himself the undisputed head of his household, as do his sons, no matter how much evidence to the contrary their wives give them.

Occasionally, when she thought I was getting too hardheaded and confrontational, Mother would tell me about her grandmother, who did not see the necessity of women's rights. In her world, any woman who was worth her salt could always get her own way by manipulating her man with a combination of sex and sweet talk.

"But I've seen you and Daddy fight," I once protested.

"Only when I intend to let him win," she had said with a knowing grin.

I savored another taste of my lumpy guacamole and said, "I guess there's a comfort in knowing your place in the universe."

" 'He for God only, she for God in him,' " Jamie said, wrapping a warm tortilla around her steak and peppers.

"Shakespeare?" I asked.

"Milton."

I laughed. "No wonder you got on Candace Bradshaw's nerves. I bet she never even heard of Milton."

"A whole bunch of women never heard of Milton, sweetie," she said. "And that didn't drive 'em into Danny Creedmore's bed."

"Anyhow," said Portland, "my cleaning woman says that Marian McKinney's taking piano lessons so her husband will never again have to depend on some uppity woman."

■ ■ ■ ■

Back at the courthouse, I was happy to hear that the civil case over the smashed swimming pool had settled amicably. The insurance company would pay for a new pool and fence and for filling half the pool. The pool owner dropped his claims for punitive damages.

I seemed to have hit the trifecta that day. Two cases asked for continuances with legitimate reasons and two more settled. By two-thirty, I was technically done for the day. I suppose I could have asked some of my colleagues if they wanted help, but before I could get involved in something else, I called Will and asked if he'd spoken to his friend at the consignment shop about that earring I'd seen in Daddy's hand on Friday.

When Will heard I had the afternoon free, he said he'd swing by in his van and pick me up and tell me all about it on the way out to Candace Bradshaw's house.

"What?"

"Yeah. Dwight and his people have finished with it, so Cameron Bradshaw called me and asked if I'd go take a look at the place, see about maybe making him an offer on the contents of the house, which is what Dee wanted me to do. But first he wants me to box up her dollhouse. He's going to donate it to the shelter for battered women so the children can play with it."

Okay, okay. I really shouldn't have agreed to this, but I admit that I was curious about the house Candace had bought herself and if, as Will had assured me, Dwight and his people had finished with it, I wouldn't be compromising anything.

As we drove out to the development, Will told me what he'd learned from his talk with Dave Carter.

"I swear, sometimes I think Daddy's had dealings with everybody in the whole damn county," he said, leaning on his horn for a motorist who seemed to have fallen asleep at the light. "Dave says Daddy floated a loan for his mother to start the business. She was a widow with nothing more than good taste and a network of elderly aunts who had some family jewelry they needed to sell. He wouldn't talk till he made me promise it wouldn't get back to Daddy, so you gotta keep your mouth shut, too, okay?"

"Hey, I'm the one told you and Amy and Dwight not to go blabbing this around the family, okay?"

"Okay. And yeah, they were real diamonds.

He told me that if the matching earring was the same quality, he could offer Daddy twenty thousand for the pair. The stones were absolutely flawless and set in platinum. Circa 1920. That seemed to be important to Daddy, for some reason."

"That the diamonds were flawless or that the earring was old?"

"That it was definitely old and that any competent appraiser would recognize that it was old from the way the diamonds were cut and set."

"Where on earth did he get it, Will?"

"He didn't tell Dave. Or if he did, Dave's not telling me."

"Which?"

My brother shrugged. "Daddy's always played his cards close to his chest, so I'd say Dave's telling the truth."

"Did Daddy want to sell it to him?"

"Nope. Just wanted to know how much it was worth and if it was really old."

We kicked it back and forth until we got to the upscale development where Candace's house was one of those in a far corner of the site, surrounded on the roadside and the back by thick privacy hedges. Candace's lot looked to be no more than a half acre here, so she had practiced what she preached: lots of rooftops on small lots.

Many trees had been carefully spared when the sites were cleared, and banks of azaleas bloomed beneath the dogwoods and pines. Thick rows of yellow and pink pansies edged the circular driveway.

"Nice," I said, when Will stopped his van behind a dark blue Lincoln.

"And you'll note that this is one of the smaller houses," he said.

Cameron Bradshaw must have been watching from inside, because the door opened before Will could ring the bell.

He wore what was probably casual dress for a man of his background — dark slacks, tie and white shirt, and a maroon cardigan. Despite a warm smile, his face was haggard as he welcomed us with old-fashioned courtesy.

Although they had spoken over the phone, he and my brother had never met, nor had I met him, so there were introductions all around and I told him how sorry we were for his double loss. Bradshaw knew who I was and seemed a bit confused as to why I was there.

"She's going to help me pack up the dollhouse," Will said breezily as he pulled flattened cardboard boxes and a roll of strapping tape from the back of the van.

This was news to me, but no surprise.

320

Around the courthouse, I'm treated with a modicum of respect as a district court judge. It's "yes, ma'am" this and "Your Honor" that and "Permission to approach?" But to my brothers, I'm still the kid sister who can be ordered around and told what to do.

Bradshaw walked us through the house to give Will an overall view before getting down to details, pointing out along the way the history of various ornaments and knick-knacks that Candace had valued. Although decorated in an excessively feminine style with lots of floral upholstery, it was a bright and cheerful place. Daylight flooded the rooms through large windows and artfully placed skylights and bounced off the white carpet. The overall impression was of frothy pink and red and white.

Until we got to Candace's bathroom.

"Wow!" I said.

Bradshaw looked a little embarrassed. "This was her favorite place in the house. She used to say that hot water was our country's greatest achievement."

He must have seen my raised eyebrows because he said, "You and I may take hot water for granted, Judge Knott, but we have to remember that Candace grew up without it. That's why she treated herself to this."

"This" was a room where almost every single surface was mirrored. Walls, countertops, cabinet doors, shower stall, even the ceiling. Only the rose-patterned floor tiles and ceramic sink and the rose toilet were exempt.

I'm comfortable with my body and Dwight seems to like it, too, but damn! How could any woman love her body so much that she'd want to see it reflected every hour of the day from groggy early morning to exhausted night? I knew Candace seemed to think she was hot stuff, but looking at this altar to vanity, she must have thought she sizzled. She was what? Early forties? How much would she have liked this room when she hit sixty and everything began to sag?

The other two bedrooms and bath lay at the far end of the house. Dee's bedroom was a shambles — clothes and shoes flung everywhere, the mattress half off its box springs, the coverlet and pillows tossed, the drawers and closet doors ajar.

"She was starting to pack up her things," Cameron Bradshaw said defensively. He touched the lacy white camisole that hung from the doorknob, then his fingers convulsed around it and for a minute, I thought he was going to break down.

Tears moistened my own eyes and I reached out to him impulsively. "We're so sorry, Mr. Bradshaw."

With a visible effort, he reined in his emotions and closed the door on his daughter's room, then showed us into Candace's immaculate and blatantly feminine office — frothy white sheers under rose damask drapes, a floral-patterned area rug atop the white Berber carpet.

Like the rest of the house, there were no books on these shelves either. Instead, they held numerous brightly colored porcelain flowers, the kind of "collectible" sold to people with more money than taste.

"The SBI agents took her computer and most of the file folders from the cabinet there," said Bradshaw. "And that's the dollhouse. She loved it so much that Dee wanted to keep it. I just hope that some scared little girls can lose themselves in it, too."

The dollhouse was at least three feet tall and looked like Tara. It sat on a wooden base that had been painted green and decorated to look like a lawn with flowering shrubs and pots of flowers on the porch. Beneath were casters that let the whole house be easily moved. Some tiny pots and pans lay on the floor next to a shoebox, along with a kitchen butcher's block and some bar stools, all to the same scale. I assumed Dee had begun to take the house apart in preparation for its move.

Will taped together some small cartons and handed me a thick stack of tissue paper and a handful of pint-sized plastic zip bags. I was given instructions to wrap the delicate furniture and carefully place the items in the boxes so they wouldn't smash. I meekly agreed, but as soon as he and Bradshaw left to look at the rest of the house, I was right over to the file cabinet, where I paused to look at the silver-framed photographs on top of it. All of them seemed to feature Candace looking up adoringly to whichever man of power stood next to her — the movers and shakers of the region and, as Jamie Jacobson had pointed out, no women. I was amused to see that she had her hand on G. Hooks Talbert's as they cut the ribbon to open the Grayson Village Inn.

Unfortunately though, the SBI agents had been way too thorough. Anything of interest once held by those four drawers must now be at the SBI headquarters in Garner. Ditto the desk.

There was nothing for it but to dismantle the three-story dollhouse. I knelt down on the rose-patterned rug that overlay the white carpet and began with the nursery on the top floor. A spindly rocking chair, a crib with a tiny baby doll inside, a high chair — each piece was soon nested into its own cocoon of tissue. The child's bedroom followed, then the master bedroom. I was amazed to see that the lamps even had tiny wires and realized that there was a small transformer that stepped down regular house current so that the lamps and chandeliers in the dollhouse could actually light up. I couldn't resist rolling it over to a nearby socket and plugging it in. Some of the furnishings were truly exquisite: there was a mahogany grandfather clock that showed the correct time, ticking away with the help of a watch battery. A gilded birdcage held a pair of lovebirds and a silver tea service sat on the dining room buffet.

Amazing.

A whole lifestyle in miniature.

I never had a dollhouse. Never wanted one. But kneeling there beside that one, for the first time, I could understand the allure, and I couldn't help wondering if this was an appropriate gift for a battered women's shelter. These delicate pieces would be destroyed within weeks by the traumatized toddlers and children who cycle in and out of the place with their mothers. Bradshaw's call, of course, even though it seemed a waste.

By now, I had finished packing up all the rooms except the kitchen, which was the least interesting to me.

While most of the dollhouse was furnished in contemporary modern, the kitchen on the bottom level was almost like a space-age laboratory. Stainless steel refrigerator, range, and dishwasher. Stainless steel cabinets above the range and —

Huh?

I looked closer at the object my groping fingers had found at the rear of the kitchen. What appeared to be a stainless steel cabinet resting atop the side-by-side refrigerator and Sub-Zero freezer was actually an aluminum-clad flash drive.

CHAPTER 21

. . . I cannot account for the purpose
Of the simple life I did not choose.
— *Paul's Hill,* by Shelby Stephenson

I know, I know. I should have left that flash drive exactly where I found it and immediately called Dwight.

I should not have turned it over and over in my hand while I considered all the possibilities.

And for damn sure, I should never have slid it into my purse and then gone back to packing up the dollhouse furniture as if nothing had happened.

On the other hand, if Candace Bradshaw had somehow found out why our Republican governor had appointed me to the bench, I wanted to be the first to know it.

"You're going to tamper with evidence in a double murder?" asked the preacher, drawing himself up in righteous disapproval.

"Not tamper," the pragmatist said nervously. *"Just look."*

"And if you find?"

"We'll cross that bridge when we come to it."

"Yeah, and blow it up if I know you."

When Will and Cameron Bradshaw returned, Will had a signed authorization in his hand to inventory and remove the saleable items in the house.

"Mr. Bradshaw," I said. "It's none of my business, but this is a very valuable dollhouse full of delicate and fragile collectibles. It's really an adult's toy, not a child's, and I'm sure my brother could get top dollar for it, right, Will?"

"At least seven or eight hundred, if not more," he readily agreed.

"Instead of giving it directly to the shelter where everything will probably get broken and scattered, you might want to let him sell it and then donate the money to the shelter in your wife's name. That way they could buy toys and books that are more appropriate for small children."

"You're right," he sighed. "Candace never let any little ones play with it. Not even Dee. She always said it was hers and she was going to be selfish with it."

Most people, my friend Jamie included, seemed to think that Candace had cared more about power than money, but I was sensing a woman who certainly cared about the things money could buy, beginning with this expensive dollhouse. Yes, it had been a present from her husband, but she had bought herself a lot of presents these past two years. A new car, a fancy house, and a hedonistic custom-built bathroom with three shower heads to spray herself with hot water, our country's "greatest achievement."

Hot water? Give me a break.

"I'll help you load the van," I told Will. I figured that if the dollhouse was at his warehouse, I had a better chance of sneaking that flash drive back into the little kitchen than if it stayed here until Will moved everything.

On the drive back through Dobbs, Will was excited about the contents of Candace's house. "The only thing Bradshaw wants to keep is a Thomas Day chest that belonged to a nineteenth-century great-great-grandfather. I think he plans to donate it to the Museum of History. Candace took several other important pieces when they separated, but he doesn't want to keep them even though they've been in the family three

329

or four generations. Says he lived without them these last few years and they might as well go somewhere else now that Dee's gone and his line has come to an end."

"It's so sad," I said, thinking how unlikely this was to happen in our family anytime soon.

"Sad for him, good for me," said Will.

He's really not as heartless as he sounds, but he does tend to view events through the lens of self-interest.

"I'll have inquiries from Philadelphia to Atlanta when I get the word out about what I'm selling. With a little luck, I can finally hire a full-time assistant."

"Mr. Bradshaw have any idea why Dee was killed?"

"No, but one odd thing. Whoever shot her didn't take any of the jewelry — and Candace and Dee both had some nice pieces — but they did take her laptop."

"Oh?"

"Yeah. Bradshaw said that the SBI agents who searched the house specifically asked him if Dee had one and he said she did. When we took a closer look at her room, I saw the cord on her bed. It's still plugged into the wall socket, but the laptop itself is gone."

To me, that could only mean that the killer

knew Dee had Candace's flash drive. I could almost see Dee finding it in the dollhouse, taking a quick look at the contents on her own computer, and realizing that the data was potential dynamite. With all the foolhardiness of youth, had Dee hidden the drive and then gotten in touch with her killer, not realizing the danger? Her computer was gone, so no way to know if the contact was by e-mail or cell phone.

Who did she call that night?

Who had called her?

Will dropped me at the courthouse, saying he'd see me later.

"Later?"

"Dwight said y'all were coming to Jackson's game this evening. You forget?"

"Oh, right."

Will's son is eighteen and plays shortstop on their high school varsity team. Jackson's so good that he's won a baseball scholarship to Florida State next fall, so if we want to see him play without having to travel all around the southeast, these last few months are it.

As I started up the courthouse steps, I met my cousin John Claude Lee, who was on his way back to his office, a much-remodeled 1867 white clapboard a half block away that had served the firm of Lee and Stephenson since the nineteen-twenties.

"Ah, Deborah. Good," he said. "I have the draft of your wills if you want to pick them up."

"That was quick," I said. I'd only called him yesterday morning after talking over the main points with Dwight.

"Everything to each other with Cal the residual beneficiary? Nothing complicated there."

John Claude has had snow-white hair from my earliest memory of him. He's sedate and dignified and one of the most thoroughly ethical attorneys I've ever known, with a dry sense of humor and an old-fashioned set of manners. He offered his arm to me, and as we walked over to his office, he took the outside edge of the sidewalk in case any carriages should try to spatter mud on my long petticoats and high-button shoes. Never mind that there have been no carriages or mud puddles on the streets of Dobbs in fifty years, and that it hadn't rained in over a week.

"Well, hey, stranger," said Sherry Cobb, the firm's office manager, when we entered the reception area. Small and dark-haired, she flashed me a smile that was genuinely welcoming.

For a moment, a wave of regretful nostalgia swept over me, even though Sherry used to drive me up the wall with her bossiness and incessant chatter when I was in practice here. Except for a year in the DA's office, this had been my home from the time I passed the bar till I was appointed to the bench, and a lot of good memories were housed in these rooms.

Now she handed me the draft of the wills and gave John Claude a list of the calls he needed to return.

He kissed my cheek with a cousinly sweetness and said, "Now you let me know if there are any changes you want," then went into his office and closed the door.

I paused to chat with Sherry for a minute and to hear about her newest boyfriend. As she shut down her computer and tidied her desk, I suddenly remembered what had been nagging at the back of my mind since reading Linsey Thomas's files on Sunday.

"Greg Turner," I said.

Sherry stooped to retrieve a paper clip from the floor. "What about him?"

"Wasn't he opposing counsel on one of John Claude's civil cases last year?"

"Hockaday versus the Town of Black Creek," she said promptly with a slightly sour expression on her face. "He was the town's attorney in a zoning change. Mr. Hockaday was fighting the change from residential to industrial, remember? He didn't want his old homeplace to wind up in the middle of a strip mall."

"And he lost, right?"

Sherry gave a small tight nod. "He lost. It was real frustrating to Mr. Lee. He thought he had a good chance of winning, but it was like every single argument he made, Greg Turner was there with a sharp answer. Mr. Lee said it was almost like Turner was standing behind him and reading over his shoulder."

"Yeah, I know the feeling," I said. "He did it to me the last case I argued against him. He's one sharp attorney, all right."

By then it was almost five, so I walked back to the parking lot, got in my car, and switched on my phone to see if I'd missed any calls. Candace's flash drive was burning a hole in my purse and I couldn't wait to plug it into a computer, but I had a feeling that wasn't going to happen any time soon, not if I was committed to a ball game that evening.

Like it or not, I needed to sit on my curiosity until I knew I would have some alone time at home. I've always been open with Dwight about almost everything and it bothers me that I can't tell him about this, but I certainly don't plan to in this lifetime. Confession may be good for the confessor's soul, but it can play havoc with the heart and soul of the person forced to hear that confession. I've seen a lot of good marriages collapse because the husbands or wives were driven by their guilty consciences to confess to a single aberrant fling.

I can rationalize from now till the trumpet blows that I've tried to be worthy of the office and to act ethically; that I haven't taken bribes and that my judgments have all been based on the law and a sense of what is right and fair, not from self-interest or to benefit someone belonging to me. Nevertheless, come Judgment Day, I will have to look my rationalizations in the eye and admit that my first appointment was tainted.

Till then, it's a matter of "Don't do the crime if you can't do the time." I had let Daddy squeeze G. Hooks Talbert with my eyes wide open, so I don't get to unburden my soul on Dwight's.

Whose number popped up on the screen as soon as I switched on my phone.

"Hey," he said. "Did I catch you before you left town?"

"Just got in the car," I told him.

"Good. Cal and I are fixing to ride in with Zach and his kids. Why don't you meet us by the concession stand at the ball field? I'll treat you to a hot dog all the way."

"All the way" means coleslaw, mustard, onions, and Texas Pete chili.

"Make it two and you've got a deal," I said and asked him to bring me a T-shirt and sweater. I keep sneakers in the car, but two hot dogs and an evening of cheering for Jackson would probably wreck the beautiful turquoise silk shirt I was wearing.

Chapter 22

I wish I could have been there when they
    courted.
        — *The Persimmon Tree Carol,*
            by Shelby Stephenson

By the time my guys arrived at the Dobbs
High School ball field, I was hungry enough
to gnaw on the back leg of a rabbit hound.
It didn't help that Will and Amy kept offer-
ing me bites of their chili dogs, although I
did let Will buy me an iced Pepsi. I was early
enough to get a hug from Jackson before
his team took the field to warm up. He's
tall and rangy like all the Stephenson males
from Mother's side of the family and he
loped across the field like a young pony feeling his oats.

We staked claim to some lower rows of
seats between third and home where we
could cheer for his every play.

My niece Annie Sue arrived a few minutes

later, pushing her daddy's wheelchair. Herman is Haywood's twin, one of the "big twins," as opposed to Zach and Adam, the "little twins," so called because they're several years younger even though they're actually taller. But Herman and Haywood are a lot broader, although Herman is a little thinner now that he's confined to a wheelchair.

Like his twin, Herman has no inhibitions and as soon as he spotted us, a big grin broke across his broad face. "Guess what, y'all?" he hollered.

"Oh, Dad!" Annie Sue protested.

"What?" Amy called back.

"She's got her 'lectrician's license!"

We erupted from our seats in hugs and laughter and congratulations. There had been a time when Herman was less than thrilled at the idea of his baby daughter following in his footsteps, but it finally penetrated his thick skull that she was the only one of his four children with a natural talent for electricity and a real love for the work. Immediately after high school, she had enrolled at the community college and taken all the necessary courses to become a licensed electrician herself, acing the tests and graduating at the head of the department.

"So are you changing the name of your business to Knott and Daughter?" Amy asked with a mischievous grin.

"Naw, she won't let me," said Herman.

Annie Sue shrugged her sturdy shoulders. "No point rubbing Reese's nose in it."

"Hell, girl," said Will. "He's gonna be working for you someday, idn't he?"

"I hope it'll be a partnership, Uncle Will. We sure don't want him to quit. He's a good electrician and he's pulling his share of the load. This way, he can work off my license, too, now."

Herman's oldest child, Edward, is a white-collar office worker out in Charlotte. Ditto Denise in Greensboro. Reese and Denise are twins and Annie Sue was an "oops" baby. Reese is still single, but he's never been one to crack the books. As long as he can earn enough to pay for his truck, his trailer, and his tall ones, it doesn't seem to much matter to him who's higher in the pecking order. All the same, it was so like Annie Sue to consider his male pride. If and when Herman turns the business over to them, I'm sure it'll be on equal terms.

Dwight and Zach arrived in the middle of our spontaneous celebration and offered to treat her to the supper of her choice — hot dogs, popcorn, ice cream, or tacos. I took the T-shirt Dwight had brought me and headed to the restroom to change.

When I got back to the hot dog stand, I saw Dwight in conversation with his deputy, Mayleen Richards. Standing beside her was a good-looking Latino in jeans, hand-tooled boots, a large silver belt buckle, and a black Stetson. Without the boots and hat, he was probably only about a half-inch taller than she, but he had an easy air of confidence that was at odds with her self-conscious awkwardness.

And at the moment, she looked more self-conscious than usual and had flushed until her fair skin was the same shade as her freckles. As I joined them, she took a deep breath, lifted her chin, and said, "Good to see you, ma'am. I'd like you to meet my friend Mike Diaz. Mike, this is Judge Knott, Major Bryant's wife."

"We've met before, I believe," I said, shaking the hand he held out to me. He had once come to court to speak for one of his compatriots.

"*Si,*" said Diaz, "but this time is better. Mayleen says I must learn baseball if I want to be a true American."

"But surely you've seen baseball in Mexico," I said.

"Oh yes. Half the major league teams here

have Mexican players, but she says I have to see it like a native." He lifted his hot dog and made a wry face. "Tacos are better, but when in Rome . . ."

We all laughed and Mayleen's face was almost its natural shade by the time we parted for separate sections of the field.

"I like him," I told Dwight when we returned to the family with drinks and dogs for everyone. "Does this mean Mayleen's going to go against her family for him?"

He had told me about how conflicted she was over this relationship and how her family had threatened to disown her if she did not break it off.

"Don't know, honey," Dwight said. "But if she's coming out in public with him around town here and introducing him to folks, it must mean something."

We distributed the food and drinks. Cal took his and immediately joined some younger kids standing down by the fence behind home plate.

At the end of the first inning, the score was one–zip in favor of the visitors and that's the way it stayed till the bottom of the ninth when Jackson reached first for the third time in the game and a teammate smashed one over the fence.

2–1 Dobbs!

■ ■ ■ ■

On the drive home, Dwight said that they had come up with a name for Candace's cousin and that someone would probably be eyeballing her old car tomorrow if the cousin still owned it.

I told him about going to her house with Will. "Did you see that bathroom?"

"Pretty fancy, huh? Mirrors on a bedroom ceiling's one thing. I'm not real sure I'd want that many in the bathroom."

"Bradshaw told Will that Dee's laptop was stolen?"

"Yeah. Sort of confirms that the two deaths are linked. The Ginsburg twins think that Dee might have found the flash drive that Candace used and that's why she was killed."

"Really?" I was suddenly and uncomfortably reminded that the flash drive everyone was so anxious to find was probably the one in my purse.

Cal had fallen asleep in the backseat. Overhead, the stars blazed down from a cloudless sky. Very romantic. Dwight smiled over at me. "Remember when all cars had bench seats instead of buckets?"

I smiled back. Unfortunately, there was a

console and a gearshift between us.

But he was in a talkative mood and told me about the phone calls Dee Bradshaw had made the evening she was killed: two to Gracie Farmer about the dollhouse and Farmer's umbrella, one to her boyfriend, who was too drunk to talk, one to Will to ask him to come out and make her an offer, one to Roger Flackman about the possibility that her mother had been skimming the company's take, and one to Danny Creedmore, who claimed that she had ended the conversation shortly after eight because someone was at the door.

"And Greg Turner says she left a three-minute message on his answering machine, but he swears she said nothing important and he immediately erased it."

"You think one of them killed her?" I asked.

"Still up in the air," he said. "I don't know how the office manager would benefit unless she was in on some skimming, but Flackman says the books are in perfect order and we're welcome to audit them."

"Are you?"

"Hell, yes."

"What about the others?"

"Well, we don't think Will had a reason to do it," he teased. "And Danny Creedmore's been pretty open about the relationship. Oh, he doesn't admit in so many words that he put her in place and has told her what to do from the beginning, but we've never heard a word of disagreement between them and he seems to have eased her over to Woody Galloway."

"To take his body or take his seat?"

He laughed. "I don't think he cared which. Woody's a pretty empty suit as far as the county's benefited, but he doesn't take orders from Danny, so maybe backing her for the state senate wasn't just going to be a holding action."

"If Woody gets knocked out of the governor's race, will he still keep his seat now?"

"I expect so, don't you?"

"Yeah. He's not totally dumb. If we've heard rumors that Candace wanted to run for real, he must have, too. Sounds like a decent enough reason for murder."

"Except that he was in conference in Raleigh with a half-dozen senators when Candace was killed."

"Greg Turner wasn't in their pocket," I said. "He's a Democrat and often voted against the others. He and Jamie Jacobson both."

"Yeah, but you read what Linsey Thomas wrote about him. Maybe Candace and

Danny helped keep it quiet about him dipping into a client's funds." He hit the steering wheel in frustration. "I just wish to hell we could find her flash drive."

"It's bound to turn up sooner or later," I said soothingly.

"You think?" He slowed to turn in to our drive. "If the killer took it, it's probably been smashed with a hammer and thrown in Possum Creek."

Now there was a thought.

CHAPTER 23

I don't know what's happening,
and I don't know how to say it.
— *Paul's Hill,* by Shelby Stephenson

Weekday mornings are normally harried and a rush to get Dwight off to work and Cal off to school, but Wednesday morning seemed to move on snail legs. Cal's backpack was sitting by the kitchen door at least twenty minutes before he needed to leave with Dwight to catch the bus at the end of our long drive and he had already bicycled down and back with the morning paper.

There was plenty of time for him to show us the new trick he had taught Bandit. I've always liked dogs, but I became particularly fond of this one after he helped get me out of a very tight spot last winter.

"Watch, y'all!" said Cal.

He told the little dog to sit, then gave an upward swoop of his hand.

346

Immediately, Bandit rose on his hind feet and bobbled across the kitchen floor.

Dwight laughed and I shook my head. "All that dog needs is an opposable thumb and he could be people."

Cal beamed and gave Bandit a small morsel of food as a reward.

He performed twice more, then it was finally time for them to go meet the bus.

"Lunch?" I asked Dwight as they headed out to the truck.

"Buzz me," he said. "I don't know what the day's going to be like."

Once I was sure they were really gone, I rushed to my computer and popped the flash drive into one of the side ports.

To my total chagrin, the thing was password-protected. Who the hell protects a flash drive?

"Someone with something juicy to hide," said the pragmatist, looking up from the morning paper.

"So give it to Dwight and take your punish-ment," said the preacher. *"You're never going to get into it."*

"Oh, don't be such a pessimist," said the pragmatist, laying aside the paper. *"You like puzzles. Maybe you can solve this one your-self. It's worth a try."*

I started with the obvious things — variations of her name and the company's name, her daughter's name, Danny Creedmore's, Woody Galloway's, the Colleton Board of Commissioners, with A-B-C or 1-2-3 before and after each one. Nothing.

By the time I was ready to bang my head against the screen, I had to quit to get dressed and go to work, but I put the flash drive in my purse and a notebook and pen on the passenger seat beside me. On the drive to the courthouse, I jotted down everything I could think of that Candace might have used as her password.

At the break, I found a computer down in the clerk of court's office that wasn't being used and ran through my list in about four minutes flat.

No luck.

As I slowly returned to my courtroom, I had to admit to myself that I had only three choices at this point: smash this stubborn piece of aluminum, plastic, and memory circuits to bits, give it to Dwight, or slip it back in the dollhouse. I was pretty sure it would fit inside the miniature freezer and I could suddenly "remember" that I had heard the freezer clunk after I'd wrapped it and then got so distracted when Will and Mr. Bradshaw came back, that I hadn't unwrapped it to see what caused the clunk.

Okay, that was weak. Dwight knows how seldom I let my curiosity go unsatisfied, but maybe he'd be so glad to get the damn thing that he'd overlook how it actually turned up.

Besides, if Candace had recorded anything about Daddy, Talbert, and me, his knowing I'd palmed it would be the least of my concerns.

When I buzzed Dwight at noon, he was too tied up to meet me. I took that as an omen that it was okay to implement my third option and to drive over to Will's warehouse.

On my way out of the courthouse, I was surprised to see Daddy coming up the steps with a man I didn't recognize.

"Daddy! Hey. Were you coming to look for me?" I asked.

"Naw," he said. "I just got a little business needs tending to."

I looked at the other man inquiringly and Daddy reluctantly introduced us. "This is my daughter Deb'rah, Mr. McKinney. Deb'rah, Mr. McKinney's the preacher at that new church over near us."

"The Church of Jesus Christ Eternal?" A sour taste rose in my throat. This was the pompous bastard who used scripture to humiliate his wife and keep the women of his church in check?

"Brother Kezzie's told me a lot about you, Judge Knott," he said, taking my hand in a two-handed clasp that was no doubt meant to convey warmth and pleasure in the meeting.

Brother Kezzie? All of Maidie's forebodings rushed back to me. Was Daddy trusting this control freak to get himself straight with the Lord?

I was speechless, and when I looked at Daddy there was an odd expression on his face that I couldn't quite interpret.

"Sorry, Deb'rah, but we ain't got time to stand here a-chitter-chattering," he said briskly.

McKinney told me again how really nice it was to meet me, then they were gone, striding across the lobby to a hallway that led to the tax offices and to our register of deeds.

Register of deeds?

For a moment I was tempted to dash after them and demand to know what was going on. I've heard that McKinney has a silver tongue when it comes to talking the elderly into giving parcels of their land to the church so that he could do the Lord's work. The catch to that is that the church is his personal property, which means that all the deeds are registered in his name. It's said he sold some of the donated land to finance a used-car dealership that was supposed to turn a profit for the church, but so far there's been nothing to show for the prosperity except a nicer-than-usual parsonage and the well-cut suits that McKinney wore.

Surely Daddy wasn't about to turn over some of his land to McKinney?

"And what if he is?" said the pragmatist in my head. *"It's his, isn't it?"*

The preacher was silent.

As Judith Viorst once put it, this was turning into a terrible, horrible, no good, very bad day.

When I pulled up at the side door of Will's warehouse, I did get a small break. There was no sign of his van and a small, hand-lettered card in the door window informed the world that he expected to be back by one-thirty. I tried the door. Locked, of course, but with a little more luck, he had only pulled the door to without bothering to throw the dead bolt on the upper lock. One of my nephews had showed me the credit card trick and the simple lock opened on my first try.

Just to be safe, though, I called out as soon

as I was inside. "Will? Anyone here?"

The office was empty, so I passed on into the warehouse proper and called again.

My luck was still holding. There was no response.

Will had left a few lights on, but they did little to cut the gloom and the floor space was so jammed with boxes, furniture, and bric-a-brac that it took me a few minutes to locate the dollhouse. When I did, I was surprised to see that half the furnishings had been unwrapped and lay strewn across the tabletop where the dollhouse sat. Happily, Will hadn't gotten to the kitchen things yet. I'd wrapped them last and put them near the top of the second, smaller, cardboard box. I soon found the little freezer and, as I'd hoped, once the shelves were removed, the flash drive ought to fit perfectly. I took it out of my pocket, but before I could slide it inside, I thought I heard something rustle behind me.

Trying to look innocent, I turned with the drive and freezer in my hands and said, "Will? Guess what I've found?"

But I saw no one and realized that I was letting my guilty conscience spook me.

I turned back, intending to wrap up the freezer and put it back in the box because I wanted Will here when I made my great discovery. But as I reached for the paper, two things happened. I heard a shot and my left arm immediately felt as if it'd been stung by a very angry hornet. What the hell?

A second shot zinged past my head so close it almost singed my hair.

I dropped everything and dived for cover behind a chest of drawers just as another shot buried itself in the wood.

I eeled along the floor till I was behind a tall wardrobe. My arm was on fire and when I looked down, I saw that the sleeve of my white linen jacket was red with blood and I had left a trail of bright drops on the floor. Bleeding like a stuck pig, where could I hide? The shooter was between me and the only way out. Beyond the office were roll-up garage-type doors, but even if I could get there without being seen, they would be locked and I wouldn't have time to figure out how to unlock them before the shooter heard me.

Frantically, I looked around for a safe haven and saw a heavy metal door standing ajar nearby. Of course! The warehouse toilet!

Clutching my burning arm, I made a desperate sprint for it. Another shot rang out and ricocheted off the metal door. As I slipped inside, I glanced back.

Halfway down the cluttered aisle, a shadowy figure held the little gun with two hands braced on a wingback chair.

Terrified, I slammed the door shut and rammed the sturdy lockbolt in place.

An instant later, the door rattled and banged in manic frustration.

"Go away!" I screamed inanely.

Something heavy crashed against the door but the metal held firm.

With my ear against the door, I thought I heard footsteps click away, but it could have been a trick. Didn't matter to me at that point because no way was I coming out before Will got back.

If the warehouse was poorly lit, this place was even darker, and the smell of urine and cheap pine cleansers almost gagged me. The single window was small and dirty and no bigger than a legal pad. Hinged at the bottom, it was probably meant for ventilation before air-conditioning. For the moment, I was glad it was at least twelve feet above my head so that I didn't have to worry about being attacked from the outside. Too, it let me see a light switch by the door.

The bulb hanging down from the ceiling must have been a forty-watter, but I didn't care. It was enough to show me the sink. Also filthy. I tried to wipe it out with liquid soap on a paper towel, but by now the pain was so intense that I quit dithering about germs. Easing off my jacket, I soaked it in cold water and held it to the oozing gash the bullet had made in my arm. Ah! Better. Much better. The wound still hurt like hell, but it didn't seem to be spurting. Not spurting was good, wasn't it? Meant no major vessel had been hit? I tried to remember the first-aid instruction Portland and I got when we gave Girl Scouts a brief try a million years ago.

Irrelevant thoughts and disconnected images tumbled through my head in kaleidoscopic turmoil as the adrenaline that had been pumping through my veins slowed down and leveled off. Throughout it all, I worried with the identity of who had shot me. In the dim light, that face had looked vaguely familiar, like a face I might have seen around town without ever putting a name to it.

Whether it was the adrenaline rush or the loss of blood, I felt myself getting light-headed and sank down on the floor. Random and almost incoherent thoughts flicked in and out of my mind — the dollhouse . . . the flash drive . . . Dwight . . . Candace Bradshaw's irritating giggles . . . insider information . . . power plays . . . playing loose and dirty . . . this dirty floor . . .

Candace's shining clean bathroom and this filthy, stinking hole . . .

I don't know if I actually passed out, but when my head cleared again, I thought I knew who that face was and why Candace and Dee had been killed. If I was right, it explained how John Claude had lost that big case to Greg Turner and why Jamie's presentation didn't win her the contract for Grayson Village.

I looked at my watch. Ten till one and I was due back at the courthouse at one. Forget that. Call Dwight. Tell him —

Oh. Right. Phone's in my purse and it must have slipped from my shoulder when that first shot hit me.

Well, it would have to stay out there. Sooner or later someone would come and then —

Abruptly, I realized it wasn't just the odor of pine cleanser and urine that was making me cough. Smoke seemed to be seeping in around the edges of the door.

I managed to stand and quietly slide back the bolt, then eased the door open slowly, half expecting gunfire. Instead, I heard the crackle of flames. Horrified, I saw a wall of fire blocking my way to the doors, and clouds of smoke billowed toward me.

CHAPTER 24

The preacher rushes
into his sermon, suffering
happiness in the tears
that drop
in his understanding
of our miserable lot.
— *Middle Creek Poems,*
by Shelby Stephenson

In the register of deeds office, the clerk smiled and handed over the receipt for the fees the office charged to register new deeds. "Good thing for y'all that there's no transfer tax in Colleton County yet."

The two men smiled and thanked her for her help.

Outside they shook hands.

"I can rest easy now," Kezzie Knott said, hefting the small carrying case in his hands. "Can't nobody ever dig up that man's body now and I know you'll use this for the good of the Lord."

To Faison McKinney's dismay, the old man opened the case right there on the sidewalk for all the curious world to see had the world been looking. April sunlight gleamed and flashed on the tangle of bright metal and faceted gemstones within.

"Since these here earrings ain't worth all that much, I reckon you won't mind if I keep 'em for a souvenir," he said and drew out the glittering pair that he had given McKinney to prove that his story was as genuine as those diamonds.

McKinney bit back his protest. No point being greedy. Not when he was getting a pile of gems worth five or six million in exchange for land and goods worth half that. "Not a bit, Brother Kezzie."

"I surely do thank you for all your help, Preacher. And you don't have to worry 'bout me ever saying a word of this to anybody."

"Same here, Brother Kezzie. When we do the Lord's work, we don't need to tell the devil."

As they parted, each man to his own vehicle, Kezzie wondered what he was going to do with that failing used-car dealership.

He wished there were a way to see McKinney's face when his jeweler friend told him that the bag contained only costume jewelry. Good-quality costume jewelry, but worth no more than five or six hundred dollars for the whole bag.

Well, a man can't have everything, he told himself philosophically, and drove to the outlet mall, where a black Lincoln with tinted windows sat all alone at the far end of the parking lot. He stopped beside the car and waited till the man in the backseat joined him in the truck's cab.

"Everything go okay?"

"Hook, line, and sinker," he said. "Just got to know what bait to use." He dug in his pocket and pulled out the diamond earrings. "And them here was better'n red wigglers or crickets. You want that used-car place? It ain't worth much and I got no use for it."

G. Hooks Talbert gave a sour laugh of grudging admiration. "Damn! You got that, too?"

"Yeah. I figured as long as we was scraping him clean, might as well."

"Do what you like with it. I don't want my name on anything connected to this."

As Kezzie drove back through town, sirens seemed to be coming from every direction.

The cars ahead were pulling over to the curb and he did the same. Two fire trucks and an ambulance went flying past and in his rearview mirror he saw several police cars weave in and out around them, all headed in the same direction.

CHAPTER 25

Clutching dear life so thin
The stubborn holding on . . .
  — *Paul's Hill,* by Shelby Stephenson

Choking and coughing as smoke swirled around me, my first impulse was to retreat to the bathroom again, to slam the door shut and cram the cracks around it with wet paper towels. Instead, I got as close to the floor as I could, where the smoke was slightly thinner, pulled my wet jacket away from my arm, and tied the sleeves behind my head so that my mouth and nose were covered.

The wound began to ooze blood again and smoke burned my eyes, but somehow I forced myself to crawl toward the fire, which must have begun up closer to the front. I was disoriented and couldn't remember exactly which way I had come until I saw the trail of my blood on the concrete floor.

I followed it on hands and knees. The crawl seemed to take forever, and I could feel the heat building toward me as I finally rounded the wardrobe I had cowered behind only a short time ago. Another few feet and I reached the dollhouse.

The flash drive was gone, of course, and so was my purse. I almost whimpered in fear and desperation, but as I turned to crawl back to the toilet, I caught a glimpse of the leather strap under the edge of a chest where I must have kicked it in my haste to get away from the bullets. I yanked at it and it caught on the foot.

The fire was getting ever nearer. I felt my skin drying and somewhere close by something exploded with a shower of glass that sprinkled down on me, shards catching in my hair. Every instinct screamed at me to leave it and go, but I couldn't give up.

A lateral tug and the purse popped out. I slung the strap over my head and made like an inchworm trying to break the world speed record.

Once I was back inside the toilet with the steel door closed and my wet jacket plugging the crack at the floor, I heard sirens from outside. Someone must finally have given the alarm.

I almost dropped my phone in my haste

to turn it on and push the speed dial for Dwight's number.

He answered on the first ring and before I could speak, he yelled, "Deb'rah? Where the hell are you? Will's warehouse is on fire and he says your car's there."

I told him as concisely as I could, trying not to babble hysterically, "Look for a small high window and oh, Dwight, please hurry!"

"Stay on the phone," he said. "Don't hang up. We'll get you out."

More sirens outside, and now I heard them through the phone wherever Dwight was. I could also hear him barking orders and then he was back on the line.

"We're almost there now. I can see the warehouse."

The front part must have been engulfed with flames by then, for I heard him groan. "Oh, my God! *Deb'rah!* You still all right?"

I was trying not to panic but now that help was so close I was terrified that they would not get to me in time. The walls were built of concrete blocks. Built to last. Like a brick oven. And me the loaf of bread dough.

"Talk to me, Deb'rah," he said and his voice was suddenly calm and reassuring.

"I'm scared, darling. Really scared."

"It's gonna be okay. I promise. We're here. Get as far from that window as you can and turn your back. They're gonna smash it open."

No sooner had he said that than bits of glass showered down. I looked up and there was the face of a fireman who called to me and said, "What we're gonna do, ma'am, is pull this wall down, so you stay back as far as you can and put this over you."

"This" was a bulky insulated fireman's coat that he pushed through the broken window. I grabbed it and cowered beneath its comforting weight, my arm throbbing with pain.

A grappling hook on a cable caught the bottom edge of the opening and soon a chunk of concrete blocks broke away. Pieces of mortar fell and bounced off the sink, but the heavy coat protected me from the few chips that reached me.

As fresh air poured in, smoke rushed in from cracks at the top of the door. Then the hook was back and another small section of blocks tumbled away.

"One more ought to do it," said Dwight's voice in my ear. "How you doing, shug?"

"Hanging in," I managed to say before another fit of coughing took my voice.

Seconds later, a fireman appeared in the now-sizeable opening. This one wore a face mask against all the swirling smoke. He slid a ladder over the wall and lowered it to the floor on my side. "Can you make it yourself, ma'am, or — ?"

Before he could finish his sentence, I had shucked off that coat and was halfway up the ladder, choking and gasping till I reached the top. He grabbed me and guided me over the broken wall to his own ladder and down into blessed fresh air. My purse was still around my neck and one grimy hand still clutched the phone to my ear until Dwight took me from the fireman and gently loosened my fingers.

"It's okay, now," he said, as I hugged him wordlessly. "It's okay."

CHAPTER 26

You knew loss and ambiguity.
Divorce, wars, and the untouched area
   memory
Fails to get ready for the direct answer.
   — *Paul's Hill,* by Shelby Stephenson

Three hours later, my arm had been stitched and bandaged. I had brushed the glass from my hair and Nadine and Herman let me use their bathroom there in Dobbs to scrub away all the dirt and filth and smoke odor. When I was squeaky clean once more, I put on the fresh underwear, jeans, and T-shirt that Annie Sue had laid out for me. Except for the bra, which Dwight had to hook for me because of my arm, she and I were almost the same size.

Will's warehouse was a total loss, a sodden shell of charred rubble. The fire was out, but everything of value was destroyed, including that exquisite dollhouse that Candace had loved, a dollhouse where she had hidden her flash drive within easy access of her laptop. She had never let her daughter play with it and in the end, it had led to Dee's death.

From the moment he saw all the blood, Dwight had barely let me out of his sight and now I sat in Bo's crowded office to give an official statement.

The order for Gracie Farmer's arrest went out within five minutes after I was rescued.

"No cushy retirement in Costa Rica for her," Dwight growled.

So far, the charges included first-degree murder in the death of Candace Bradshaw, second-degree murder in the death of Dee Bradshaw, attempted murder (me), and arson.

"And if she didn't smash that flash drive as soon as she got her hands on it —"

"The Ginsburg twins have it now," Terry assured me.

"— then there's probably evidence that she and Candace ransacked the files of the offices where they have the cleaning contract. Candace wasn't just checking up on her cleaning crews, she was using that flash drive to copy any unprotected computer files that looked interesting or could help her cronies.

"Bradshaw did say she was always asking him about hypothetical scenarios," said Dwight. "If we pin him down, we may learn that some of those scenarios had nothing to do with her commissioner's agenda."

I nodded. "Every office has a copier of some sort these days and I'm willing to bet good money that she or Farmer printed out John Claude's memos and trial preparation notes and sold them to Greg Turner. Probably one of my old cases, too. Jamie Jacobson said another advertising firm came up with an almost identical presentation for the Grayson Village project, so I'm guessing there'll be other instances of selling a firm's work product to interested parties."

"Including Danny Creedmore?" asked Bo Poole with a sardonic glance at Doug Woodall.

Our DA was sitting there with a stunned expression on his face. I could almost see the wheels turning as he tried to figure out how this was going to affect his race for the governor's mansion.

Mayleen Richards was there at Bradshaw Management when Gracie Farmer was arrested. "Her assistant told me that a week or so ago, one of their clients — a caterer — accused them of selling his customer list to his main competitor so that the competition could undercut them. She said Mrs. Farmer managed to convince him that it was a coincidence, but that was the second time this month a client had complained. Candace Bradshaw must have gotten a little careless."

"Or greedy," said Bo. "We thought her letter was an apology for misusing her public office. Instead it was Gracie's attempt to throw all the blame on Candace for misusing her business office. Even if it did almost get you killed, Deb'rah, it's a good thing you remembered hearing that — what was it? A toy freezer? — rattle."

"Yeah, wasn't it?" Dwight said, his voice carefully neutral.

I knew he didn't totally buy my story, but he wasn't ready to cross-examine me in front of his colleagues.

Sensing that my throat was still raw and parched, Mayleen Richards handed me a bottle of orange juice from the vending machine down the hall. For the first time, my presence didn't seem to make her self-conscious and she was finally treating me normally. "Mr. Bradshaw said that when he mentioned to Farmer that your brother had taken the dollhouse back to his warehouse yesterday, she suddenly remembered a lunch appointment. What she really remembered was that Dee Bradshaw was probably packing it up right before she called to ask about some of the stuff she'd read on the flash drive. Farmer's not talking yet, but I seriously doubt if her phone conversation with Dee was about umbrellas. Besides, Dee knew the password and her computer's still missing."

"She knew her mother's password?" I asked as innocently as I could.

"Yeah. She told us last week that she was the one that showed her mom how to use a flash drive and also how to use a digital shredder to delete the cache files from her hard drive. She even set up the password for her — hot water. Run together as one word."

Hotwater? Of course! "Our country's greatest achievement." And I'd even seen that bathroom.

"Hot water?" Terry grinned. "That's where a lot of people in this county are gonna be finding themselves, don't you reckon?"

CHAPTER 27

. . . the world's so finely
balanced a beetle could push it along.
— Fiddledeedee, by Shelby Stephenson

Thursday morning (eight days later)
With heads rolling all around the county
and rumors and promises of indictments to
come in the wake of the Bradshaw murders,
the burning of a warehouse and the near-
murder of his very own daughter, Kezzie
Knott was not surprised to see that the story
of an embezzling preacher received only
three or four inches of print in *The News &
Observer,* but he did think that the *Ledger*
would have had more to say about it.

One disillusioned member of the Church
of Jesus Christ Eternal was quoted as saying, "Guess you can't really call it embezzling if it's all in his own name, but I sure
did think we were giving our dollars to the
Lord, not to Faison McKinney."

"Looks like the bank's gonna take the church house," said another fallen-away member. "They say there's not enough in the treasury to pay the light bill."

"What you reckon happened to the money?"

"I heard it all went up his nose."

"You know not!"

"Well you've seen him preach. We thought he was hopped up on the Holy Spirit, but what if it was drugs?"

"Not drugs," someone said firmly. "My wife said she heard Marian McKinney all but say he's got a gambling problem."

The biggest media stories centered around the murders and the alleged malfeasance of the Colleton County Board of Commissioners, now being investigated by the SBI and the district attorney's office. Two commissioners had already resigned and there was talk that Danny Creedmore had hired himself one of the best lawyers in Raleigh.

John Claude Lee and two other attorneys were suing that brilliant young legal star Greg Turner, and the bar association had begun its own investigation. Some of the cases Turner had won were in danger of having the judgments reversed and he faced the distinct possibility of disbarment.

Despite a cornucopia of Pulitzer-worthy

material right there in its own backyard, *The Dobbs Ledger* managed to resist any in-depth coverage of those juicy tidbits. Instead, the paper, which came out three times a week, had devoted most of its news pages to the significance of Candace Bradshaw's Toyota being found down in Augusta, Georgia. It ran a long interview with Sheriff Bowman Poole, who stopped just short of drawing a straight line from the dead commissioner's car to the hit-and-run death of Linsey Thomas, the *Ledger*'s late and much-beloved editor.

"The crime lab hasn't finished comparing her car with the evidence found at the crime scene," said Poole, "but the rough findings are quite significant."

"Yes," said Ruby Dixon, the current editor, when asked to confirm a probable motive for her former boss's death. "Linsey Thomas believed in sunshine and paper trails and he planned to roll up the window shades on Mrs. Bradshaw and her tenure as chair of the board. She knew it, too, because he tried to interview her a few days before he died and she blew him off."

When asked if she would put more reporters on the board stories now, Dixon took a swallow of the orange juice that was ever-present on her desk and allowed as how maybe she would wait to see what Sheriff Poole came up with.

All in all though, thought Kezzie Knott, maybe it was just as well people weren't paying too much attention to the Church of Jesus Christ Eternal. He had sworn the six people involved to secrecy before handing them back the title to their lands, but even though the registrar of deeds was a good ol' fishing buddy, transferring property was a matter of public record.

"We don't necessarily have to open the page in the right deed books where something's recorded," he told Kezzie, "but I can't sequester the books either."

"Ain't asking you to," Kezzie told him. "I don't reckon they's all that many people interested anyhow."

"It really was all legal, wadn' it, Kezzie?"

"He look to you like a man with a knife to his throat?"

"Naw, can't say he did. In fact, best I remember, he was real cheerful."

"Well, there you go, then. A willing seller taking what a buyer was willing to pay."

"So, which one were you, Kezzie?"

The old man smiled and shook his head. "Hard to say, ain't it?"

James Ennis pulled his small black truck in

behind a late-model SUV that was parked on the shoulder of woodlands that were back in his family again, only this time it was his mother's name on the deed and not his grandmother's, despite the older woman's self-pitying indignation that she no longer had a say in how the land was to be used or dispersed. She trotted out the Biblical commandment to honor thy father *and* thy mother, "and this does me dishonor," she told her daughter.

"Sorry, Mama," Mary Pritchard Ennis had said. "You gave our land away once. You don't get a chance to do it twice. After I'm gone, it's going to my boys."

Before he got out of the truck, Ennis made a note of the SUV's license plate. One bumper sticker read JESUS LOVES YOU; the other THIS CAR HAS GPS — GOD'S PROTECTIVE SALVATION.

He lifted his .22 rifle from the gun rack across the rear window, stepped onto the pavement, and studied the ditch bank until he saw where someone had gone into the woods. The trail was easy to follow. A hippopotamus could not have trampled down a wider swath of weeds and briars, and dead limbs had been knocked off some of the pines to make for easier passage.

A wren scolded from its perch on a wild

cherry branch in lacy white bloom and a brown thrasher flew up from a clump of dried broom sedge still standing from last fall.

About fifty feet into the woods, where the land began to slope down to a stream, he saw an oak that had come down in one of the hurricanes to create a rough clearing beyond the pines. A chunky-looking white man labored there with a shovel. He wore dark blue slacks, a blue-and-white striped open-necked polo shirt, and shiny polished town shoes that had probably started off a lot shinier than they were right now. As Ennis watched, he saw the man wipe his face with a large white handkerchief that he stuffed back into his pocket before climbing down into the hole he had dug. It was waist-deep on the man and as damp dirt flew up from the hole, Ennis could hear him puffing with the unaccustomed effort of digging through rocks and roots.

He moved out of shadows into the sunlight, the rifle held loosely in the crook of his arm, and looked down on the man. "Mind telling me what you're doing, mister?"

Startled, the man stepped back with the shovel across his chest as if for protection, slipped, and went down heavily on his rump. Sweat poured from his soft face and his eyes widened as he looked up and saw the rifle.

"This is private property, mister, and you're trespassing," James Ennis said, standing over the trench the man had dug. "How come you're out here digging?"

"This your land?" The voice changed to warm molasses. "Then you must be one of Sister Frances's grandsons, right?"

Ennis gave a tight nod.

"I'm —"

"I know who you are, Preacher, and you don't own one square inch out here any more, so I ask you for the last time" — he shifted the rifle significantly in his hands — "what are you digging for?"

Faison McKinney pulled out his handkerchief again and looked at it distastefully. It had begun the day ironed and neatly folded just as he liked his handkerchiefs, but now it was so streaked with dirt and sweat stains Marian might never get it clean. Nevertheless he wiped his face, then used the shovel to hoist himself to his feet. There was only wet sandy clay beneath his shoes. No parachute, no bones, no sign that this soil had ever been disturbed.

"You ever get left all night at the end of a long dirty ditch holding a bag?"

"No, sir, can't say as I have."

"Well, this here's the ditch and I'm the fool that thought it was full of snipe."

G. Hooks Talbert finished ordering and handed the elaborate menu back to the waiter. Located off Glenwood Avenue, this was one of Raleigh's best restaurants, the food adventurous, the service impeccable. Tonight, the tables would be filled. Here at lunchtime, however, he and the plainly dressed woman seated across the table from him had a corner of the room to themselves, which was precisely why he had chosen it.

Talbert considered himself a connoisseur of beautiful women and this woman would never be beautiful, but with better clothes, an expert hairstylist, and proper makeup, she could be striking.

She looked like hell, he thought, but his words were kindly when he said, "I wish you didn't have to dress like one of those born-again cult women."

"I am born again, but our church is no cult."

"Then why dress like it? There are lots of good religious women who don't consider it a sin to wear nice things. You don't have to look like all your clothes came from a Goodwill store."

"If you'll recall, Hooks, I didn't grow up with silks and satins. After the divorce, Mother was lucky if she could keep me in denim and cotton." She was not complaining, merely stating the facts.

"You may not have had it so plush as a kid, but you got a generous inheritance. Don't tell me it's all gone?"

The younger woman shrugged and Talbert shook his head in disbelief.

"But I offered to invest it for you, to give you security."

"I invested it in my marriage." She smiled serenely as he gave an involuntary scornful humph. "How many wives have you gone through now, Hooks? Three?"

When he didn't answer, she said, "Our father had four."

She smiled a thank-you to the waiter who set butter and a woven silver basket of freshly baked yeast rolls before them, then turned back to her older half brother. "I'm still married to the only man I ever gave myself to." She took one of the warm rolls, breathed in its fragrance, and reached for the butter.

"And what kind of marriage is it, Marian?" he asked, unable to control his dismay. "You drink his spit. Do you eat his shit, too?"

"If he asked me to."

"Jesus Christ!"

"You will not take the Lord's name in vain," she said, speaking sharply for the first time. "My husband's a righteous man, Hooks, and he has it in him to do good work. If he gets a little zealous at times —"

"Your husband's a fool who fell for one of the oldest scams in the book if what you've told me are the facts. Traded all your assets for a bag of fake jewelry because a bootlegger with a grade school education conned him into thinking they were real? He spent half of your inheritance when you two went off to — where was it? Patagonia? Syria?"

"Lebanon," she murmured, buttering another piece of her roll.

"To Lebanon to convert the Muslims. Then he takes the rest of your money to build this church, bankrupts it, and now you come asking me to bail him out?"

He heard the anger in his voice and realized this was not the way to move her. "Even if he does mean well, haven't you had enough, honey? You deserve so much better than this. Hasn't he embarrassed you enough? No wonder he's ashamed to say what happened to the money. I can understand that he'd rather people think he's a crook than think him a fool, but that's what

380

he is and he's pulling you down with him. Just say the word and I'll get you the best and most discreet attorney in the country. I'll even give him a settlement to let him get a fresh start somewhere else. Please, Marian."

The waiter returned with the bisque they had ordered and Talbert was so distraught that he was almost oblivious to the appetizing aroma of lobster and well-seasoned cream. He gave it a ritual taste and then accepted a light sprinkle of pepper from the waiter's grinder, but it was only a formality.

Marian McKinney shook her head when it was offered to her.

"I can't leave him, Hooks. I love him and I believe in what he's doing. This whole experience has humbled him and he needs me now more than ever. Yes, he was prideful before. And yes, maybe he wasn't thinking clearly when he used me to make a point about following God's commandments. He thought he didn't care for worldly glory. But when temptation came, he was weak and he yielded. He really did think of all the good he could do if those jewels had been real. But he knows now that he was also thinking about the glory to himself, not to God. I'm glad this has happened!"

Her eyes sparkled with the intensity of her

emotions. "I'm glad because now that he's stumbled, now that he's admitted his weakness to me and to God, he understands how frail we all are when we don't trust God to give us the strength to resist the worst in our own natures. He's changed, Hooks, and he can lead others to change. That's why I'm pleading with you to help me help him save our church."

He looked at her in sorrow that was tinged with exasperation. In his world, he was used to giving orders and having them followed — his wives, his sons, his employees, the associates who were bound to him with golden chains. But this sister!

"I'm sorry," he said.

"You'd pay for the best attorney in the country to get me a divorce but you won't pay a dime to save my marriage?"

"Please. Eat your soup while it's still hot."

Obediently, she dipped her spoon into the thick creamy bisque and ate quietly for a few minutes.

He had finished his soup and sat silently stewing in his own thoughts until the waiter removed their bowls and brought them salad.

"Did I get a fair inheritance, Hooks?"

"What?"

"You heard me. Did I get a fair share of

our father's estate?"

He shrugged. "How should I know? He told his attorney what to write and he signed the will while 'of sound and disposing mind.' Considering that your mother didn't like to let you visit us, I'm sure he thought it was commensurate with the circumstances."

"Circumstances he created when he kicked her out after five years of marriage for a little whore half his age."

"Granted Cheryl was a whore," he agreed mildly, "but as I recall, your own mother was only half his age herself."

"Stop evading the question. Did I get a fair share?"

"Even if you had, it would be gone now, too."

"Then you admit that Father's will was unfair?"

"I don't admit a damn thing except that you're married to a bastard who humiliates you in front of a whole congregation and you don't have enough backbone to tell him to go fuck himself!"

She leaned back in her chair and gave him a long level look.

He held her gaze for a moment, then gave a resigned sigh and apologized.

"I'm sorry, Marian. There's no excuse for

that kind of language."

She continued to look at him without speaking.

"What?" he said irritably.

"It's not me that's been humiliated, is it, Hooks? It's you."

"Don't be stupid."

"Whoever told you about what happened Easter Sunday knows that I'm your sister. You're the one it humiliated when you heard it." Her quiet voice taunted him. "The great G. Hooks Talbert, the millionaire who tells governors and senators what to do, and his sister drank the spit water of a man he himself wouldn't spit on."

He glared at her with clenched jaws.

"A hundred thousand will save the church, Hooks."

"What?"

"Or maybe I'll write a magazine article, give a few interviews."

"Are you blackmailing me?"

"A hundred thousand."

Her eyes did not drop beneath his glare and he could see her resolve growing firmer until it hardened into marble.

"A hundred thousand, Hooks. You can take it out of petty cash."

Defeated, he shook his head and, with a wry smile, reached for the checkbook in the breast pocket of his jacket. "If I give you a hundred and ten, will you put some windows in that damn church? And a decent lighting system?"

Her answering smile was serene. "I'll ask," she promised.

CHAPTER 28

There are two conversations.
The other one is the other one.
    — *Paul's Hill,* by Shelby Stephenson

"Hey," Dwight said when I got home a little before six that Thursday evening. He was frying chicken strips to top a green-beans-and-rice dish he had invented.

Before he could say anything else, Cal piped up. "Blue's dead, Deborah. We found him in the lane when we came home."

"What?"

"Yeah," said Dwight, turning the chicken strips to brown them evenly. "I don't know if he was hit by a car first or just died of old age."

"Does Daddy know?"

He nodded. "We took him over to the house and I dug the grave."

"How's he taking it?"

"Okay, I guess. After all, it's not the first

dog he's had die."

True. Nonetheless, when I went to change clothes and he said that supper would be ready in about ten minutes, I told them to go ahead without me. "I think I'll run over there for a little while."

Five minutes later, I was driving through the rutted lanes to the homeplace, absently scratching at the bandage on my arm. Despite all the blood, it had only been a flesh wound and was healing very nicely. I would have a scar, but the doctor assured me it wouldn't be too noticeable.

I seemed to have lucked out all around. Ten days now since Candace Bradshaw's flash drive had been found and the contents transcribed, and it would appear that there was absolutely nothing about Talbert, Daddy, or me on it. Nothing that wasn't already public knowledge anyhow.

(*"The wicked flee when no man pursueth,"* the preacher murmured.)

If I had thought it through a little more carefully, I probably could have handed it over to Dwight as soon as I found it and saved myself a lot of grief. Daddy was not going to talk about it, Talbert had no reason to, and I'd certainly never told a soul nor written anything down for Candace to find when she rifled the law firm's records.

Besides, if what I'd heard about her the last few weeks was true, she wasn't all that clever about extrapolating from incomplete data.

I was trying not to extrapolate too much myself, but I had put in a few hours at the computer that week and I had questions for Daddy that had nothing to do with Blue's death.

He was sitting on the porch swing when I got there and Ladybelle was sprawled on the wooden floor nearby. She stood up as I approached. I know we give human attributes to our animals much too easily, but I swear it seemed to me that her tail did not wag as vigorously as usual.

"Hey, Daddy," I said, shaking my head in sympathy. "I was real sorry to hear about Blue."

"Yeah, I reckon his heart just wore out. Twelve years old last Thanksgiving."

He sighed and moved over so I could sit down beside him on the swing, but I took the top step instead so I could pet Ladybelle, who put her nose under my hand to get me to scratch her ears.

There were almost two hours of daylight left and we could easily see the graveyard down the slope from the porch, where family members have been getting buried for over a hundred years. My mother's there and so is the mother of the older boys. Inside the fence there are formal stones, stones with proper names and dates, but outside the fence is a long row of rough stones, some no bigger than a football, others big enough to sit on. None of them are chiseled, but there are names in black paint and every spring, when my brothers and I get together to clean off the weeds and trim back the rosebushes, someone will get out the can of black paint to touch up the letters, and we'll start remembering the various animals that have shared our lives.

"I guess you put him down there?"

"Yeah. Dwight dug the grave hole and Andrew fetched a rock from the creek."

I remember when Blue arrived. He was a Christmas present from Andrew, who traded two of his rabbit dogs to a breeder down in South Carolina for the little blue-speckled puppy. Daddy swore he was never going to have another house dog after the redtick he'd had for eight years was bitten by a cottonmouth, but it had been six months and Andrew rightly figured he was ready.

When Andrew handed him that puppy on Christmas morning, Daddy handed it right back.

"Didn't I say I won't gonna have another house dog?"

But by the time the fruitcake and coffee went around for the last time that night, the pup was sound asleep in his lap and when Andrew said, "You want me to take him on home with me?" Daddy said, "Naw, ain't no need to wake him up."

I should have realized that he would take Blue's death in stride. When you've seen that many well-loved dogs arrive as puppies, live a dog's long life, then die, I guess it gives you perspective.

I was pretty sure that there would be another new puppy to keep Ladybelle company before the year was out, and that the cycle would continue.

I leaned back against the rail post to face Daddy and said, "Guess you heard about your friend losing all the assets of his church."

He gave me a wary look. "My friend?"

"McKinney. The preacher at the Church of Jesus Christ Eternal."

"He ain't my friend."

"He was calling you Brother Kezzie when you introduced us the other day at the courthouse."

"That was just preacher talk." His voice turned stern. "You trying to tend to my business, Deb'rah?"

"No, sir, but did you know that most of the documents that pass through the register of deeds office are online?"

"What's that mean?"

"Means that I can sit at my computer at my house and look up the deed holders of every piece of property in the county."

He frowned. "Anybody can do that or just judges?"

"Anybody," I said.

He pulled a pack of cigarettes from his shirt pocket and lit one. The swing rocked gently back and forth, making a small squeak.

"I gotta get up there with my oil can," he said.

I didn't respond and the silence stretched between us.

I blinked first. "So how come he signed over to you practically everything he had? What did he think he was getting in return?"

Daddy didn't answer.

"If you got his land fair and square, how come he doesn't just tell people he sold it to you?"

"You see any dollar amounts on them deeds?"

"Just the one dollar everybody says when they don't want to tell how much money's changing hands."

"Well, then. He must know about that computer stuff, too, and how people can go poking their noses in other people's business so easy. If it didn't worry him, I don't know why it's worrying you."

"I'm not worrying, Daddy, and I'm not trying to mind your business, but when I see you with a shark like Faison McKinney —"

"Oh, he won't much of a shark, shug. More like a little ol' goldfish. Besides, if you read them deeds, then you seen I didn't keep none of the ones he give me."

"I know. But why would he bankrupt himself and his church for nothing?"

"Well, now, maybe he felt like he was getting a good trade."

A sudden thought chilled me. "You have something on him? You blackmail him into giving back those deeds?"

"I'm done talking about this, Deb'rah. You got questions, you go ask that preacher."

"I'm sorry, Daddy. But I thought maybe he'd fast-talked you into thinking he could help you get straight with the Lord."

"Me and the Lord's doing just fine." His tone was mild, but it was clear he did not plan to talk about land deeds or Faison McKinney any more. He stood up and said,

"Let me get the paint 'fore it gets dark."

He stepped inside the house and was back a few minutes later with a rag, a can of black paint, and a small trim brush.

As we walked down the slope with Ladybelle at our heels, the sun was still three fingers above the western horizon and the sweet smell of wild crab apples hung in the air.

The stone that Andrew had brought for Blue's grave was about the size and shape of a five-gallon bucket. Daddy sat on a nearby rock and pried up the lid of the paint can.

With the rag, he brushed the dirt away from a fairly flat area on the stone and dipped his brush in the paint.

"Do you believe in a life after this?" I asked him from my perch on a rock that marked the grave of Aunt Sister's ugly pet goat. "In heaven?"

"Wings and halos and streets of gold?" He smiled and shook his head. "Naw, that never made much sense to me."

"What do you believe in then?"

He shrugged. "Just because I don't believe in heaven don't mean I believe there ain't nothing after this. We can't never know, can we? I used to study on it, 'specially when your mama was dying. Now I've quit worrying about it. If being alive's a accident, then we're the luckiest accident in the universe, ain't we?"

He finished lettering Blue's name and the day's date, then capped the can and leaned back against the fence to watch the sun slip lower. A light breeze brushed our faces and ruffled his white hair.

"You ever think about them stories your mama used to read y'all? Stories from all over the world about old gods?"

"The myths?" I asked, surprised that he recalled them.

"I reckon. One of 'em was about a chief in one of them cold countries where they have mead halls. Adam wanted to know what a mead hall was. Your mama said it was where they had big feasts, with singing and laughing and beer made with honey."

I smiled, having no memory of this.

"Anyhow, somebody asked the chief if there was anything after this and the chief pointed to a moth up near the roof timbers that'd got in and was flying down the length of the mead hall. He said that moth was like life. It comes in out of the darkness, it stays awhile to see the feasting and laughing and song-making and storytelling and then it flies back out into the darkness. We can't see in the darkness, but the moth flies on like there might be something better a little further on out there."

"Is that what you believe, Daddy?"

He stubbed out his cigarette with the toe of a scuffed brogan and smiled over at me. "Well, shug, I got to say it makes more sense than angel wings and streets of gold."

The sun sank below the horizon in a blaze of reds and purples and oranges. "But for right now, this is one mighty fine mead hall, ain't it?"

ABOUT THE AUTHOR

Margaret Maron grew up on a farm near Raleigh, North Carolina, but for many years lived in Brooklyn, New York. When she returned to her North Carolina roots with her artist-husband, Joe, she began a series based on her own background. The first book, *Bootlegger's Daughter,* became a *Washington Post* bestseller that swept the top mystery awards for its year and is among the 100 Favorite Mysteries of the Century as selected by the Independent Mystery Booksellers Association. Later Deborah Knott novels *Up Jumps the Devil* and *Storm Track* each won the Agatha Award for Best Novel. To find out more about the author, you can visit www.MargaretMaron.com.

We hope you have enjoyed this Large Print book. Other Thorndike, Wheeler, and Chivers Press Large Print books are available at your library or directly from the publishers.

For information about current and upcoming titles, please call or write, without obligation, to:

Publisher
Thorndike Press
295 Kennedy Memorial Drive
Waterville, ME 04901
Tel. (800) 223-1244

or visit our Web site at:

http://gale.cengage.com/thorndike

OR

Chivers Large Print
published by BBC Audiobooks Ltd
St James House, The Square
Lower Bristol Road
Bath BA2 3SB
England
Tel. +44(0) 800 136919
email: bbcaudiobooks@bbc.co.uk
www.bbcaudiobooks.co.uk

All our Large Print titles are designed for easy reading, and all our books are made to last.